D0761404

TOUCH OF MAGIC

ALSO BY ALICIA MONTGOMERY

THE TRUE MATES SERIES

Fated Mates

Blood Moon

Romancing the Alpha

Witch's Mate

Taming the Beast

Tempted by the Wolf

THE LONE WOLF DEFENDERS SERIES

Killian's Secret

Loving Quinn

All for Connor

THE TRUE MATES STANDALONE NOVELS

Holly Jolly Lycan Christmas

A Mate for Jackson: Bad Alpha Dads

TRUE MATES GENERATIONS

A Twist of Fate

Claiming the Alpha

Alpha Ascending

A Witch in Time

Highland Wolf

Daughter of the Dragon

Shadow Wolf

A Touch of Magic

Heart of the Wolf

THE BLACKSTONE MOUNTAIN SERIES

The Blackstone Dragon Heir

The Blackstone Bad Dragon

The Blackstone Bear

The Blackstone Wolf

The Blackstone Lion

The Blackstone She-Wolf

The Blackstone She-Bear

The Blackstone She-Dragon

This is a work of fiction. Names, characters, businesses, places, events, locales, and incidents are either the products of the author's imagination or used in a fictitious manner. Any resemblance to actual persons, living or dead, or actual events is purely coincidental.

COPYRIGHT © 2020 ALICIA MONTGOMERY
EDITED BY LAVERNE CLARK
COVER BY JACQUELINE SWEET
032520

ALL RIGHTS RESERVED.

TOUCH OF MAGIC

TRUE MATES GENERATIONS BOOK 8

ALICIA MONTGOMERY

PROLOGUE

THREE YEARS AGO ...

The call came at three o'clock in the morning, and anyone who's ever been woken up by their phone at that time *knows* that such a call would be important. That's why Cross Jonasson immediately picked up the cell from his bedside table and answered it.

"It's me."

The sound of his father's voice made him sit up. As hybrid—part Lycan, part warlock—his eyes naturally adjusted to the darkness so he didn't need to reach for the light. His wolf, too, heard the urgency in his father's voice and was immediately on alert.

"What's wrong? Is it Mom?"

"No, it's Gunnar." The words came out short and clipped, his father's accent becoming more pronounced. "Come *now*."

"I'll be there."

Rolling out of bed, he grabbed his discarded clothes from last night and quickly shrugged them on. From the dead seriousness of his father's tone, he knew there would be no time to wash up or even gulp down a cup of coffee, even if he could make it himself on the go. Of course, while most people made coffee by brewing grounds, he could literally make coffee from thin air, via transmogrification, one of the powers he'd inherited from his warlock father.

As he grabbed a rubber band to tie up his messy blond locks, he focused his thoughts on Gunnar's location. He'd been there numerous times, so it wasn't difficult to transport himself there using the other power he'd inherited from his father—teleportation across long distances.

In seconds, he transported himself from his Lower East Side apartment in New York to the middle of nowhere in the Shenandoah Valley. He appeared in the corner of the living area of the sparse cabin, a spot he and his father had designated as their transport spot. Teleportation, after all, was a tricky power. He needed to have been somewhere before to transport there, or have a clear idea of the location and view of the place. Even then, it was dangerous as he could accidentally materialize inside a tree or piece of furniture. It was so dangerous that he didn't even attempt it until he had been studying with his father for at least a decade.

"What's wrong?" he asked as he strode into the cabin's lone bedroom.

Daric stood by the bed, his hand on his son's shoulder as he looked to Cross with those blue-green eyes so much like his own. "It happened again."

Though Gunnar had his face buried in his hands as he sat at the edge of the bed, Cross could tell from the tense lines of his body that something was *very* wrong. Not as bad as the last time—the incident that lead him to live like a hermit in this remote cabin—but this seemed grave nonetheless. Moving closer, he mirrored his father's gesture and placed his hand on his brother's other shoulder. "Gunnar, are you okay?"

Slowly, Gunnar turned his face up. His skin was pale and his brown eyes had a glazed-over look. "It was awful, Cross. Terrible. We ... you ... Dad ... Mom ... everyone dies."

Daric's eyes turned stormy. "He's had another premonition."

And that was the gift his younger brother had inherited from their father. The ability to see the future. However, unlike Daric's power—which relied on touch—Gunnar's was more spontaneous. He didn't need to touch anyone to see their future. He just saw it.

Cross knelt beside him. "Was it clear?" Gunnar nodded. "Have you told Dad?" Another nod. "Can you tell me?"

There was a moment of hesitation in Gunnar's face, but he took a short, sharp breath and began to speak. "It was so clear ... so many there ... you, Dad, Mom. Astrid. And Nick Vrost ..." He shook his head. "No, it wasn't Nick, this guy was younger. Maybe one of his sons. One of the twins or the eldest one. Also ... Julianna Anderson, and Elise, and two more men I don't recognize."

"What were they—we doing?" Cross asked.

"A white marble table. Two things on top—a small sword and a pendant. There were hooded figures all around. Red robes. Red eyes."

Gunnar became even paler, and Cross knew why. Though he'd never seen one before, he knew his history well.

Red robes and red eyes. It could only mean one thing—mages. "And then?"

"There was a ceremony or something. They were chanting. You came up, trying to stop them, but you couldn't."

"Why not?"

"Because they had ... there was a woman. White-blonde hair. Unusual eyes. Blue—no, they're like amethysts. And she's wearing a ring. It's silver with a small red stone in the middle. She takes the sword and the pendant and then ... and then ..."

Daric's grip tightens. "Go ahead, tell him."

Gunnar's lower lip trembles. "She falls to the floor. You're holding her and whisper something in her ear. There's fighting around you. A man with long white hair wearing a red hooded robe slips the ring on his finger, raises the dagger and the necklace over his head. He takes all the three objects and disappears. You're all lying on the ground. Then everyone's dead ... you're dead. She's dead. Mom. Dad. Astrid. Everyone dies. And they take over ... armies ... cities burned to the ground ... humans in chains ... death. I can't ... stop!" His fingers gripped his short blond hair, pulling at it. "I can't—"

"It's all right, son." Daric rubbed at his back. "Why don't you lie down?"

Gunnar lay his head on the pillow and curled up into a ball. When he closed his eyes, Daric motioned for Cross to follow him out to the living area.

"Was anyone hurt this time?" Cross asked when he shut the door behind him.

"No, but that's why he stays out here."

Since the accident over three years ago, the first time Gunnar's premonition powers manifested. He'd been at the club in The Village he co-owned, and the magic he bled out was so powerful, it knocked everyone unconscious. That's why he'd been living here. Well, that was the short version.

"He's never had another bad episode since the first time. Why now?"

"I think the more important thing here is *what* he predicted."

Cross glanced back at the door to the bedroom, wondering if Gunnar was all right. These horrific visions he had ... it tormented him. But Daric was right. What he saw was concerning, because Gunnar's visions had never been wrong yet. "The mages are back." He never thought he'd say such words out loud. "Or they will be."

"That's what I'm afraid of." His father's brows drew together. "We must warn the Alpha."

"Grant Anderson is no fool." Cross rubbed his temple. "I don't think he entirely believed us when we said Gunnar had an accident with some potions that mixed together in his pocket. If he finds out about what really happened—"

"He won't," Daric said. "I'll make sure of it. *We'll* make sure of it."

Cross swallowed audibly. If Grant Anderson knew Gunnar's powers were out of control, he would have no choice but to tell the Lycan High Council. And the council—who were already prejudiced against hybrids in the first place —could order his brother put down if he were deemed a danger. However, Cross also knew that the situation was so grave that Daric was willing to risk exposing his son.

"What will we tell him?"

So, they came up with a plan, and by sunrise, they were back in New York. Though they could easily teleport into Grant Anderson's office, they opted to go through his assistant, Jared, and they were shown in right away.

"And what was this matter you needed to talk to me about?" the Alpha asked. "It must be important enough for you to come all the way to see me."

"Alpha," Daric bowed his head with respect. Although not a Lycan himself, the warlock had pledged to the clan long ago. "I've had a vision, and my mother, she had the same one as well."

And they relayed to him what Gunnar had seen, under the guise of Daric and Signe's powers. As non-Lycans, they would not be subject to the Lycan High Council's influence.

The Alpha listened to them, not saying a word until they finished. The silence in the room was thick and heavy, until he did speak. "You haven't spoken of your visions in a long time, Daric. And neither has your mother."

"Anything we've seen in the last couple of decades haven't been important enough to share." The lie slid out of Daric's mouth so smoothly that Cross would have believed it too.

"All right." Grant folded his hands over his massive oak desk. "There's nothing else you can tell me about your vision? How far into the future is it? Where did it take place?" Daric shook his head. "No clue at all?"

"I'm sorry ... I'm just relaying the vision to you. I can't control it."

Grant's jaw hardened. "I can't just act on a vision—reliable as it may be. But I think we need to learn more."

"I completely agree, Alpha," Daric said. "That's why I'm

going to send Cross on a mission. To find out more about the objects in the vision."

The Alpha turned to him, his emerald green eyes turning dark. "And you're okay with this? What about your work at Lone Wolf?"

Like most of the people in his extended family, Cross worked at his uncles' private security firm, Lone Wolf Security, which was an offshoot of the larger Creed Security Corporation. "We're going to tell them that Dad is sending me on an extended training session to help me gain more control of my powers," he replied. The lie would be believable enough. After all, because his gifts were so complicated, he'd been studying and training with his father since he was thirteen. Daric himself had started when he was much younger, but then those were different circumstances. "I'm sure Uncle Killian and Sebastian will understand."

Grant thought for a moment. "All right. You can go on this fact-finding mission, but this needs to stay between us. While we don't want the same thing to happen as last time, we can't get everyone into a panic. The Lycan High Council should be notified as well."

"You're right of course," Daric said. "But maybe we should wait until we have solid proof before informing the council."

"Hmmm." Grant tapped his fingers on the desk. "All right, proof first."

After conferring on a few more details, Daric and Cross left, reappearing back in Gunnar's cabin.

"Are you ready for this, Cross?" Daric asked.

If he were honest—not really. "You've trained me well, Dad."

His father cracked a genuine smile. "And you've been an excellent student. I have every confidence in you. Now, let's go see if Gunnar feels well enough to tell us more."

When they walked into the bedroom, his brother was walking out of the bathroom, freshly showered and shaved. "How about some breakfast, son?" Daric asked. "What would you like?"

Gunnar rubbed a towel down his face. "Chinese food. Emerald Dragon's egg rolls."

"We'll have it ready for you by the time you finish getting dressed."

So they did, and as they ate, Gunnar gave them as much detail as he could about his vision. When they finished, Daric stood up. "I think I may have an idea where you can begin looking, Cross. But I need to check something out first. Don't worry, we'll take care of all of this." With that, their father disappeared.

"Do you need me to stay or get you anything, Gunnar?"

"Cross." His brother's hand snaked out and grabbed his wrist. "There's something ..."

Gunnar's grip was deathly tight. "What is it? What's wrong? You can tell me."

"I ... I didn't tell you everything. About the vision."

"What? Why would you keep anything from me and Dad?"

"It's not you ... it's Dad." He withdrew his hand and curled his shoulders inward, bent his head down. "I thought ... I wasn't sure if I should have told you, but I think you should know something."

"What is it?"

Gunnar slowly lifted his head. "Cross ... that woman. In the vision."

"What about her?"

"She's there because of you."

"Why?"

His whiskey-brown eyes turned dark. "Because she's yours."

"Mine?" His heart thudded in his chest. "What do you mean, mine?"

"Your True Mate."

———

Three months later ...

Despite being called The City That Never Sleeps, Cross knew that New York, did in fact, sleep, at least pockets of it did. On this particular September early morning, this part of the Upper West Side was waking up—the garbage truck was chugging along, collecting bins left on the street, workers at the corner coffee shop were coming in for their morning shift, and of course, right on time—Deedee Creed was hopping down the steps of her brownstone home, about to head into work. It had been months since he'd seen his best friend or even talked to her, so he thought he might surprise her and take her out to breakfast. Then maybe they could make plans for dinner with his sister Astrid. Growing up, they'd been a tightly-knit trio, and he'd missed their company after being away for so long.

She was just across the street, walking toward the subway

stop on Eighty-Sixth, so he crossed the street and stepped onto the sidewalk, making a beeline for—

"Whoops! Pardon me."

Someone had bumped right into him as he tried to cross the street. He whipped around and saw that someone walking away from him, going the opposite direction as Deedee. At first, he turned back to chase after Deedee, who had nearly reached the corner, but something made him turn around. It was the scent of apple cider and fresh snow. It made his inner wolf freeze, then raise its head in the air, sniffing for more of that delicious scent. The person that bumped into him—a woman, he realized—was nearing the other end of the street.

Before he knew it, he was walking behind her. She was wearing a light trench coat, and her hair was hidden under a cap. She turned uptown, and he followed her for a few more blocks, taking the trace scents of her, following it like breadcrumbs leading to ... what exactly?

He stopped, realizing that he'd walked over ten city blocks following this woman. Some might say he was acting like a stalker. Rubbing a hand down his face, he made a motion to turn around when she stopped, then walked into one of the coffee shops along Amsterdam Avenue.

His wolf urged him forward, and he found himself reaching for the shop's door when he looked up at the sign overhead. "Wicked Brew," he muttered to himself. The logo of the coffee shop had, of all things, a silhouette of a witch on a broomstick.

Instead of going in, he withdrew his hand and stepped aside when someone behind him cleared their throat. However, he couldn't help but glance inside the shop. He saw the trench coat draped over the back of a chair in the corner, but no sign of the woman.

Quickly, he pivoted on his heel and walked away. His wolf scratched and whined at him. *What is it?* But his wolf didn't exactly talk back. As he moved farther and farther away from the coffee shop, it quieted down, so he continued to walk, trying to clear his head of the apple cider and snow scent. He didn't realize how far he'd walked or how late it was until he saw Columbus Circle up ahead.

"Damn." Checking his watch, he knew he was going to be late for his meeting with his father and the Alpha unless he left right this moment. He ducked into the Time Warner Center, then headed towards the bathrooms and into one of the stalls. He pictured the Alpha's office in his mind, imagining that spot behind him with the large windows that faced Central Park. And in seconds, he was there.

"Apologies, Primul," he said, using the traditional honorific a Lycan used for his Alpha. "I was running late."

The leather chair swiveled around to face him. "No worries, Cross," he said. "Have a seat."

Daric, not surprisingly, was already there, sitting on the chair opposite Grant Anderson. He merely lifted a blond brow, but said nothing as Cross sat next to him. "I know you're busy, so I'll get right to it. As you know, I've been looking through the archives of several libraries around the world."

"Did you find any more information?"

He looked at Daric, who gave him a slight nod. "Yes, Alpha. And I have reason to believe that the things that were in G—Grandmother's and Dad's vision are three artifacts that were owned by a powerful mage named Magus Aurelius."

"Magus Aurelius?" Grant's brows snapped together. "Never heard of him."

"He lived over a thousand years ago, according to the texts I've read, though we can't really take 'thousand' literally as the English translations can be tricky. It could be much older than that."

"All right, so tell me more about this Magus Aurelius and those artifacts."

"A long time ago, Magus Aurelius controlled a large chunk of what we know now as Central and Eastern Europe. However, his subjects were rising up against him, with the help of the Lycans. He knew his reign was about to end, and so he hatched a plan to infuse his magic into three objects."

"Why three?" the Alpha asked.

"Three is an important number in magic," Daric said. "But please go on, Cross."

"Magus Aurelius chose three objects and then sacrificed three hundred humans and three hundred Lycans so he could bind his powers into these objects."

The Alpha leaned forward. "Then what happened?"

"I haven't found the exact answer, but it seems he was defeated by the Lycans and the humans, but the artifacts were lost. However, they seem to resurface every now and then, and I've narrowed it down to three possible objects—a necklace, a blade, and a ring. Each one on its own has different properties and powers."

"What kind of powers?"

Cross took out his phone and lay it on the table. He opened up his photo library and expanded an image he had taken from St. Catherine's in Egypt of a pendant on an ancient papyrus scroll. "The necklace is said to be able to control a person." Swiping to the next image, he zoomed in on a drawing of a short sword on delicate yellowed paper. "This was from the *Khizanat al Qarawiyyin* in Fez from one of their oldest books. The blade can create portals that can cross the world." His finger hovered over the screen.

"And?" the Alpha said. "The ring?"

"I don't have much on the ring." Cross swiped to the next image. It was a picture of a large book propped up against a shelf that was filled with chained books. "But this book written by a monk from the twelve hundreds talks about a ring found in a village in Gaul. The people reported some mysterious events that no one could explain."

"What kind of events?"

"Little things. Crops dying overnight, and then a few hours later, it was like nothing happened. Farm animals being found dead in the fields, but the next day they'd be roaming around again. They traced it to a woman in the village, whom they saw out in the middle of the woods. Witnesses say she had her hands over a dead deer, when the animal suddenly jumped up and ran away. They rounded her up and accused her of witchcraft. Said she had found a ring in one of the ancient cemeteries. Unfortunately, she mysteriously died, and that was the last we've heard of the ring."

"So, this ring ... it has the power of death?"

"Not just death," Daric began. "Death *and* life."

"If we're even sure this is *the* ring." The Alpha rested his elbows on the table and steepled his fingers. "You'll need to find out more."

Cross nodded. "I already have some leads."

"But, good job on the rest, Cross." Grant rubbed the bridge of his nose with his thumb and forefinger. "I thought we had this mage business done and over with. We need to start making plans. Now, I haven't spoken to anyone else about this except Frankie and Lucas, but I'm thinking it's time for me to retire."

"Retire?" Daric seemed taken aback. "But the Alpha is a lifetime position."

"It's rare for an Alpha to retire, but it's not unheard of. You have to remember, in the past, with so many wars and battles over territory, not many Alphas survived very long. Though if there is trouble brewing ahead ..." His expression turned dark. "Frankie and I will have to have a long talk."

"I'll do my best, Primul."

"I know you will, Cross. If anyone can find the ring, it's the two of you. And once we have the artifacts"—the Alpha's eyes grew dark—"we need to destroy them."

Something about his words made Cross uncomfortable. But he knew it had to be done.

"Now." Grant picked up his phone. "If you don't mind ..."

"Not at all, Alpha." Daric gave him a quick bow of the head and turned to Cross. "Son, shall we head home and go over a few things?"

"I ... need to take care of something at my apartment." he said. "I'll come by for dinner and surprise Mom. I'll be here for a couple more days."

"All right, son, I'll see you later."

Cross waited for his father to disappear before he himself left. However, instead of transporting himself to his apartment, he reappeared in a small alleyway between a

Chinese restaurant and a supermarket on Eighty-Third Street. He traced his way back to Wicked Brew and hurried inside the door. The smells of coffee, pastries, sweat, and various colognes lingered in the air, making it hard to ferret out the scent of apple cider and snow. His wolf whined in disappointment.

It was silly anyway. Walking out of the coffee shop, he intended to go back to the alleyway where he first appeared, but then changed his mind and walked toward the subway. After three months, it was nice to be back in the city. Truth be told, he'd never used his powers as much as he did while he was away traveling, so it was nice to just take his time. A long subway ride could be just the thing he needed.

His wolf didn't like the dark, confined space of the underground station, but it was comforting in a way. There was a lot more to be done; his job wasn't finished, and he couldn't be distracted now.

————

"Good morning, welcome to Wicked Brew." The cheerful young woman manning the cashier smiled as Cross stepped up to the front of the line. "Oh, welcome back. Just the usual?"

"Yes, please."

"How about a pastry?"

He shook his head. "Just the coffee, please."

She picked up a cup and scribbled on the side. "Black brew, no sugar, and just a bit of cream," she repeated.

Cross handed her a bill. "Keep the change," he said as he stepped aside. When the barista called out his order, he grabbed his cup and sat down on the empty chair in the far corner of the dining area.

This was crazy. He told himself that over and over again. He told *his wolf* that this was insane, but still, he found himself coming here every morning, for the last four days. It was a long way to come for a cup of coffee, but when he tried to reason with his wolf, it just wouldn't listen.

You don't even know if she'll come back here. She might have gone in here on a whim. Still, the animal didn't care.

He sipped his coffee, the minutes ticking by. By midmorning after he'd had his second cup, he decided it was time to leave. Not just the coffee shop, but New York. He'd had dinner with his parents every night since he got here, and Astrid even made an appearance last night when they all went to see Gunnar. Of course, she and their mother spent half the night bickering, but Cross knew it was because they were too much alike. When Astrid had to leave early because she worked night shifts as a security guard, Meredith started to moan and complain why she can't just hold a regular job or go back to school, which of course irritated his sister. Astrid led an unconventional lifestyle, to say the least, but she had always marched to the beat of her own drum.

Yes, it was nice coming back and spending time with his family, but there was work to be done. His contact from the Malatestiana Library in Italy had found that book he'd been searching for and asked him to come right away.

Ignoring the pleading whines of his wolf, he tossed the empty cup into the trash and strode toward the door. He pushed it open, but he was so distracted he didn't see that someone had pulled on it from the other side at the same time.

"Whoa!"

Objects clattered to the ground as he collided into the other person, who stepped back. Peering down, he saw an easel, an empty canvas, and a bag that had fallen over on its side and spilled various paintbrushes and tubes of paint.

"Sorry, sorry," he murmured as he bent down to pick up the various items.

"No, it's my fault," said the feminine voice. "I wasn't looking where I was going. I had this spark of inspiration, you see. The sky, it's so blue, and it made me think of pansies. My thoughts tend to wander, but that's how I get my inspiration. Like I said, it just came to me. Like a spark. Ever had one of those?"

They reached for the same tube of paint at the same time, and their fingers brushed together. A strange bolt of electricity ran up his arm. His wolf suddenly perked up.

"Oh. No. Not quite that kind of spark. Must be static, though." She swept the tube back into the bag. "Damn. I hope I didn't miss anything." She glanced around her. "That yellow ochre was my last tube. They always run out of it. You'd think Van Gogh and his sunflowers were coming back in vogue or something."

"Miss?" The sun shone behind her, momentarily blinding him. However, the familiar scent of cider and freshly-fallen snow entered his nostrils, and his wolf howled in delight. *It was her.*

"Hmmm?"

He hadn't seen her face the other day, and even now, her features were obscured by the large sunglasses she wore, and a large hat covered most of her head. But that perfume was all he needed to recognize her. "Sorry, I wasn't looking where I was going." He picked up the easel and canvas. "Are you an artist?"

"Well, trying to be," she said. "Um, thank you." She tried to get the easel and canvas from him, but he held it firmly. "Uh, can I have my things back please?"

"No. I mean ..." God, what was wrong with him? While he wasn't smooth with the ladies, he was never tongue-tied around them. "I'm really sorry for knocking all your things over. Can I get you a cup of coffee as an apology?"

Her tongue darted out of her mouth to lick at her lips, a move that sent a surge of desire straight to his gut. "I suppose so." She nodded. "Okay. If you don't mind carrying—"

"Not at all." He gestured for her to go in first, and he followed behind her. She headed for one of the tables in the corner and took off her trench coat, draping it behind the chair before she whipped her hat off. Long, lustrous locks of white-blonde hair tumbled down her shoulders.

A strange feeling came over him—something like déjà vu, but not quite. It was something else gnawing at him, or had been gnawing at him all these months. And that something was Gunnar's voice, ringing in his head.

White-blonde hair.

Surely that wasn't an unusual hair color. He gripped the back of the other chair so hard he heard the wood creak. "What would you like?"

"Hmmm ... I don't know what I'm in the mood for. Something sweet, maybe. I always need something sweet." She sat down and put her bag on the floor beside her, then took off her sunglasses, placing them on the table. "Caramel macchiato. Yes, that's it. A caramel macchiato, please," she said as she looked up to him. Her porcelain skin made her light eyes—a true violet color—stand out even more. "Um, are you all right?"

"I'm fine."

Unusual eyes. Gunnar's voice grew louder in his ear. *Blue —no, they're like amethysts.*

He pivoted and headed for the cashier, giving her his order. Time seemed to slow down, and there was a pounding in his temple as a vice-like grip wrapped around his chest. It was like walking in a dream, he couldn't even remember picking up her drink and walking back to the table.

Her eyes went wide as he sat down and pushed the cup toward her. "Thank you."

You're holding her and whisper something in her ear.

"Uh, are you okay?" Her soft voice knocked him out of his daze, and he stared down at her. She was so lovely it made him ache. Softly rounded cheeks, delicate brows, sweeping lashes, and a straight, pert nose. The only imperfection marring her face was a mole under the right side of her mouth, but that only seemed to add character to her face.

"You have interesting eyes, you know," she began.

"I do?"

"Mm-hmm." A dreamy expression crossed her face. "I'm trying to figure out what colors I'd use to get them just right. I think turquoise ... no azure, with a touch of emerald. I'd have to try a couple of times to get the shade just right. And—" Her hand went to her mouth. "I'm rambling again, aren't I? I always do that when I'm nervous ... er, you know, you uh, you don't have to sit here with me ... I mean, unless you want to." A blush swept across her cheeks. "You're more than welcome to, ah ..."

"Cross." He sat down on the empty chair in front of her. "My name's Cross. And you are?"

She's there because of you.

"Sabrina." She held out her hand. "Nice to meet you, Cross."

She's yours.

Taking her offered hand, he squeezed it firmly. He ignored the frisson of electricity racing up his arm because he could only focus on one thing.

On her ring finger was a silver band with a stone in the middle the color of blood.

Everyone dies.

CHAPTER ONE

PRESENT TIME ...

Shouldn't have come here. This is wrong. A mistake. The words repeated in Cross's head over and over again. Words he'd been telling himself for nearly three years now, but still, he couldn't resist the pull. Couldn't resist *her*. And so, he went.

It was early yet, and the sky was still in that stage between blue, pink, and yellow, the sun peeking out from between the high rises. She was a heavy sleeper, so she didn't notice him when he appeared by her bedside.

Each time, he told himself it would only be a few seconds, a minute, tops. But each time he ended up staying longer. Just watching her usually. But today, the ache was so bad. He had to touch her, so he bent down and placed his palms over hers, lightly brushing his hands over her delicate skin. Feeling bold, he threaded his fingers through hers. This would have to be enough for now, to stave off that deep loneliness in his very soul.

She was like an addiction; one he just couldn't break. God that *scent*. It was etched into his brain so deep, he could live to a million years old and he'd never forget it. Even now, it lingered on him, calming him and his wolf. It was the only time the animal seemed content.

He stared down at their linked fingers, anger bubbling up as that damned *thing* wrapped around her ring finger mocked him. Taunted him. Reminding him of *why* he couldn't be here.

A soft moan made him start, and he let go, quickly backing away from the bed. But he couldn't leave yet. His heartbeat picked up as he waited. Maybe just one more second but ... no! He shouldn't have touched her hand. As her lashes began to flutter, he shut his eyes tight and transported himself to the building across the street where he had a clear vantage point of the large loft apartment. What he'd give to be able to look into those eyes again ...

She stretched, rolled over, and sat up, looking around her. With a shake of her head, she rose from the bed and made her way to the bathroom. He watched her through the large windows of the loft studio, going about her morning routine. Coffee. Toast. News on the TV, which she never really paid attention to, because all she needed was the noise. Then to her studio, where she would sit and paint and—

Shit. How long had he been there? The sun was already high in the sky. What time was it? He was late. With one last glance across the street, he closed his eyes and thought of the place where he should have been ten minutes ago.

"Apologies for the delay."

Grant—no, he corrected himself—Lucas Anderson's office was more crowded than usual. The new Alpha had asked him to come back for a meeting because they had some special guests. According to his father, Marc Delacroix had reunited with his long-lost family. They had always known he was a hybrid of some sort, seeing as he had the power to disappear in the shadows, but it turned out he was a member of a coven of witches and warlocks that they had never even heard of before.

"I had some business to attend to." He strode toward the middle of the room. "Primul," he said to Lucas. "I have—"

A high-pitched shriek cut him off. "You too!"

A girl—no, a teenager—with dark eyes looked him up and down before fixing her gaze on his hands.

"What's wrong?" someone said.

The young woman cocked her head as she moved two steps toward him. "He's ... he's ..." There was power emanating from her, something with a dark tinge to it, similar to what he'd felt when he met Delacroix. "You've touched something bad," she said accusingly.

"No, only *I* have touched the dagger." It was his father who spoke.

"But his hands," the girl cried. "His hands." Those dark eyes were magnetic and he couldn't turn away. "You've touched it too and ..." She frowned. "What's wrong with your glow?"

Glow?

"She's right." He managed to pull his gaze away from the girl, toward another unfamiliar figure in the room—an old woman with long white flowing hair, whose dark eyes had turned to him. "You've touched something very powerful. It's similar to what stains the warlock's hand, but different."

"Cross?" Tension laced the Alpha's voice. "What is she saying?"

"Son." His father walked toward him, and suddenly, he felt like an animal trapped by its prey. "What's the meaning of this?"

He had to stay calm. There's no way they could possibly know ... "I don't know what you're talking about."

"She"—the Alpha nodded at the young girl—"can detect traces of magic. And she knows you've touched it."

"Touched what?" A bead of sweat formed on his temple.

"The *artifact*, son." His father rarely raised his voice, not even when he was scolding his children. Shouting was more his mom's thing. But now, he could feel Daric's temper bubbling. "You've touched the ring of Magus Aurelius, haven't you?"

"You have it?"

Cross's wolf cowered as power radiated from Lucas in waves. Though his own wolf was strong and dominant in its own right, it recognized its Alpha. There was no way he could fight it; it was either bend or break.

The Alpha's eyes glowed, a signal that his wolf was very close to surfacing. "All this time, you've had it?" he snarled.

The air was too thick, and it was hard to breathe. His wolf urged him to submit. To confess. "It's not ... it's not what you think."

"What the hell are we supposed to think?" The Alpha moved toward him. "You've been keeping it from us and—"

"I'm sorry." They could never find out. The truth would be

the end of them. He turned to the one person in the room who he could really trust, beseeching him. "But you have to understand ..." Then he focused on the farthest place he could think of, disappearing into thin air as a vicious growl echoed in his ear.

He staggered back as he realized that he'd landed on uneven ground. The wind on top of the cliff was bitingly cold, but his Lycan side would help him adjust. The chill felt good on his skin, almost calming, as was the sight of the Northern Lights in the distance. This had been his father's childhood home, at least, that valley right under the lights was. Daric had taken him here, the first time he tried his powers. It felt safe here, and would give him time to think—

"What did you do?"

He spun around. Of course his father knew he would come here. "I ... Dad, please. You have to trust—"

"Trust you?" Daric said incredulously. "Why should I trust you when you've been hiding the ring all this time? Where is it?"

"I can't ... I can't give it to you."

A vein pulsed in his father's neck. "And why not?"

"I ... I don't have it on me." *Not a lie.* Then he thought of the first place that came to his head when he thought of safety.

"Then go get it and—No!"

His father lunged for him, but he disappeared just in time. Back to New York, to his childhood bedroom. It was the first place he could think of. His parents had provided him a safe and loving home, after all. And he could just sit and decide—

"Cross, what have you done?"

His father materialized by the bed. Daric knew him too well. "Just ... I need time to ..."

"We have to go back, son," he said. "The Alpha is demanding your head. I cannot protect you if—"

"I can't let you do that!" This was life and death. They could never know. He had to get out of here. So, he focused his thoughts on the farthest place he could think of.

He took a deep breath as he reappeared on top of a mountain top along the Annapurna mountains in Nepal. The air here was thin, and made him lightheaded and lose his balance. Stumbling forward, he dropped to his knees.

"What do you mean you can't let me do that?" Daric's voice cut into his oxygen-deprived brain.

How the heck did he know—no time to think on that. His body was beginning to recover, so he whisked himself away. To an abandoned island in the middle of the Caribbean. He waited for a minute, letting out a sigh as he plonked down on the sand.

What to do now? Come up with a plan, he guessed.

As the waves washed over his feet and legs, his thoughts strayed to her, as they always did. The last three years of his life had been devoted to protecting her, making sure no one suspected she existed or what she meant to him.

He sunk his hands into the wet sand. *Focus.* Minutes ticked by, but it was hard to tell how much time had passed out here. It was times like this that made him wonder about the past and the decisions he'd made that brought him here.

There's no other way, Cross. You know it.

His eyes shut tight. Had there been no other choice at the time? Could there really have been no alternative?

"I'm sorry, son, we have to take you in."

Cross turned his head toward the sound of the voice, then shot up to his feet. *Fuck.* Daric was there again, and he wasn't alone. Delacroix and Jacob stood behind him; their faces drawn into serious expressions.

But *how?* Daric's control on his teleportation powers were far superior to Cross's, not just because he was more experienced but because he had traveled to more places. In fact, when he first started using his powers, he was only allowed to transport to places Daric had shown him first. But this beach ... Cross had never been with his father here. How did he know about this place?

"You must come with us, *mon ami*," the Cajun said. "We promise, no harm will come to you."

"C'mon, Cross," Jacob added. "You can't run forever."

He weighed his options. There was no way he was just going to come with them, so what was their plan? His gaze moved from his father, to Delacroix, and to Jacob. Then he saw something in the Cajun's hand. A silver bracelet. *So that was their plan.*

"I can't let you take me in," he said, keeping his eye on the bracelet. His father had shown it to him before—it was a special bangle that prevented a witch or warlock from using their powers. "And I won't let you put that on me!" He closed his eyes and disappeared.

Egypt. Montenegro. Tierra del Fuego. Beijing. London. He skipped from one place to another, but it didn't seem to matter. Daric, Jacob, and Delacroix were there on his tail. As they stood on the edge of a cliff on the Amalfi Coast, he turned toward the sea. Fatigue was weighing him down. He didn't think he could feel this tired seeing as he was Lycan, but magic always had a price. His father too, was getting tired; he could see it as he swayed on his feet as he took a step forward.

"Cross!"

Daric's voice echoed as he disappeared and went to the next place he could think of where he could find refuge. It was a gamble, but what choice did he have?

The cool winds of the coast turned into dry heat. The desert sun blazed high above him, scorching his skin and temporarily blinding him. It had been over a year since he'd been to this place, and nothing had changed much, though they did fix that giant hole on the balcony floor. Focusing his senses, he could hear the cry of an infant from the other side of the door.

"You must tell me where it is."

He started as his father and his companions appeared a few feet away. *Damn!* How the fuck did they keep following him?

Daric's eyes blazed like liquid fire. "Do you think Deedee will give you sanctuary, when you're hiding the one thing that could destroy us all? That could mean harm to her mate and child? King Karim will burn you first."

"I'm not trying to hide!" God, this was a mess. "I need time! Just stop following me—shit!" It was then he realized how they were tracking him. Reaching into his shirt, he grabbed the medallion hanging from the chain around his neck. Every member of the Guardian Initiative task force had one on them. He and Daric enchanted it themselves so they could always track anyone who wore one and whisk them away from danger.

"Son, don't—"

But he ripped it from his neck and flung it far away. "I'm sorry, Dad," he said solemnly. "I'm so sorry."

His father's face faded away as he used one last surge of energy to transport himself to a hotel room in the Baixa district in Lisbon. It was empty, thank God, so he teetered toward the bed and collapsed in exhaustion.

———

Cross woke up with a start. How long had he been out? He wasn't even sure what time he'd arrived here. Though he didn't feel as drained as when he first arrived, his body still hadn't fully recovered, and it took him a moment to remember where he was. *Lisbon*. The Avenida Central Hotel.

Hauling his legs off the mattress, he sat on the edge of the bed and ran his hand down his face. *God, what a mess.* But hopefully he could hunker down here for a few days until he figured out what to do.

A vibration coming from his jacket pocket made his body stiffen. That's what had woken him up. Fishing his phone out, he read the preview of the first message on the screen.

Leave.

What was that about? Unlocking the phone, he scrolled through the messages.

Run.

They all came from a company called Acme Escape Artists.

Tracking you down. Stalled as long as I could. They made me do it.

That company name ... *Lizzie!* His cousin was trying to warn him.

Another message popped in.

They're in the hotel. Destroy the phone and get out NOW!

"Fuck!" He crushed the phone in his hands and then used his power to turn what was left into dust. Where to go ... where to go. He could stay on the run forever, survive in the woods or somewhere, but that wasn't a viable long-term plan. For one thing, Gunnar hadn't said if his vision had changed; if anything, the predictions he'd been having about the mage attacks only seemed to solidify his original vision. And in three years, Cross still couldn't find the solution to his problem: how to save his clan and his *mate*.

His enhanced hearing could pick up footsteps down the hallway. He had to decide now. Every single place and contact he had; his father knew about. All their clans, their allies, their family and friends. It would have to be somewhere the New York clan had no connections to.

Ransom.

The name popped into his head just as the door to his room flew open, and Jacob burst in. "Stop, Cross!"

Fuck! His brain scrambled for the location of the last place he'd seen Ransom. What was the name of that garage?

The moment's hesitation was enough for Jacob to stretch his hand forward and throw a ball of fire at him. Cross screamed in agony as the flames hit his shoulder, burning his clothes away and searing his flesh.

"No!" Daric shouted as he dashed inside. He reached out to Cross, but it was too late. His surroundings shimmered, and he disappeared from the hotel room.

His arm was still aflame, so he beat at it with his hand.

"*Argghh!*" The pain was so unbearable that it made him lose his balance, so he dropped face down on the rough asphalt. The smell of his burned flesh was magnified to his sensitive nose, making him want to pass out. *Can't give up yet.*

Lifting his head, relief sluiced through him when he saw the words Bucky's Garage painted on the side of the single story brickwork structure. He forced himself up on his feet despite the dizziness threatening to overpower him.

"Hello?" He rapped on the door. "Anyone here?"

There was a shuffling inside before the door opened. "Whaddaya want?" the old man asked, his weathered face wrinkling up as he frowned and sniffed the air. "Holy shit, sonny!" His eyes grew wide as he saw Cross's shoulder. "I'll call nine-one-one—"

"No!" He pushed past the man and hurried inside. "Call Ransom. Please."

The old man hesitated, then let out a harrumph. "Fine." He turned around and fished a phone from his pocket, then tapped on the screen and put it to his ear. "Yeah, it's me. There's someone here lookin' fer ya ... no, doesn't look like anyone I'd seen before ... tall fella. Just showed up, bleedin' all over my garage. Looks like one of them goddamn Vikings." The man's face changed. "All right." He handed Cross the phone. "He wants to talk to you."

"Ransom, it's Cross," he said.

"Damn, I thought it was one of my buddies from the slammer." The voice was gruff, not that Cross expected a warm greeting. "What do you want?"

"I'm in trouble."

"And so?"

"Yes ... and I just need to lie low for a few days. Can I crash with you?"

There was a pause. "I'm not sure that's a good idea."

"Look, I promise I won't be any trouble. I just need a place to sleep and think."

"Cross, you know—"

"You owe me." He didn't want to bring up that night, but what choice did he have? "Please."

There was a low growl followed by a grunt. "Fine. You need a ride?"

"I ..." The pain was too much, and he dropped the phone. The world swirled around him, and a wave of nausea hit him.

"Sonny!" The voice seemed far away. "Sonny! Don't—"

His vision went black, and the only thing he was aware of was the cold cement floor underneath him. What was wrong? His body should be healing by now, not getting worse.

Give it to us.

"Who said that?" he slurred. "What do you want?"

The dagger. Give us the dagger.

"You can't!"

Give us the dagger. Or your mate dies.

"No!" He sat up, grasping at the sheets around him. *Sheets?* Where was he? The smell of pine was the first thing he noticed, then the feel of a firm mattress underneath him. Grabbing his shoulder, he winced at the twinge of pain, but it wasn't as bad as before, and someone had dressed the wound in a white bandage.

"Finally up, huh?" came the low, gravelly voice.

His head turned to the sound of the voice. It was dark inside this place, and his tired eyes were having trouble focusing on the shadowy figure in the corner. A shaft of moonlight, however, shone through a window and illuminated a pair of black leather boots. "Ransom, is that you?" he rasped. Why was his throat so scratchy? "Did I pass out?"

The boots sounded heavy on the wooden floor as their wearer stepped forward, revealing his face. "You've been asleep for hours."

He looked up, his vision focusing on the man hovering above him. Gold-green hazel eyes regarded him, and there was no mistaking who it was. "Hours?"

"Yeah." Ransom knelt down to his level. "You okay, buddy? That was a nasty burn."

"Yeah I ..."

"It's healing now. Dressed it myself." When Cross tried to roll out of bed, Ransom placed a hand on his good shoulder. "Stay put, get a couple more hours—"

"No." He couldn't delay, not after that message. It was obvious who it came from. The mages. His father had told him that his old master, Stefan, was able to send him telepathic messages. Somehow the new mages had found a way to do it, and now they were blackmailing him into giving them the dagger.

He pushed Ransom aside and got up, wincing as he felt his singed flesh protest. It was definitely better than before, but it wasn't quite done. Lycan healing was a hell of a lot faster that a human's, but it wasn't instant. It would maybe take another day or two for the burn to completely heal. "I have to go."

"Go?" A dark blond brow lifted up. "After you made me risk everything by bringing you here?"

"Shit. Sorry. But"—he stretched out to full height—"I have to go back."

"Back where?"

"New York," he said. His thoughts were already focusing on where he had to go. It wasn't hard, because his thoughts always brought him back to her.

CHAPTER TWO

You can do this. It's not a big deal. The store's not far away.

Sabrina Strohen repeated the words to herself like a mantra. Taking a deep breath, she wiped off the sweat forming on her palms down her jeans and then reached for the door.

Every single time she had to leave the house, the struggle nearly overwhelmed her. *Well, that's probably why I don't leave the house.* Why bother when everything could be delivered to her loft apartment? Or she could always have her agent, Barbara, or her father bring it for her when they came around. No, there was no need to ever leave the safety of her home. And she hadn't, not for the last three years. Not since the bus accident.

But there were times when there was an emergency, and she had no choice but to leave. Like today. She was making a cup of coffee during her afternoon painting break when she realized she was out of her favorite cookies.

Damn her sweet tooth.

She had tried to ignore the craving for the sweets. Distracted herself. Told herself she didn't *really* need them. Her hips and her chunky thighs certainly didn't need extra padding. But now the need for them was screaming at her, and she couldn't even pick up a paint brush.

I'm going to get those damned cookies, even if it kills me!

The lump in her throat had grown too large to swallow. Going out wasn't going to kill her, she *knew* that. But the crippling anxiety weighed her down, as it always did when she attempted to take even one step outside.

"You can do this!" she hissed and grabbed the door. Turning the knob, she pushed her body out as if an outside force was propelling her. The loud slam seemed to portend her doom, but it was too late now. She took one step forward, and another, and another, until she got to the elevator. She hit the call button and waited; the air stuck in her lungs.

The doors opened and she let out a loud sigh. *Oh, thank goodness!* There was no one else inside. She would have taken the stairs, except it was six floors down and would only prolong her sojourn outside. Thankfully, the elevator continued to the first floor without stopping and as soon as the doors opened, she made a run for the exit, bursting through the double doors and out into the street.

The Meatpacking District in New York was a cacophony of sounds as well as smells and sights. The blare of car horns. The smell of grilled meat from a nearby food cart. The seemingly endless parade of people as a tour group crossed her path. It assaulted her senses, making her dizzy.

The doctor at the hospital said it was psychosomatic, that there was nothing wrong with her. It was all in her head, Dr. Stevens had prognosed. But she knew it wasn't and insisted that all these physical symptoms were real. Her father had been so furious that he took her out of the doctor's care and that hospital immediately. Since then, she hadn't seen him or any other doctor. But that was fine because she was fully healed from the bus accident, physically anyway.

As the wave of dizziness passed, she made a beeline for the corner store. The minimart wasn't crowded at this time of the day, so she was able to zip toward the snack aisle for her cookies. The sour-faced man at the register didn't try to make small talk, and she did her best to avoid looking into his eyes. After tapping her debit card on the machine to pay, she grabbed her stuff and scampered back to her building. Her stomach tied up in knots when she saw the people waiting for the elevator, so she did a one-eighty turn and headed for the stairs.

Six flights up later, she was finally inside her apartment. Sure, her lungs nearly gave out, but she was here, safe and sound. Her fingers played with the silver ring on her right finger, twisting it around. Though she'd had the ring for what seemed like forever, it was a nervous habit she'd developed in the past three years, as if it were some magic charm, protecting her from whatever harm her brain had cooked up since the accident.

Why couldn't she just be normal? She sank back against the door and buried her face in her hands. How come everyone else could leave their homes every day and not have a panic attack? Why were they able to go about their day interacting with other people without anxiety creeping in on them?

Minutes ticked by before she finally found the will to get up, then headed toward the kitchen. Her loft took up an entire floor of the building and had one large living area in the front that flowed into the kitchen and dining room, while the rear part was where her bedroom and studio were located. Her coffee was no longer hot, but she didn't bother to reheat it. Instead, she ripped into a box of cookies and scarfed two down before swallowing a gulp of the leftover brew.

The loud buzzing of the doorbell made her slam the cup down in surprise. It was five thirty, so it could only be one person.

"Hi, Dad," she greeted as she opened the door. "You have a key, you know, you can always come in anytime. You do own this loft, though one day you're going to let me buy it off you or at least pay you some rent."

As always, Jonathan S. Strohen looked immaculately groomed and dressed in his tailored navy suit, his white hair combed back. He smiled at his daughter, his brown eyes turning soft. "I told you, this place is yours. And I wouldn't dream of intruding on your privacy, sweetheart." He leaned down and kissed her on the cheek, his mustache tickling her. "How are you today?"

"Oh, you know." She stepped aside to let him inside. "The same."

There was a flash of sadness across her father's face, but he quickly pasted on a smile. "How's the latest work going?"

"It's going. Want to see?"

He nodded, and she led him to her spacious, light-filled studio. Several paintings were propped up on easels around the room in varying states of doneness. Usually, she worked on one painting at a time, but all of these just seemed to come out of her brain together.

"These are beautiful, sweetheart." Jonathan took his time

looking at each painting as he always did. "I don't see a theme, though."

"Um, there's no theme, really. Just stuff that came to me."

There was a painting of a bench from Central Park that was almost done, while beside it was the beginnings of a scene from one of her favorite coffee shops. Then there was one of the subway stop on Eighth Avenue, and another of the interior of her studio. Actually, there were three canvases that featured scenes from her loft, including one that she painted back when she had a lot of plants. When she came back from the hospital after the accident, she had found her loft bare, and her father said he had to get rid of most of them because they had died while she was away.

She sighed and fiddled with her ring nervously. "I don't even know if I'll show them. Barbara wasn't too enthusiastic when she saw them." Compared to her other works—usually dazzling landscapes or thought-provoking portraits—these seemed almost mundane. There was also a hint of sadness in them, like there was something lacking, but she couldn't quite put her finger on what that was.

"Well ..." He turned to her. "I'm sure they'll turn out great once you're done. And your next show will be another smashing success."

"You're supposed to say that. You're my dad," she said wryly.

He harrumphed. "I'm so proud of you, Sabrina." He placed his hands on her shoulders. "You're so talented. I bet your mother would have been so proud too ..." His voice broke off, as it usually did when talking about her mother.

Melanie Strohen died shortly after Sabrina had been born, and though she was sad that she never knew her mother, she didn't know what it was like to have her around. Jonathan, however, still grieved her loss and must have loved her because he never remarried.

"I don't know ... do you ... do you think she'd be proud of me despite me being so ... you know."

Jonathan pursed his lips. "Being what?"

"I mean ... I can't leave the house without having a complete breakdown. I can't talk to anyone. It's like something's wrong and—"

"Sweetheart, no." He gripped her shoulders harder. "There's nothing wrong with you okay? It was the accident."

Yes, that was it. The day everything changed, at least, that's what she was told. "But why can't I remember it, Dad?" Her anxiety began to rise as it always did when she tried to recall what happened. Her right hand closed into a fist, and she used her thumb to rub her ring. "I remember everything before that. But why can't I recall—"

"It's probably some kind of safety mechanism in your brain," he reasoned. "Blocking out the trauma. It was a terrible accident. All those people ..." He *tsked* and shook his head. "You must have seen some terrible things when your bus overturned. You were the only survivor."

She'd heard the story over and over again. Yet, nothing clicked in her brain. There wasn't even a glimmer of a memory in her mind of that time, only before or after. She couldn't even remember which bus it was or where she was going. It was like her life stopped and skipped a whole section. But then again, maybe he was right. She'd read books and articles about selective amnesia, and how trauma could somehow trigger memory loss, along with a host of other conditions like anxiety and depression. "I ... maybe someday ... I mean, today I managed to get out."

"Y-you did?" His eyes widened.

"Yes. I ran out of cookies, and you know I had to go and—"

"You shouldn't—I mean, sweetheart, next time just give me call, okay? I can run over and bring you whatever—"

"*Daaaaad*." She removed his hands from her shoulders. "You run a multinational corporation. I don't think your shareholders would appreciate a CEO who runs out of the office in the middle of the day to run errands."

He harrumphed. "You're my daughter and my number one priority."

She turned away from him, hoping to hide her face. "I know, Dad, I know." That was the kind of father he was. He'd never missed a recital, a school play, or a graduation while she was growing up. She enjoyed the attention, of course, being an only child and him being her only parent, though after the accident, he seemed to get even more protective. Even suffocating in some ways.

"And what's this? New project?"

She whirled around, her eyes widening in horror as her father reached for the curtain that partitioned off one corner of her studio. "Dad, no!" she cried as she practically flew across the room to get between him and the curtain. "I mean, I'm not ready to show that yet."

His brows snapped together. "Are you all right, Sabrina? You look pale."

"I ..." The blood indeed, felt like it was draining from her face. "I'm just you know ... tired."

He placed a hand over her forehead, like he did back

when she was a little girl and complained of a fever. "You don't have a temperature or anything. You need to get rest, sweetheart."

"I do, I sleep pretty soundly, though"—she couldn't help the chuckle bursting from her lips—"I think the ghost is back."

"The ghost?"

Relieved that her father had forgotten about what was behind the curtain, she linked her arm through his and led him back into the living area. "Oh, I guess I haven't told you," she said. "Well, I didn't want you to worry about your investment. If you ever do think of kicking me out, it might be hard to sell this place once your prospective buyers find out it's haunted."

Now it was father who turned pale. "Haunted?"

"Yeah ... sometimes things move in the middle of the night." They sat on the couch and she smoothed her hands across the buttery soft suede. "Like, I'll leave a cup of tea by my bedside, and the next morning, it'll be knocked over on the floor. Or sometimes I'll fall asleep here on the couch, and when I wake up, I'll have a blanket on top of me." And then there was that scent that seemed to linger ... chocolate with a hint of mint, like the smell of her favorite cookies. It happened again yesterday morning. There was a lingering scent in the air, like someone had been there next to her bed.

"I'm sure it's just you being forgetful, sweetheart." He took his phone out, and tapped on the screen. "So, what do you want for dinner? I can have my driver pick up anything you want."

"Oh." Food. Yes, that would be nice. Her ghost momentarily forgotten; she tapped her finger on her chin.

"How about Chinese? From the usual place?" She kept telling herself that one of these days she was going to start to diet, but since she never really went out or even saw anyone other than Jonathan or Barbara, there didn't seem to be any immediate need for her to lose weight.

"Egg rolls, right?"

"Yes, please."

As her father called his driver, she glanced back at her studio. The tension from her shoulders drained, but still, it had been too close for comfort. Jonathan could have pulled the curtain aside, and well, she just wasn't ready for him to see *those*. It was hard enough for her to display that first painting for an exhibition, and even then, she couldn't part with it. Barbara had called her up, told her some rich royal wanted it and was willing to pay a mind-boggling amount, but she couldn't sell it. It was too ... personal.

She mentally shook her head. No one—not Jonathan, Barbara, or anyone else—would see what was behind that curtain, not if she could help it.

———

"This was great as always, Dad," Sabrina said as she opened the front door. "Thanks."

"Of course, sweetheart." He placed a kiss on her forehead. "If you need anything—"

"I know, Dad." She brushed a stray lock of hair from his forehead. "I love you."

"Love you too." With a final wave goodbye, her father stepped into the elevator, and she shut the door, locking in the deadbolt and chain for good measure.

Dinners with her father were one of the few things she looked forward to, and while she knew he couldn't come every night, Jonathan did his best and came over at least thrice a week. It was their time to catch up, and for a few moments, Sabrina forgot that she lived the life of a shut-in.

With a deep sigh, she picked up the half-empty boxes of food and stuck them into the fridge, then put the plates and glasses in the dishwasher. She was about to head into the bedroom when she stopped, turned, and headed to her studio.

Maybe I should just start over again. Those paintings were missing something. Why did she feel the need to make them anyway? It was like a chronological depiction of how pathetic her life had become—while she used to enjoy things like going out to Central Park or Wicked Brew, now she was stuck here, in a prison that she seemingly made herself.

An odd chill crawled up her arm. It was like she wasn't alone. Rubbing her hands on her arms, she turned and walked out of the studio. Another chill blasted through her.

"W-who's there?" she said, then cursed silently. That was stupid of her, because if someone was out there, now they knew *she* knew they were there.

A shuffling sound made her start, and her heart went wild. *Someone was in here!* Without a second thought, she dashed to the bathroom and locked the door. "Oh God, oh God!" Frantically, she glanced around, wondering if there was anything she could use for a weapon. If only she'd thought to grab a knife in the kitchen or something. Flattening herself against the sink, she stared at the door, watching the light from under the small gap between the floor and the door.

Shadows crept in, blocking the light. She released the breath she was holding. "Whoever you are, you better leave! I've just called the police." Crap, she should have gotten her phone. Hopefully the intruder hadn't seen it on the kitchen counter.

The door jiggled.

"L-l-leave me alone!" she cried. "I have jewelry and cash in the drawer next to the bed. Y-y-you can have it all." Slowly, she slid to the floor and hugged her arms around her knees. "Please." A squeak escaped her mouth, and her eyes shut tight when she heard a loud crash.

"Sabrina."

That voice.

She was sure she'd never heard that voice before, so why did her heart skip a beat? Why did a strange, warm sensation pool in her stomach? Slowly, she lifted her head.

Oh.

Eyes the color of the sea stared down at her. There was something about them ... it was more than that they looked familiar. No, it was like she *knew* those eyes. And that nose, those cheekbones, and that mouth. That face! This was ...

It couldn't be!

A lightheaded feeling came over her. *No, no, no.* But how could it be? How could *he* be standing here, in the flesh?

"Sabrina. You need to come with me."

She bolted up to her feet, ignoring the sudden rush of blood to her brain. "E-e-excuse me?"

"I don't have any time to explain." He ran his hand through his golden hair—he'd shaved the sides, though. "You're in danger, and I can't let you fall into their hands."

"Danger?" she echoed. "From whom?" His mere

presence overwhelmed her in this tiny space, and she tried to move aside, but he caught her hand. Electricity shot up through her arm, like a really strong shock of static. There was a flicker of acknowledgement in his blue-green eyes. "You felt that too?"

"Sabrina—"

She yanked her hand away. "And how do you ... how did you ... how *could* you ..."

He frowned. "How could I what? Know your name?"

This was a stranger who had somehow broken into her home, but she didn't feel scared or threatened. No, instead there was a hum of excitement in the air, tinged with longing.

"Please, Sabrina." The low timbre of his voice was like a caress. "Come with me."

A sudden surge of boldness sent her heart beating like mad. "No, I won't come with you! Not until you tell me w-w-why ..."

"Why what?"

She dashed around him, running through the doorway and out to the living area. He called her name, but she didn't stop as she ran all the way to her studio. Was she doing the right thing? Well, she was going to find out.

Just as she expected, he followed her, his footsteps coming closer. She halted by the curtained partition and spun around. "Tell me why!"

"Why what?"

Grasping the curtain, she flung it aside. It was obvious from the way his eyes grew wide and his mouth hung open that he was shocked. She couldn't move, not even to look behind her. Not that she needed to. "Why ... why do I keep painting *you*?"

"Sabrina ..." His voice came out in a whispered choke.

"That's you, right?" She gestured wildly to the dozen or so paintings behind her. "That's you!" A portrait of him in Central Park, sitting on a bench. "And that one too." Standing on Fifth Avenue, hailing a cab. "And that one." It was a half-formed bust in clay, not very good because sculpting hadn't been her best subject in art school, but she'd managed to capture his bone structure. "And this one ..." The very first one she painted. He was dressed in a white linen shirt, with a wall of cliffs behind him. When his face first took shape on the canvas, she thought he looked like a Viking, so she researched fjords and came up with that background based on a photo of a remote village in Norway she had seen.

"I can explain."

"Then *do it*!" Her voice rose a few decibels, but she couldn't help herself. Her head began to throb and her vision shimmered. It was like her brain was fighting something. But what?

"If you come with me, I'll do my best."

"Come with you? Are you crazy?" She waved her hands in the air. "I don't even *know* you."

There was a flash of pain in his face, so fleeting she almost thought she imagined it. "There's no time for this." He made a grab for her, but she sidestepped him. "Sabrina!"

She sprinted out of the studio and headed toward the kitchen, then grabbed the butcher's knife out of the block. Spinning around, she held the knife in front of her. "Where are you?" Carefully, she crept into the living area. Was he still in the studio? There was no time to lose. Although her stomach turned at the thought of leaving the apartment, what choice did she have? And so, she made a mad dash for the front door. Lunging forward, she reached for the chain, but something jerked her back, like an invisible force.

"Don't even think of escaping."

It was not the blond man who spoke. No, this voice brought a cold chill to her veins, and something inside her screamed danger. "Who ... who's there?" Her body pivoted on its own, like a puppet hanging from strings. "You ..."

The bald man cracked a smile, his skin breaking like cracked porcelain. "Sabrina Strohen," he said, lifting a gnarled, ashen hand tipped with long fingernails. "You will be of good use to us." He wore a blood red robe, and three more people wearing similar robes stood behind him. "Don't worry, we won't kill you ... yet. Why would we, when you can help us hit two birds with one stone?"

"What are you talking about?" She gasped when her body refused to move. "What did you do?"

He moved closer to her. "We need you, Sabrina. There's no escape."

Oh God, what the hell was happening here? How did all these people get into her apartment without unlocking or breaking down her dead bolted and chained door?

A thunderous sound from behind the robed men made her freeze. Then, a large white blur burst out from the doorway to the studio.

"Insolent cur!" the bald man screamed, spittle spraying from his mouth. "Get him!"

"What the—" Surely she was seeing things. Did those men drug her or maybe there was a gas leak in the loft? Because she just couldn't believe that a large white wolf was standing in the middle of her living room.

One of the men swung around and lifted his hand to

throw something at the wolf, but the animal dodged to the left, then lunged forward. Its great maw opened, baring large teeth that sunk down on its would-be attacker's arm. The man let out a scream as the wolf easily flung him aside.

"Dirty dog! You—Ah!" The bald man was flung aside and hit the wall.

Whatever bonds were around her loosened unexpectedly, but it was too late to stop her body from collapsing. The floor vibrated as the sound of claws clicking on the hardwood came harder and as she looked up, she saw the giant wolf lunging toward her.

"No!" She put her hands up to her face and braced herself. The wolf's body slammed against her, and she waited for the impact of the door on her back, but instead, tumbled backwards. Furry limbs wrapped her up, as they continued tumbling on the damp, grassy ground.

Grass?

She landed on top of the wolf with a loud, "Oomph!" and that's when the smell hit her. Chocolate, with a touch of mint. *That scent ...*

Swiftly, she rolled off him and scrambled to her feet. Oh God, she must be hallucinating but it all felt real—the night breeze, the soil under her bare feet, and the fact the she was outdoors for some reason.

What the hell was going on?

CHAPTER THREE

Cross knew it wouldn't be easy convincing Sabrina to go with him, but he didn't expect things to go south as they did. Maybe he should have planned things better, but if he had taken his time, the mages would have gotten to her first. In retrospect, there really was no other choice.

She stood there, frozen, eyes wide as she watched him warily. He was still in wolf form. He hadn't intended for her to see him this way, but when he heard the mages arrive back in her loft, he knew it was the only way he could surprise and overpower them. In his dealings with the mages in the last year, he learned never to underestimate them. They always carried potions and recruited some truly powerful blessed witches and warlocks on their side. He and Daric barely made it out alive of that last mission in Russia.

"Don't kill me, please," she whispered.

The fear in her voice slashed at him, and so he made a decision. A rash one, for sure, but he didn't have much of a choice. So, he put his wolf away, tucking it deep inside him as he transformed back to his human form. Thankfully, he had done this so many times that it was automatic for him to recreate his clothes as he shifted so he wasn't buck naked in front of her once he was fully human again.

"Y-y-you ..."

"Sabrina, I can explain." Though she flinched when he used her name, she didn't run away, which was a good thing.

"I don't understand!" She threw her hands up. "What's going on? What ... who were those men, and what are you?"

Where to begin? "Those men wanted to hurt you. That's why I asked you to come with me."

"And you? You're not going to hurt me too?" she accused.

"I would never hurt you." His chest squeezed tight. "Please believe me."

"I need to get back ... wait, where are we?"

"We're in Kentucky," he said. "At a friend's place." Well, he and Ransom weren't friends per se, but it was easier to explain it that way. "You'll be safe here."

"Oh, my God! How did we get here? My dad ... he'll be worried." Her hands shook as she buried her face in them.

As her body began to shiver, he realized she was freezing. So, with a wave of his hand, he conjured a soft, cashmere blanket around her. "Better?"

"What the hell?" Her hands grasped the blanket. "How did you do that?"

"Er, magic."

"Magic? Oh, my God ..."

She began to sway, so he quickly grabbed her arms to steady her. Wrong move, because it gave him a good whiff of her intoxicating scent. *Get a grip*. The last thing she needed was him acting like a randy teenage boy while he turned her world upside down. *Again.*

"Let me try to explain it from the beginning, but first, we should get you indoors." He nodded to the cabin behind her. "Why don't we go inside and you can sit down? I can make you coffee."

"Why should I come with you?"

He could tell her that there was no way in hell he was going to let her leave now, but that would only make her even more scared. "Look, I know you're confused. But how about you ask me questions, and I'll do my best to answer them, then you can decide what to do. What have you got to lose?"

"You mean, what choice do I have?" There was that defiant spark in her eyes, that fire he knew she had inside her.

He held his hand out. "Please? I told you, I won't hurt you." *You know this. Search deep inside you, Sabrina, you know it.*

His heart seemed to stop as she contemplated his hand. Finally, she took it, and his heart beat wildly at her touch. "All right."

He led her into the cabin that Ransom had initially put him in when he was injured. Ransom would not be happy, but Cross had no other choice. There was no other place where he or Sabrina would be safe. The cabin was sparsely furnished, with only a double bed, a table, chairs, and a small kitchenette in the corner. The only other room was the bathroom. But it was clean and had all the necessities.

"Have a seat." He gestured to the table. As soon as she sat down, he conjured up a cup of coffee and a plate of her favorite cookies.

She started. "What the hell? How did you ..." Picking up a cookie, she took a sniff. "Magic, right?"

He took the seat opposite her. "Yes. Now, why don't you ask me any question?"

"Um ..." She seemed to ruminate as she took a bite of the cookie, then washed it down with a sip of coffee. "How do you know me, but I don't remember you?"

The question was so unexpected that he wasn't sure what to say. She'd been attacked by mages, seen him shift, and was teleported to another state, but that was the first thing she asks?

"No, wait! I mean, how many questions do I get? Only one? Two? Three?" Fingers drummed nervously on her chin. "I mean, it's obvious why I don't know you."

"It is?"

"Yes. The accident."

Oh. Yes. The *accident.*

"About three years ago, I was in a bus when it crashed." Her nose wrinkled. "And ... everyone died except me. But I lost my memory. I can't remember anything that happened that day at all. And before that ... well some things are fuzzy. But you ..." Her lips pursed as her violet gaze landed on him. "We must have met right before the accident, right?"

"I ..." He knew he should stop this now. Telling her the truth now would only lead to hurt. But then again, if the mages ever got to her, none of it would matter anyway. So, he took a deep breath. "If you have amnesia, then maybe you shouldn't attempt to look into your past. Maybe your brain is trying to shield you from the trauma—"

"No!" Coffee sloshed over the side of the cup as she slammed it down on the table. "Stop it! That's what everyone says but ... I need to know. And y-you promised me that you would answer my question."

He let out a sigh. "All right." One little detail won't hurt her, he supposed. "Yes, we met before your accident."

"How? When? Where?" She fired the questions rapidly. "And why haven't you visited me before?"

The inside of his cheek nearly bled as he stopped himself from denying that last statement. "Let's start from the beginning. We met at Wicked Brew."

"Oh." Her eyes lit up. "That's my favorite coffee shop. I go there whenever I paint in Central Park." Her gaze lowered and her shoulders sank. "I mean, I used to. Before ..."

"We bumped into each other," he said quickly. "And I knocked you over and spilled all your painting supplies. I felt terrible, so I offered to get you a cup of coffee ..."

Three years ago ...

"It's nice to meet you too, Sabrina." Cross focused on her face, particularly on her plump lips on the edge of the white cup as she took a sip of her caramel macchiato.

A pretty blush spread across her cheeks. "Thank you for the coffee. I know it's got sugar and I don't really need the extra calories ..." Her brows drew together. "These drinks go straight to my hips and as you can see, they don't need any more padding."

What was she talking about? "It's the least I can do after knocking your stuff over." His gaze flickered to the easel and canvas. "So, you said you're trying to be a painter? What does that mean?"

"Well ..." She lowered the cup. "I've always loved to paint, so I went to art school. I graduated from the Rhode Island School of Design two years ago and got my bachelor's in Art, then stayed there for another year, then came back last summer. I've been painting here and there, sold a couple of pieces, though that was mostly to my dad's friends." She sat up straighter. "But I had an agent come to my loft a couple of weeks ago, and she thinks she can help me sell my stuff and maybe even have a show of my own."

"Are you any good?"

Her brows snapped together, but a second later, her eyes lit up, and a smile spread on her lips. "You're teasing me."

"I was," he said. "I'm sure you're very good."

A blonde brow lifted. "Are you just saying that because you feel sorry that you knocked me over?"

Now he felt bad for questioning her talents. "I didn't mean—" He stopped short when he realized she was biting her lips to keep from smiling. "Now *you're* teasing me."

"I couldn't help it." Her laugh reminded him of tinkling bells. "But, why don't you find out for yourself? I'm headed to Central Park to paint. You can watch me."

"You're inviting me to watch you paint?"

"Mm-hmm." Her silvery hair caught shafts of sunlight as she nodded.

"Are you sure? I could be an axe murderer."

"So could I."

"Right." He wagged a finger at her. "I guess I shouldn't trust you."

She rolled her eyes at him, grabbed her bag, and opened it. "See for yourself, no axes in here. Just paint and brushes."

He peered into the canvas bag, which was filled with

multi-colored tubes, brushes, palette knives, and other painting paraphernalia. "True, but I haven't seen the bottom of the bag yet." It was so easy to tease her, and he loved watching the play of emotion on her face.

"All right ... we could have a truce then. No chopping up each other's bodies for today."

"It's a deal."

————

Sabrina's face had turned pale, so Cross stopped his story. "What's wrong?"

"I can't ... I can't believe ..." She blew out a breath. "I don't remember any of that. But how do you know all those things about me? Where I went to school and what Barbara said."

"Because we know each other."

"And I invited you to watch me paint?"

He nodded.

"Cross." The color came back to her cheeks. "That's your name."

"Yes." He swallowed hard as his stomach tightened into a knot. For the last three years, he'd been imagining her saying his name again, never knowing that this would be the moment he'd hear it from her lips.

"Cross ... were we friends?"

"You could say that."

"More than friends?" Hopeful violet eyes looked at a him.

"I ..." He stood up. "You're probably tired. Why don't you get some sleep? The cabin has everything you need." While he was telling her the story, he'd already conjured a few basics for her, like pajamas, some snacks in the fridge, and a few bathroom essentials. "I'll be back with a hot breakfast tomorrow."

Her lips parted but they quickly shut. She didn't say anything as he pivoted toward the door. His wolf growled angrily, not wanting to leave her behind, but he ignored it and reached for the door.

Leaving her was difficult, but he put one foot in front of the other, walking farther and farther away. How far would he have to be so he wouldn't be tempted to go back in there and take her in his arms and tell her the entire truth? Well, maybe Mars would be far enough.

He took deep, calming breaths, inhaling as much of the cool mountain air as he could. It managed to calm him and clear his senses of her intoxicating scent so he could think. Looking ahead, he saw the main cabin at the top of the hill. Now there was another conversation he wasn't looking forward to, but he knew it had to be done. He jogged over to the front of the cabin and knocked on the front door. "It's me," he called.

A few seconds later, the door opened. "You're back," Ransom said. There was a weariness in his gold-green eyes that Cross hadn't seen before.

"Can I come in? You busy? Or have company?" Ransom was only wearing his jeans, and his hair was mussed up. Though he had numerous tattoos all over his arms and chest, it was the wolf tattoo over his hip that stood out—the one that marked him as a Lone Wolf, a Lycan who didn't have a clan of his own.

"Ha." He took a step back and motioned for him to come

in. "Drink?" A bottle of rum and a single glass sat on top of the coffee table.

Cross shook his head. "I need to talk to you."

Ransom grabbed a leather vest from the back of an armchair and slipped it on. Stitched on the back of the vest was the head of a wolf with its jaw opened and above the image read "Savage Wolves MC."

When he turned around, Cross noticed a new patch on the front: President. "You got a promotion."

"Pop died, so, yeah."

"I'm sorry." He'd only met the older Lycan once, but he seemed like a good man and father to Ransom and his sister. "What happened?"

The other man said nothing as he plopped back down on the leather couch, grabbed the bottle and glass, then put his booted feet on top of the table. "What do you want?"

Cross wasn't sure how to say it, so he began with, "About that cabin ... I'm gonna need it for a few days."

Ransom poured some rum into the glass and knocked back the entire thing. "I figured. Did you want my bike too? And my truck? Hell, just fucking move in here and take everything."

"Yeah about that. I'll need to crash in here, too."

"The fuck?" Ransom roared as his booted feet pushed the coffee table forward, the legs scraping loudly on the floor. "What do you need my guest cabin for? Stashing some illegal shit in there?"

There was no way he would be able to hide Sabrina from Ransom, so he had to fess up. "No, a friend. She's in trouble."

"Shit." Ransom took another shot, then got to his feet. "You're risking my neck for a piece of ass?"

Cross gritted his teeth, trying not to react to the other man's taunts. His wolf, however, growled so loud he could feel it rumble in his chest. "Some people are trying to hurt her, nearly killed her tonight. I got to her in time."

There was a flicker of conflict in Ransom's eyes. "Why can't you stash her somewhere else?" he asked. "You could bring her to Timbuktu and no one'll find her."

"She's scared. And I can't just leave her alone in a strange place. What would I do if she wandered off?" That, and he couldn't be alone with her.

"And you? You wanna tell me why you showed up at Bucky's half-dead?" He pointed his chin at his shoulder.

"You wanna tell me why I found you floating in the Hudson last year?" he challenged back.

Green-gold eyes turned dark. "Fair enough."

"Look," he brushed his palm down his face, "I just need some time to figure stuff out. But that means I have to go and check on a couple of things, and in the meantime, she needs a safe place to stay. You don't have to do anything, just make sure no one gets to her. She can't leave the cabin."

"What, did you put a spell on her or something?"

His jaw hardened. "She just won't, okay? Look, I don't have anyone else I can trust. I swear, and I'll take care of her."

"I don't run a fucking B and B, so of course you take care of her," Ransom said gruffly. "All right. You can keep your girl here. But after this"—he pointed at Cross with the bottle in his hand—"we're even."

He breathed a sigh of relief. "Thank you."

Ransom kicked the table aside and marched toward the stairs. "You take the couch," he said without looking back.

"What, I don't get towels?"

"Fuck you." The boots stomped louder as he ascended the stairs. He turned the corner on the landing and disappeared, then a few seconds later, a door slammed loudly.

Weariness sank into him, replacing the adrenaline that was now seeping out of his system. He plopped down on the chair wishing he'd taken up Ransom's offer of a drink. Even a few seconds of a buzz would have been welcome right now.

Taking off his shirt, he winced as the fabric abraded his injured shoulder. The skin was still red and angry, but much better than it had been a few hours ago. With a wave of his hand, he covered it with fresh bandages and some burn salve from a recipe Signe had taught him. His brows drew together at the thought of his grandmother and all those summers he spent with her, learning how to make potions and activate them with simple spells. But thoughts of Signe always brought him back to that one particular summer and one particular lesson he could never forget. The irony was not lost on him.

Putting those thoughts aside, he concentrated on getting comfortable. Rest would help, and he could get it out here. No one would be able to track him anymore, not here. The Savage Wolves MC kept to themselves and had no alliances or allegiances; after all, no one liked associating with Lone Wolves. Most who turned Lone Wolf were outcasts or simply had no place in Lycan society. Though they were not allowed to hold territory and were required by Lycan law to register with the high council, there wasn't much oversight, and as long as they kept out of trouble and wore a tattoo to signify their status, no one bothered them much. It wasn't usual for Lone Wolves to come together; it was rare, and so was forming some kind of club. He supposed The Savage Wolves were able to skirt rules about territory because they were technically a motorcycle club and not a clan.

Leaning back on the couch, he closed his eyes. *Just a couple of hours.* Uninterrupted sleep should help him figure out what to do next.

CHAPTER FOUR

WITHOUT A WATCH OR HER PHONE, SABRINA DIDN'T know what time it was when she woke up. For just a second, she thought she'd dreamt it all. A bunch of people appeared in her loft in New York and tried to kill her, then she was rescued by a man she couldn't remember meeting who turned into a giant white wolf and could also teleport, and now they were in Kentucky. But, when she found herself inside the cabin, wearing the flannel pajamas she'd found folded on the bed, she knew it hadn't been a dream.

She lay in bed, her fingers twisting her ring as she contemplated the events of last night. Her life had changed overnight, and she had more questions than answers. But these answers wouldn't come easy, and maybe for now, she'd just have to roll with it.

Sitting up, she crawled toward the window next to the bed. The early morning sun was peeking out from behind the mountains, bathing the valley in a soft light. Her fingers itched to paint it. If only she had her painting supplies. Well, she thought, she'd have to go outside first, but the thought of stepping out of the door made her nervous.

After doing her business in the cramped bathroom, she headed toward the kitchen. Her heart slammed into her ribcage when she realized Cross was sitting at the table.

"Did you sleep all right?"

"I, uh ..." Her tongue found it difficult to move as she fully took in Cross's presence. Despite being seated, he still seemed to take up a lot of space in the cabin. Last night, she'd been so distracted by, well, all the stuff that happened, that she didn't notice how tall or large he was. He must be at least half a foot over six feet, which made her feel small. His shoulders were broad but not overly large, and tattoos peeked from under the collar of his white shirt and down his arms. And that face ... strong features, piercing eyes, firm lips which not even his beard could conceal. His hair, she realized, though kept long was shaved down the sides, unlike in her paintings. It was funny how she'd spent a year painting him and yet, she still felt like she'd been hit by a Mack truck just from staring at him.

"Sabrina?" Blue-green eyes looked at her with concern. "Did you want to eat? If you don't like any of this stuff, I can get you something else."

"Huh?" It was then she realized that the table was, indeed, laden with food—platters of eggs, a pile of toast, crispy bacon, pancakes smothered in syrup, bagels and smoked fish, coffee and tea. Everything looked freshly made too.

Heat crept up her face as she sat down. She'd been too busy ogling him to notice. No wonder he didn't answer when she asked if they were "more than friends" last night. He was an Adonis and could probably get any girl he wanted, so why would he want anything to do with her? Cross was way out of her league, and for once, she was glad she had amnesia, because that meant she'd never know if she threw herself at him and he rejected her. She wanted to cringe just thinking about it.

"Did you want—"

"No, this is great. Just great," she said, trying to sound cheerful as she spooned some eggs onto a plate and grabbed a piece of bacon. "Just great." The food was delicious, and she didn't realize how hungry she was until she gobbled down all the eggs and bacon, plus two pieces of toast, which she washed down with coffee. "Thank you."

He opened his mouth to speak but was interrupted when the cabin door opened. "Well, as I live and breathe," came the feminine voice. "I thought Ransom was pulling my leg when he said you were here."

Two people entered the cabin; the first, a gorgeous, slim redhead who gave Cross a big smile. Her flannel shirt, slim jeans, and knee-high boots clung to her curves and made Sabrina feel horribly underdressed in her loose pajamas.

Behind her was a tall man, not as tall as Cross, but much broader. He wore a black leather vest over his flannel shirt, but she could see tattoos extending from his elbows to his wrists. Though his beard was a shade darker, his dark brown hair with highlights set off his golden eyes. No wait, they were green. Or both?

Cross stiffened, then got up and turned around. "Hello, Silke. Ransom."

The redhead sauntered up to Cross and pulled him into a hug, and Sabrina felt a hot, tight ball curl in her chest. *Who was this woman, and why did she have her hands all over Cross?* Sabrina felt an urge to scratch her eyes out.

"You've finally decided we were worth a visit, huh?" she asked.

He eyed the other man. "You told her?"

"Hey." The man held his hands up. "It's her place. I can't hide nothing from her."

She turned to Sabrina, her emerald eyes going warm. "Hi there, I'm Silke Walker," she said, walking toward her and holding her hand out.

Sabrina stared at it for a moment before taking it. "I'm Sabrina."

The redhead clasped both hands over hers. "Ransom— that's my brother over there"—she tossed her head back to the man in the leather vest—"told me that you needed a place to crash because you've got some bad people after you." Her lips pulled back, and Sabrina noticed a long, thin scar that extended from the right edge of her lip all the way to the tip of her cheekbone. "Is it a husband? Boyfriend? Dad?"

"I, uh …"

Silke shook her head. "You don't have to tell me, sugar. But, please, stay as long as you need."

Sabrina was speechless, and she felt shame that she'd judged Silke too harshly. "Thank you. I don't know how long I'll be staying, but I'll try not to be too much trouble."

"Thank you, Silke," Cross said. "I appreciate it."

"No trouble at all," she said, which earned a snort from Ransom. "You're one to talk. This man saved your life—"

Cross cleared his throat. "We just need a couple of days, and then we'll be out of your hair."

"I'm sorry we don't have much in here," Silke said,

gesturing around the cabin. "It's not really meant for long stays. We would put you in one of the guest lodges or rooms, but we have other people staying there and they're at the front part of the property, closer to the highway."

"Other people?" she asked.

Silke nodded. "I run the Seven Peaks Mountain Lodge and Cabins, but don't worry, while the lodge sits on the same property as we are, they're far away enough."

"Silke owns about fifty acres of land up here," Cross explained. "And the lodge takes up about thirty. The rest is where Ransom and the MC live."

"MC?"

"Jonasson," Ransom said in a warning voice. "Just because I'm letting you stay doesn't mean you can tell everyone about our business."

"*I'm* letting her stay," Silke said, patting Sabrina's hand.

Ransom rubbed a hand down his face. "I have shit to do." Without another word, he left the cabin, the door slamming shut behind him.

"I'm sorry to be causing trouble between you two." She lowered her gaze.

"Don't let my brother's gruff exterior fool you; he's a sweetheart ... most of the time," Silke explained. "He's just ... he's had a tough year."

"You both have," Cross said. "He told me your father died. I'm sorry."

"Oh no, I didn't realize." Sabrina said. "My condolences."

Grief marred Silke's pretty face. "We weren't expecting it. And ... well, Ransom wasn't his, but Pops never treated him different, you know?"

Sabrina blinked. "Wasn't his?"

"I was a baby when his mother and Pops got together," Silke explained. "My momma died after I was born; she was the one who owned the lodge and the property."

"I never knew my mom. She died after I was born too," Sabrina said in a soft voice.

"Really?" Silke blinked and then flashed her a sad smile. "We have more in common than I thought."

"So, Ransom's your step-brother?"

"I thought that would be obvious, seeing as I'm fully human."

Sabrina looked at her with confusion. "I don't know what that means."

Silke looked up to Cross. "What's going on? Does she not know about Lycans?"

"It's a long story," he said with a sigh. "I'm sorry, Silke, for not telling you myself. I wasn't sure if you wanted to get involved in all this."

"After what you did for Ransom? Of course I want to help out." She planted her hands on her hips. "All right, I'm sure you have your reasons, but you should tell her ..." She shook her head. "I'm sorry, Sabrina, I don't mean to talk about you like you weren't here, but ..." She let out a sigh. "I have to go, but I'll come and check back on you occasionally, okay?" With a wave goodbye, she left the cabin.

"So, they're ... interesting," Sabrina said.

"Yeah." Cross sat back down across from her. "Listen, I know you have a lot of questions, still. And I promised you I would answer them if you came with me, so go ahead."

"I don't know where to begin." So far, the only thing she knew was that they knew each other before the accident, but she'd forgotten about him. How could she forget all these things? "Silke said she was fully human. That means you and Ransom aren't? Can he turn into a wolf too and do magic?"

A pulse ticked in his jaw. "Ransom can turn into a wolf, yes. He's a full Lycan, which mean both his parents were Lycan, and he can shift back and forth from human to wolf form. And no, it doesn't have anything to do with the moon, except for one exception. Silke's mother was a human, so that's why she can't shift. Usually, only two Lycans can produce a Lycan pup, but there are some exceptions." He paused. "I'm part Lycan, but also part warlock. My mom's a Lycan but my dad's a warlock, and so I'm what's called a hybrid, which is why I can do both."

A dead silence filled the air. "It's a lot to process. If I hadn't seen it with my own eyes ..." A throbbing ache began in her forehead, but she ignored it. Instead, she took another sip of coffee. "And those men who came into my apartment last night?"

He swallowed audibly. "Those men are entirely different. They're called mages, and they are my kind's sworn enemy. They want to destroy us."

"But, I'm not one of you ... why did they come after me?"

"They want ..." He paused. "They want to do something bad with you."

She gasped. "With me?" A cold chill ran through her. "What?"

"I don't know. But trust me, Sabrina." Reaching out, he took her hand in his. "I won't let them get to you."

Could she believe him? She looked him straight in the eyes. He didn't avoid her gaze nor did she feel uncomfortable. She desperately wanted to believe him. But there were so many missing pieces. "My dad," she said suddenly remembering him. "Oh, my God, he's going to worry. I need to talk to him."

"You'll put him in even bigger danger," he said. "If the mages find out he knows where you are, they might go after him. Better to keep him in the dark."

"But—"

"Think about it, Sabrina, you know I'm right. If your dad thought you were missing, he'd call the police. They'd do a search of your home and put out an APB. Your father would probably hire private detectives. When the mages who tried to kidnap you see that, then they'll know he has no idea of where you are either and will stay away from him."

Darn it, he was right. "Okay, fine. We won't tell him, but I'll have to let him know I'm okay."

His mouth thinned into a grim line. "Once the threat has passed, you can tell him yourself."

"And how long will that be?" She stood up. "And what exactly am I supposed to do? Twiddle my thumbs?"

"I'm sorry, I didn't think." He scratched his head. "I'll get you some stuff, okay? I'll be right back."

"Be right—hey!" He disappeared into thin air before she could ask anything else. She massaged her temples. Oh Lord, hopefully this headache would go away.

A sharp knock made her start. "Come in," she called.

The door swung open, and Silke strode back inside. "Hey, Sabrina, I hope you don't mind, but I figured you might not have any clothes with you. Or anything to entertain you while you're camping out here, so I brought you a few things." She held up a bag. "Cross should be able to scrounge you up some stuff too, but I see he's gone again."

"Oh, thank you." There were a few things inside,

including some sweatpants, a hoodie, and some paperback books. "You're too kind."

"Not at all," she said. "I've ... I've been where you were, you know."

"Y-y-you have?"

She nodded. "And, well, I know what it's like, wanting to escape a situation and feeling like you don't have anyone. I'm just glad I had Ransom to bail me out and ..." Her voice drifted off. "Anyway, if there's anything I can do—"

"You've done a lot already, letting me stay here."

"We owe Cross, so I'm happy to return the favor." She sat down opposite Sabrina. "He found Ransom half-dead and brought him back here to us a year ago. You know, I don't really know much about him. He came back every couple of days to make sure Ransom was recovering, but we haven't seen him since."

"So, he hasn't been back at all?"

"No, why would he?" Silke shrugged. "Anyway, I never thought he'd visit us. Not everyone wants to associate with Lone Wolves."

The throbbing in her temple intensified. "Lone Wolves?"

"I—"

"Sabrina, I'm back—oh." Cross had materialized again, this time, just by the door. "Silke, I didn't think you'd be back so soon."

The redhead got up. "I only thought to bring Sabrina some clothes and a couple of books to keep her occupied. Though I suppose that's what you brought along?" she asked, staring at the large bag in his hands.

"Yeah."

"Well, I'll be off." She patted Cross on the arm. "Don't be a stranger, okay?"

"Sure, Silke."

"I like her," Sabrina found herself admitting once Silke was gone. Then she blinked.

"What's wrong?" He crossed the room in a few strides. "Sabrina?"

"I just ..." How could she explain it to him? "Since the accident, I've had this condition, you see. I get anxiety every time I have to leave the house and meet new people. My chest tightens, and my palms get sweaty just at the thought of having to cross from the front door or meeting a neighbor in my elevator. I can count the number of times I've left the house in the last year on one hand, and I haven't interacted with anyone except for Dad or Barbara. And yet ..." Her head pulsed and throbbed again. "In the last twelve hours, I've not only left my house, but now I'm in another state and I've met three—er, two new people."

"How are you feeling?"

"That's just it ... I don't feel nervous or anxious at all." It really was puzzling. "I mean, I do have a headache right now, but I didn't turn into a nervous wreck meeting Ransom or Silke."

A strange expression flickered briefly on his face. "I can get you some pain killers for your headache."

"No, it's fine." She waved her hand at him. "But, what did you bring me?"

With a wave of his hand, he cleared the table, then placed the large canvas bag on top. "Since you don't have anything else to do, I thought I'd get you some supplies."

"Supplies?" She opened the bag and let out a small cry.

"Oh, my God!" Reaching in, she pulled out some tubes of paint. "These are my brand too!" Of course he knew what brand she used. She rooted in the bag to take out brushes, a palette knife, linseed oil, paint thinner, and a few other essentials. "Cross, I don't know what to say. Thank you." She clutched the supplies to her chest.

"The easel's outside." He jerked his thumb toward the door. "And I'll get you anything else you need."

"Oh, this is really ..." He was standing so close to her, she could smell his delicious, chocolatey smell. How could someone smell exactly like her favorite cookie, anyway?

"One more thing." Cross reached into the bag and took out a small electronic device and a speaker. "I know you like to listen to music when you're in your studio, so I got you this."

"That—wait. How did you know I like to listen to music?" She took the offered music player and pressed the play button.

A flush crept across his cheeks. "You ... you invited me to watch you paint in your studio. After that day in the park."

"I did?"

He nodded. "When you finished painting in the park, you gave me your number. I messaged you a few days later and then you invited me to your place. You were playing cello music. Said it's the only thing you could listen to while you painted."

Now *she* felt heat creeping into her cheeks. No one had ever watched her paint, except when she was studying. It had felt oddly intimate. A lightheaded feeling passed over her. "I can't believe ..." She broke off as music began to play from the speakers. Familiar music. "*Le Cygne,*" she breathed.

"The Swan," he added.

"Well, it's about a swan dying," she said wryly. "The Greeks and Romans thought the swan was the most beautiful creature on earth. It's mostly silent but—"

"When the swan is about die, it supposedly sings the most beautiful song," he completed, as those stormy blue-green eyes looked at her, seemingly seeing right into her soul. "You thought it was wonderful. And I must have looked at you in horror, but you smiled and told me, 'Everyone dies, Cross. But isn't it lovely that in the end, that swan made beautiful art after being silent her entire life?'"

"How ..." But nothing else came out of her mouth as she stared at him, listening to the cello swell in the final bars of the song before concluding and fading out. God, how could he possibly know all that, unless ...

A new song began to play on the speakers. She stood up as she recognized the arpeggiating G major chords. "That's —" She stopped as her head throbbed. But she couldn't move, couldn't breathe. Her vision blurred. Cross was saying something—calling her name, maybe—but he, along with the rest of the world, faded away.

———

Three years ago ...

"Cello music is all you ever listen to while you paint?" Cross asked.

"Yes," she said. "I don't know ... something about the strings ... it's so soothing and relaxing."

He glanced down at her music player. "Hopefully you've got other songs that doesn't involve animals dying?"

She chuckled. "No more swan songs, I promise."

"I'll let you get back to your work, then." He strode over to the windows. "What?" Cross asked.

"Mm-hmm?" She was sitting down at her stool, facing her current work in progress, but for some reason, she couldn't keep her mind on the painting, not when her gaze kept going to Cross. The way the sunlight was playing off his golden hair was distracting, among other things.

"Why are you looking at me?"

"What? Nothing." She ducked behind the canvas, hoping he wouldn't see her blush. What had possessed her to invite him here? While she really did enjoy his company at the park while she painted, she would never in a million years have thought she'd have the courage to ask him over to her studio to watch her paint. It had felt oddly intimate.

But that day at the park, there was just something about him ... something compelling that she couldn't forget. And it wasn't just that he was handsome, either. She'd been so giddy when he messaged her, and she quickly invited him over.

"I like your plants," Cross murmured as he touched a large monstera plant she had in the corner of her studio by her desk. "I noticed you had a lot, especially in your living room."

"Yeah, my mom loved plants," she said. "Orchids especially. They're difficult to keep alive, but I love caring for them. It kind of makes me feel like ... well ..."

"What?"

She blew a breath to push away a lock of hair that had

fallen on her forehead. "It kinda feels like she's here with me, you know?"

"I think I understand." He remained quiet, but looked out the window.

After a few seconds of silence from him, she went back to her painting. As she always did, she was lost in her own world while she painted. However, she didn't ignore him completely. His presence was something she couldn't ignore, and she could feel it the entire time he was there. It was not demanding, but more like a steady pulse in the background.

Finally, she was satisfied with the progress for today. When she glanced at her clock, she realized that hours had passed since he arrived. Her music playlist had cycled back and it was now playing the second song on her list—the prelude from Bach's Cello Suite No. 1 in G major. It was another favorite piece. She loved how it started with those quick arpeggios with the open G note grounding the entire section. "You must be so bored. You've been standing there for hours."

"Not at all," he said quickly, then began to walk towards her. "I just hope I'm not distracting you."

"Well, you kinda are," she said.

"Me? Distracting?" His brows drew together. "Why?"

"Oh Lord," she muttered under her breath. The way he seemed so unconscious of his attractiveness was cute. "Has anyone ever told you, you look like a Viking?"

"It makes sense. My father was from a small village in Norway."

She put her paint brush down and stood up. "Really?"

He nodded. "Yes. He was born near some fjords, actually.

But he ... moved away when he was small and went to live ... elsewhere."

As the cello piece began to shift to the dominant D chord, her finger tapped on her chin. "Hmmm ... I can definitely see you as a Viking from old times. Actually, I was thinking I could paint you by the fjords."

"Oh?" A blond brow shot up. "Would you paint me as a warrior, then?"

She thought for a moment, tracing her gaze down from his face all the way to his feet and back up again. My, he was so tall. And how did he come to stand so close to her? "No, I don't think so. I could see you as ... a farmer maybe?"

"A farmer?"

"Yes. A warrior, no." The cello's strings deepened even further, getting lower and her lips twisted in distaste. "I couldn't imagine you carrying an axe and pillaging villages and ... you know, the other stuff that Vikings supposedly did." No, definitely not. Cross seemed so gentle and kind.

"I suppose not." He stood next to her, looking at the canvas. "You really are talented. This landscape ... it seems to come alive. How is it that you can capture the sunset so well? It's like I'm looking at the sky, and not at a canvas and paint."

"I ... thank you." Those ocean-colored eyes held her gaze, and she couldn't turn away.

"Sabrina ..." He reached over to tuck a stray strand of hair behind her ear. Air caught in her throat as she waited for him to pull his hand back, but he didn't. Instead his fingers dug into her nape and his thumb touched her cheek. Her heartbeat swung back and forth, following the rhythm of the bariolage passage in the latter part of the cello suite prelude.

Her knees weakened as he leaned down and touched his lips to hers in a soft kiss.

He pulled back, his mouth barely hovering over hers. A breath escaped her, and he swooped in again. This time, his other hand came up to caress her jaw. Both hands cupped the sides of her face preventing her from moving; not that she wanted to. Oh, no, it felt like she'd been waiting for this moment forever, and it was oh so worth it. His mouth moved over hers in a gentle caress, teasing and coaxing her to open for him. A thrill of desire shot through her when his tongue licked against the seam of her mouth ...

"Sabrina! Sabrina!"

Strong hands gripped her arms and she felt herself being shaken gently.

She sucked in a breath. "Oh." After a few blinks, her vision came back into focus. The continuing notes of the prelude hummed through the speaker as the cello went up the chromatic scale, returning to the G major chord and finally resolved.

"What's wrong? What happened?" Cross asked, concern marring his face.

"I remember," she croaked. "I don't know how ..." She braced herself on the table with her sweaty palms.

"Remember what?"

"Painting in my studio ..." She took another deep breath, taking in as much air as she could. "You ... that first day ... we ..." Her fingers touched her lips. She could still remember the way he tasted. It was like her lips were still swollen. Oh, it had felt so real. Maybe because it was real and it did happen. Slowly, she looked up at him. "We kissed. That day."

An inscrutable look flashed across his face. "Sabrina ..."

"You didn't answer me when I asked if we were more than friends. I thought ..." A heat coursed through her body as more memories flashed through her mind. His large, warm hands on her skin. His breath on her neck. His tongue tracing a path between her breasts...

A dizzy wave passed over her. "Oh God ..." She sank on the chair and buried her face in her hands, shutting her eyes tight.

"Sabrina, I'm sorry ..." he choked. "I'm just ...."

Focus on breathing. Her left hand immediately went to her ring, twisting it around as she focused on the smoothness of the silver under her fingertips. Slowly, the nausea and dizziness faded away. Her body still felt hot, but at least she didn't feel like fainting anymore.

A few more seconds passed before she lifted her head. Of course he was gone. "Coward," she muttered. But why did he leave? And why was he so reluctant to tell her about that kiss?

She massaged her temples with her fingers. The headache had faded, but it was still there. The memory had been so clear in her head, like she had just lived through it again, that it couldn't have been her imagination. Did he not want to kiss her? It couldn't have been—he was the one who kissed her first. Maybe they broke up before the accident and he didn't want to tell her?

Confusion, sadness, and anger swirled in her brain like a whirlpool, threatening to overwhelm her. She crossed over to the bed and lay down, hoping her mind and body would calm down

CHAPTER FIVE

HER MEMORIES WERE COMING BACK.

Cross didn't even know that was possible. They weren't supposed to come back. But somehow, it was happening. He saw that look on her face—the sadness, surprise, shock, and confusion. That musical score always brought him back to that first kiss, but he never imagined that after all that happened, it would do the same for her. Was there a way to stop it? And more important: did he *want* to stop it?

Hope soared in his chest, but he quickly squashed it. Of course he didn't want her to remember. They didn't work this hard only for things to come crashing down again. His inner wolf, on the other hand, whined in displeasure.

"Jesus Christ, you gotta warn me if you're going to just show up like that."

He looked up from where he sat on the leather couch in the main cabin. Ransom was on the landing, staring down at him, his face drawn into a scowl.

"Sorry. Just needed to clear my head." He didn't really think about where to go, so he teleported himself back to

Ransom's. His first priority was getting out of that cabin when she started asking questions he couldn't answer.

Ransom trudged down the stairs. "I thought that's why you came here in the first place, to clear your head."

"Yeah, well ..."

"She's got your mind all twisted up." It was a statement, not a question. "Women. They're all the same."

He raised a brow. "You sound like you're talking from experience. Didn't see you as the commitment type." Actually, he didn't really know anything about Ransom's love or sex life, but from what he'd seen, the prickly Lone Wolf tended to keep everyone at arm's length, even his own sister.

Ransom grunted. "Women are good enough for a short while, but you can't let them mess with your brain."

"I'm sorry if Sabrina's made things difficult between you and Silke."

He plopped down on the couch next to him. "Silke always has to have her nose in someone's business. She ain't happy until she knows everything. Besides, this is her place. She'd have torn me a new one if I kept your girl from her. She's always helpin' out bleeding heart cases. Broken people have always been her thing."

"Sabrina's not—" He shook his head. Ransom probably didn't care, one way or another. "I'm glad Silke's okay with this. I'll owe her too."

There was a hard set to his jaw. "Just keep your girl safe, you know that's all Silke would want in return."

Cross stood up. "Well, thank you to you both all the same. If you don't mind just keeping an eye out, I need to head out for a while."

"Where're you going?"

"To see an old acquaintance." With a nod to Ransom, he closed his eyes and thought of where he needed to go. *Back to New York.*

Unsure where best to show up, he staked out the entrance of 414 Johnson Street in the financial district of Manhattan. He waited across the street for the rest of the day until he saw his target exit through the glass doors of the shiny new modern building that housed the headquarters of Strohen Industries. The target walked toward the limo where the driver was already holding the door open. As soon as he entered and the limo was on the move, Cross followed it, grateful for his Lycan speed and the slow crawl of rush hour traffic.

A few blocks later, when the vehicle stopped at a traffic light, he made his move. He rushed toward the limo, peered through the window and checked the interior, then transported himself into the empty space next to the lone passenger.

"What in the—" Jonathan S. Strohen's eyes widened, and he clutched his chest in surprise. "*You.*"

"Yes, Jonathan," he said. "It's me."

"What the hell are you doing here?" Jonathan glanced around, as if checking to see if anyone was watching. "I thought we agreed—"

"I know what we agreed to," Cross said, cutting him off. "But Sabrina's in danger. They came for her last night."

"Goddammit!" He fished for his phone. "I need to check on—"

"Don't worry, I've taken care of it. Taken care of *them.*"

Jonathan lowered his hands. "You have? How?"

"I scared them away and then took Sabrina with me."

Color rushed to his face. "What the hell do you mean *took Sabrina with you?*" he blustered. "Where have you taken her, you bastard?"

"She's safe."

"Where?"

Cross leaned back. "If you don't know, then it's safer for her. You *know* that."

The older man grumbled. "You're right. But why come see me after all this time?"

"I needed to know if you knew anything about why they came to get her."

Jonathan's face turned redder. "Arrogant asshole. Why would I let anyone harm my own daughter? I've spent my entire life protecting her from them."

Cross leaned back and waited for him to calm down. Jonathan Strohen was a man of reason, after all.

Finally, Jonathan spoke. "So, what do you want me to do? Pretend I don't know she's gone?"

"That would bring down more suspicion on you. You don't have to do anything, except go about your usual routine." Cross produced a small vial from his pocket. "And forget I came to see you."

Jonathan's lips pursed together, but took the vial from Cross's outstretched hand anyway. "I'm supposed to have dinner with her tomorrow. Should I stick to that or visit her sooner?"

"No, tomorrow works," he said.

"Fine." He uncorked the glass vial. "You sure you know what you're doing?"

He wasn't, but it didn't matter. The only thing that mattered was that Sabrina stayed alive. That was one thing he and Sabrina's father could agree on, at least. Besides, after he drank that potion, Jonathan would forget this conversation ever happened.

———

Three years ago ...

Sabrina pulled away from the kiss abruptly. "I ..."

"I'm sorry." He stepped back and ran his hands through his hair. "I shouldn't have ... I didn't mean to ..." On the other hand, his wolf thought kissing her was a step in the right direction. *No, I shouldn't have done that. Gunnar—*

"You didn't mean it?" she asked breathlessly.

"I did," he said quickly when he saw the crestfallen look on her face. "I mean, I wanted to kiss you." He had wanted to do it the first moment he saw her.

Her cheeks bloomed with a pretty blush. "Me too. I mean, I didn't think someone like you would ever ... you know, want to kiss someone like me."

"What are you talking about?" He took her hands into his and kissed each palm, making her shiver. "You're beautiful."

"But you're *perfect*," she said with a little laugh. "You belong on an underwear ad in Times Square. While I'm—" She glanced down at her body with a woeful expression.

His brows snapped together. His wolf didn't like the self-deprecating tone of her voice either. "Stop talking like that, Sabrina." Perhaps by society's standards she didn't have the "ideal" waif-like model's body, but he loved that she was all curves and bumps. Society's standards could go to hell for all he cared. "You're lovely, and you take my breath away." To show her what he meant, he pulled her into his arms and pressed a kiss to her forehead.

"This is crazy," she whispered. "We've only just met, but I feel like ... this feels right."

His chest tightened at her words, and his wolf agreed with her wholeheartedly. He inhaled her scent, and in this moment, he forgot about everything else—Gunnar's predictions, the ring on her finger, the fate of the world. There was only them and now, in this space.

"I don't want to rush things," she said. "Can we please slow down?"

Reluctantly, he released her. "Do you want to ... get to know each other?"

She nodded. "I do. How about we go out to dinner first?"

"Like a date?"

"Mm-hmm."

He'd take her out on a thousand dates if that's what she wanted. Anywhere in the world. "All right. Will you go out with me, Sabrina?"

She chuckled. "I would like that."

And so, they did go out, three times over the next week. On their first date, they had breakfast at Wicked Brew. He had to leave right after, but he walked her back to the subway station on Eighth Avenue. A few days later, they had a late lunch at a cafe not far from her loft. Though the meal had ended, it started to rain and she made some excuse about not having an umbrella so she couldn't leave and they decided to stay. They spent the entire afternoon just talking and teasing each other. It had pained him to leave her after that wonderful rainy afternoon, but before saying goodbye, they made plans for their next date.

Finally, they had their third date tonight, and Cross took her to dinner to a Peruvian restaurant on the Lower East Side. Since their first kiss, he hadn't tried to get closer to her because he didn't want to rush her. Tonight, though, he could definitely read the signals—from the way she arched her body toward him when he talked and the small touches she gave him. After dinner, he offered to share a cab with her. Though he didn't live anywhere near her place, he wanted to make sure she got home okay.

"Do you want to come in?" Sabrina asked shyly as they stood outside her building. "Maybe, have some coffee? Or a drink?"

"Sure."

He followed her inside the darkened loft apartment, anticipation humming in his veins. It was like he'd been waiting for this moment ever since that first kiss. His wolf, too, had grown impatient, wanting him to be with her all the time.

He was on tenterhooks, wondering when it would happen, and even plotting the different ways he would coax her into a kiss again. Tease her with a few touches here and there? Or maybe just push her up against the wall?

As he closed the door behind him, she said, "Did you really want that drink?"

"No. Not really."

Her mouth parted in a small sigh. "Good." She pushed him back against the door. "Because I've been waiting all night, and I'm not sure I have the patience to wait until you've finished your drink."

A chuckle escaped his lips as he bent his head down. "I've been thinking about this for forever." He captured her mouth, and she sank right into the kiss.

She moaned as her hands slid up his chest, fingers exploring his muscles. Her scent intensified, as did her arousal, and he deepened the kiss. His fingers thrust into her hair, digging into the soft locks, and pulled gently so her head bent back and her mouth opened. That taste ... it would be imprinted in his mind until he died. Sweet, with a touch of spicy desire. She wanted him, and despite the lingering thoughts of the future ahead, he was certain that them ending up in bed together would be an inevitability. His inner wolf let out a low, hungry howl, urging him to make her theirs.

Her fingers shook as she unbuttoned his shirt, and a gasp escaped his mouth when her lips moved to kiss his jaw and then his neck. With a rough growl, he moved his hands under her knees and hoisted her up. She let out a surprised laugh and planted a kiss on his cheek as he walked them back to the couch.

"My bed's over—"

"I know," he said, nipping at her lips. "Too far." He had to have her *now*. Oh, he'd have her in bed too, and every room and surface of this place. But his priority was to take her, mark her as his. If he didn't smell her need for him, he would have taken it much slower.

He lay her down on the couch, shucking off his shirt while she unbuttoned the front of her blouse. "God, you're gorgeous." His hands immediately cupped her generous breasts, covered only in a red lace and silk bra. The nipples were already poking through the fabric, and so he bent his head to suck one into his mouth through the silk.

"Cross!" Her hands dug into his shoulders and her body arched forward.

His tongue teased her nipple, while his hand found its twin. Fingers dipped into the cup and rolled the bud, torturing it with his attention. Her hips thrust up at him, and her arousal was like a thick cloud, driving his desire and making his cock strain painfully against his jeans.

With a quick motion, he pulled down her bra to display her naked breasts and puffy pink nipples. Pushing her down on the couch, he crawled over her, letting the bulge under his jeans brush against her in a torturous motion. When he looked down at her, her arms went up to cover her naked torso, but he pulled them away and pinned her wrists down on the couch with a soft growl. Why she was so self-conscious of her body, he didn't know; she was all deep dips and gently rounded curves and smooth skin—a magnificent package in one woman—the only woman, he would ever want from now on. He dipped his head, letting his tongue trace a path between her breasts, and grazing lower—

A loud buzzer sound made them both stop. Looking up at her, he saw her expression freeze, her mouth parted. "I should ..." She sat up on her elbows.

He muttered under his breath, but got up from the couch and onto his feet. As she frantically pulled her bra up and scrambled for her blouse, he put his shirt on and hastily buttoned it up. With a deep, calming breath, he tucked his shirt in as he managed to calm down his raging cock. "Are you expecting anyone?" he asked.

She worried at her lip as she smoothed her hair back. "Um, my dad sometimes comes for a visit."

"Your dad?"

Her fingers brushed away at some lint on her top. "Yeah. We, uh, only have each other, see, so we're close, and he ... kinda owns this place."

He glanced around. "Do you want me to ... to leave? Or maybe wait in the bedroom?"

She laughed as she strode toward the door. "What? No! We're not teenagers. We don't have to hide." Her steps faltered. "I mean ... if you don't want him to see you—"

"No!" he said a little too quickly. "It's fine. I mean, you're right. We're adults." While he wasn't ready to meet Sabrina's father, there was no avoiding it now.

Her face brightened. "That's—" She startled when the buzzing started again, this time more insistent. "My dad's the best, you'll see."

Somehow, he doubted Sabrina's father would be happy to find her alone at night with a man in her apartment, but as she said, they were both consenting adults.

"Dad!" Sabrina greeted brightly as she opened the door. "I wasn't expecting you."

"I called to let you know I was dropping by, but you weren't answering, sweetheart." The white-haired man who entered the apartment was impeccably dressed in a tailored black tuxedo. "I just came from the Masterson gala—oh." Brown eyes narrowed when they landed on Cross. "You're not alone."

Cross tamped down his wolf's displeasure at the presence of another male near their Sabrina.

"Uh, Dad, this is Cross Jonasson," she introduced quickly, before he could ponder on his wolf's possessiveness. "Cross, this is my father, Jonathan Strohen."

"Good evening, sir." He tried to make his tone as deferential as possible, if only for Sabrina's sake.

A white brow quirked up as he glanced at Sabrina. "Cross, is it? Are you my daughter's friend?"

"Uh—"

"*Daaad.*" She rolled her eyes, but the corner of her mouth quirked up. "Cross and I are, uh, dating." A blush spread over her cheeks as she looked up at him shyly.

There was a fierce pride that swelled in him at the way she didn't back down or try to hide who he was, even from her father. He smiled back at her and placed his hand on her lower back.

"Oh, really, now? And how come this is the first time I've heard about it?"

"We've only had a few dates, sir," Cross explained.

"And now?"

"Dad!"

Cross cleared his throat. "I would like to keep seeing your daughter. If she would like to see more of me," he said, with an emphasis on the *she* part.

"Of course I would," she added.

Jonathan harrumphed. "In that case, you wouldn't mind if I got to know you better?"

Before Sabrina could protest, he answered, "Not at all, sir." His fingers gently pressed on her back.

"Good. Let's all have dinner tomorrow, shall we? My club, say, around seven-thirty? Sabrina will know where it is."

"I look forward to it."

"Excellent. It's getting late. Why don't you see me downstairs, Cross? I could also drop you off at your home, if you like."

Sabrina sent a mortified look to her father. "That's not—"

"Of course, sir. You're right, it is rather late. But the ride won't be necessary."

"I'll wait outside the door while you say goodbye." Jonathan kissed his daughter's cheek and then walked out the door.

"I'm sorry about that," Sabrina said in a low whisper. "He's protective of me. My mom died when I was born, so it's only been him and me."

"I understand." The hand at the small of her back gently pushed her to him. "I'll see you tomorrow."

A sigh—was it of disappointment?—escaped her mouth as he pressed his lips to her temple. "I'll see you tomorrow, Cross."

He wanted to kiss her again, but he restrained himself. Because if he got another taste of her mouth, he wasn't sure he would be able to leave. Closing the door behind him, he turned to Jonathan, who was waiting by the elevators, arms crossed over his chest.

"I didn't think you'd leave with me."

Cross couldn't quite tell if the man admired him or thought him a fool. "I have an early day tomorrow; I should be headed home too."

"And where is home?"

From the cut of his clothes to the way his patrician nose looked down on him, Cross knew Strohen was one of those upper crust types who judged other people based on their zip code. "Not far." A ding told him that the elevator car had arrived and sure enough, the door opened. "After you."

The ride down with Sabrina's father was fast, and thankfully, silent.

"Are you sure I can't drop you off?"

"I'll be fine, sir."

"Call me Jonathan." They strode toward the waiting limo, where the driver was already waiting to open the door. He slipped inside and then turned back to him. "I'll see you tomorrow night, Cross."

"I'll see you then, Jonathan."

As the limo drove away, Cross contemplated Jonathan Strohen. He seemed to be an important and wealthy man, but also, a doting father. But there was something about him ... he just couldn't figure it out.

His wolf, too, eyed the man suspiciously, which was strange in itself. "There's nothing to worry about," he told it. "He's her father." The man was just being protective of his only child. Nothing more to it.

CHAPTER SIX

When Sabrina woke up the next day, she was surprised that the table was once again laden with fresh food, and she had a pile of new clothes at the foot of her bed. Of course, there was no sign of Cross, but even if he didn't leave the food or clothing, she would have known that he'd been there by the lingering scent of chocolate and mint in the air.

Hauling herself out of bed, she immediately went to the table. Her stomach growled the moment the aroma of fresh bread, pancakes, eggs, and coffee hit her nose. Though she was still furious at the man who had brought it, she wasn't about to cut off her nose to spite her face, especially when there was coffee. As she nibbled on a piece of toast, she wondered what she was supposed to do today. Most of yesterday was spent sketching and painting in the cabin. Well, rage painting anyway. She glanced at the canvas sitting in the corner furtively. Perhaps she had taken her frustration and anger out by painting, since the target of those feelings wasn't around. The painting was supposed to depict a serene river on a moonlit night, but it had turned darker. Splashes of black paint that were supposed to be shadows looked like frightening monsters lurking in the corner. Even the river looked ominous, like a fierce creature was about to rise out of its depths.

With a long sigh, she put it out of her mind and turned back to the food. However, that kiss played in her head over and over again, like a scene in a movie. It was so clear; she knew it couldn't have been a dream. Who the hell was Cross, and what was he to her? Why weren't they friends—or more than friends—anymore? Did he break up with her? Or did she break up with him?

A guilty feeling crawled into her chest. If she wasn't so confused, she'd laugh. Break up with him? It seemed impossible. He was gorgeous and not an asshole, so that already put him miles above the other guys she'd dated back in art school. If anything, she was still reeling over the fact that he would even give her a second glance. It wasn't that she didn't think herself pretty. No, she had an appeal, but she'd never attracted the jock types like Cross.

All this was making her even more confused, so she put it aside for now and ate what she could of the massive feast on the table. As she painted yesterday, she had worked on the leftovers most of the day since no one had come by to give her lunch or dinner. She guessed it would be more leftovers today too.

She grabbed the towel hanging from one of the bed posts and headed to the bathroom. A shower should help her clear her head. She stripped off her pajamas and stepped into the small, but usable stall. Maybe she'd even paint something—

She let out a screech when an unexpected blast of cold water hit her naked body. "Holy mother of—" She nearly slipped as she tumbled out of the shower. Grasping the door, she managed to regain her balance, though the icy water was still spraying at her, making her skin prickle. She reached into the stall to shut off the shower, but somehow, the handle came off in her hand.

"Damn it!" She slammed the stall door shut and scrambled out into the room. *What to do, what to do,* she thought frantically as she hopped into the fresh clothes at the foot of the bed. Was she supposed to cut off the water supply? Back in her loft, she hadn't needed to perform any kind of home repair; her dad had always taken care of that. But now, she had to figure out what to do before the entire cabin flooded.

A loud crash from the bathroom made her start, and without thinking—or even stopping to put on or search for shoes—she ran out of the cabin.

"Help!" she cried. "Anyone here?" A quick scan of the area revealed no other people or sign of civilization around her. Silke had said there was a resort of some sort on the land, but that was near the front part of the property and took up about thirty acres. How big and how far did that cover? She wasn't sure, but if she didn't want that cabin ruined, she needed to find someone fast.

And so, she ran in one direction, going up a gentle hill until finally she saw a large structure farther up. It was done in the same style as the cabin she was staying in, but was much larger and had two stories. Hopefully, that was either

Silke's or Ransom's cabin. She dashed toward it, and by the time she was climbing up the porch steps, her lungs and throat were burning like she'd swallowed fire. The last of the burst of energy she had was spent on knocking on the door furiously.

After a few seconds, the door opened. "What the—who're you?"

Unfortunately, the person who answered was neither Silke nor Ransom. *Talk about bad luck.* Though she thought this man might be a guest, he didn't look like a typical vacationer, not with his closely-shaved head, dark eyes, and large build. The hand that held the door open had a tattoo of a wolf's head, and he looked more like a biker, as he wore a leather vest over his white shirt. A patch on the chest said Vice President.

"Hardy, what's going on? Who—you?" The man stepped aside as Ransom's large frame filled the doorway. "What are you doin' here?"

She didn't know if she felt relief or fear at Ransom's chilly reception. "Uh, hi. I'm sorry, I didn't know who—"

"Cross said you wouldn't leave the cabin."

Her nostrils flared. "I didn't know I was a prisoner here."

"We don't keep prisoners, and that's not what I meant," Ransom groused. "Cross just said you—" His mouth closed shut.

Alarm bells rang in her head. "Cross said *what*?"

"Never mind. Whaddaya want?" he said, crossing his arms over his chest in a move that was probably supposed to intimated her.

Frankly, it worked, but she didn't have time to feel scared.

"The shower in the cabin. It broke. And now the water won't stop."

"The shower broke? Why the hell didn't you turn off the main valve?"

"Well, I'm sorry, no one gave me a freakin' tour before leaving me alone for a whole day!" Her hands flew to her mouth when she realized what she had said and how rude it was.

Hardy laughed which earned him a glare from Ransom. "Fine," he said. "Let's go turn that valve off."

"The thingy ... uh, the handle broke, and there's no hot water."

Ransom's scowl deepened, then he turned his head behind him. "Proby, get your tool box."

Her gaze flickered into the cabin, and she realized there were a few more people inside—about five or six men, all staring at her. God, she must look a sight, with her hair in tangles, wearing only a T-shirt and jeans with no shoes.

"Let's go, sweetheart," Hardy said, placing a hand on her elbow and edging her away from the door.

"Buncha degenerates," Ransom muttered under his breath. "You think they ain't never seen a girl before."

Hardy laughed. "Well, it's your fault for—"

Ransom sent him another withering look. "C'mon, let's get to that valve before my guest cabin turns into Lake Michigan."

The three of them hurried back to the cabin, and Hardy headed to the rear part where the main valve was located while Ransom and Sabrina went inside. By the time they got to the bathroom, the shower wasn't spewing water anymore. She let out a sigh of relief. Thank goodness it wasn't as bad as she'd thought. Although the bathroom had flooded, the water hadn't reached the main living area.

"I'll clean it up," she said, "if you just give me a bucket and a mop."

A figure appeared in the doorway, this time, a young man with a mop of curly red hair. He looked to be in his early twenties, though his baby face and freckles made his face seem much younger. "I got my tools, Prez."

Ransom jerked his thumb behind him. "In there, Proby."

He flashed Sabrina a brief smile before scurrying into the bathroom.

Ransom rubbed his chin. "Now, let's—what the hell are the rest of you doing here?" he shouted all of a sudden.

She followed his gaze toward the front door. Four faces peeked into the cabin, though they scattered away. Seconds later, one of them walked in—an older man with salt-and-pepper hair and a friendly smile.

"Oh, hey there, Ransom," he greeted with a wave of his hand. "I didn't know you had a guest. Hello, young lady," he held his hand out to Sabrina. "How're you doing? Name's Bo."

Though the man was tall and wide—which seemed to be the norm around here—his affable expression made her feel at ease. "I'm Sabrina." She shook his hand.

Bo's handshake was firm, but not intimidating. "I hope you don't mind. Me and the boys were curious, and all." He shot Ransom an inscrutable look.

Ransom rubbed a hand down his face. "It's not what it looks like."

Three more men filed in, and Sabrina realized they were all wearing similar leather vests as Ransom, Hardy, and Bo. From what she'd glanced earlier, on the back was a picture of a wolf and the words Savage Wolves MC above it.

"Well, lookie here," one of them said as he stepped closer to Sabrina. He had a wide smile on his face, and his blue eyes sparkled. "Ransom didn't tell us he had a guest."

"I thought you said 'rules are rules,' Prez," the second man behind him said.

"Yeah," the last one added. "No broads as overnight guests in the territory."

Ransom's jaw hardened. "She's not a broad," he said.

"Oh, is she gonna be your old lady then?" Blue Eyes asked.

Old lady? Her gaze shot to Ransom.

"She's not mine—"

"What the heck is going on here?"

The wall of buff men parted as Silke pushed past them, mops and a bucket in her hands. "Why are you all crowding Sabrina? Give her some space. Poor girl looks like she's gonna faint."

Sabrina didn't even realize that her palms had gone sweaty, and her heart was thumping in her chest. How she didn't *really* faint with all these new people around her was a miracle. Normally, even the thought of being in a room with so many people would have sent her anxiety into the stratosphere.

"You know her?" Bo asked Silke.

"Yeah, *I* was the one who decided she could stay," Silke said.

The men seemed mollified, and the atmosphere in the tiny room lightened.

"Uh, sorry, Prez." Blue eyes looked sheepishly at Ransom. "I just thought—"

"Next time, think with your head, not your dick, Axle," Ransom berated. "Now get outta here and go into town and pick up that package from Bucky." He glared at the other men. "And as for the rest of you, grab those mops and start cleaning up. I'm gonna head back to my cabin." With that, he marched outside.

After the men took the cleaning supplies from her, Silke linked her arm through Sabrina's. "You poor thing. C'mon, let's go outside and let the boys clean up."

They walked out to the porch. "I'm sorry I didn't check up on you yesterday, I was pretty busy."

"Oh, don't worry about me," Sabrina assured her. "I'm sure you have more things to worry about than keeping me entertained."

"Ransom said Cross would be taking care of you. Did he come back and bring you more food?"

She couldn't help but wince when Silke mentioned his name. "I'm fine. He brought me breakfast this morning."

"But you haven't seen him?"

Her shoulders dropped. "No. But it's okay. I mean, I'm used to being alone." She twisted her ring out of habit.

"Yeah, but still, he shouldn't leave you here by yourself." Silke planted her hands on her hips. "The man brought you here, after all. He damn well better take care of all your needs." Her jaw dropped as she must have realized the double meaning of her words. "I mean ... he shouldn't just leave you like a prisoner in solitary. You need stimulation." She slapped her hands on her forehead. "Sorry. It's none of my business what you and Cross are. I mean if you are, I'm not one to judge."

Mortification made her face heat up. "It's not like that." At least, she didn't know if it was like that. Or ever been like that.

"Again, not my business." She waved her hands. "But, yeah, the man should take some responsibility for you. And Ransom! My brother should have explained to the guys who you were, at least. Though those boys are nosier than my Grandma Heloise's quilting circle, I'm sure, given the chance, they'd be all over you like ants on a birthday cake," she said with a laugh.

"So ... all those guys live here?"

Silke nodded. "Yeah. They're part of the Savage Wolves Motorcycle Club. My dad and some of his Lone Wolf buddies founded it." She lowered her voice. "Technically, Lone Wolves aren't supposed to have their own territory without becoming an actual clan, but my momma owned this land and the resort, and she let Pops and the MC live on the territory."

"Oh. So, they turn into wolves, like Cross?"

"Yup." Her lips pursed. "Cross explained all that already?"

She nodded. "I saw him ... change. Then he explained it to me."

"He could get in trouble with their high council. But, I'm sure he did it for your own good."

"I don't think he had a choice," she said. "The night he rescued me, he had to turn into his wolf, and then he brought me here with his magic."

Silke cleared her throat. "Is there anything I can do to help? Who tried to hurt you?"

"It's ..." Her chest tightened, thinking of that night. A chill ran through her as she thought that she might have died —or worse—if it hadn't been for Cross.

Silke gripped her hands and squeezed. "I'm sorry, sugar. Here I am being nosy after you've gone through such a trial. Like I said, you don't have to tell me, though I'll be here when you need to talk."

"Thank you." She smiled warmly at Silke and wondered; beneath that strong, independent surface, what scars did she bear? She projected a confident exterior, but she saw the way her eyes turned dark when she asked about who tried to hurt her. Had she been hurt too? And that scar on her cheek ...

"Now." Silke took a deep breath. "The reason I was busy yesterday is that I was taking care of some check outs, and I had a group cancel for the weekend. We're actually empty until the next guests come in tomorrow."

"Oh no, I'm sorry."

"Nah, it happens. Actually, it's a good opportunity to do some maintenance stuff I couldn't manage when we're booked up." She nodded her chin back toward inside the cabin. "I have a list for the boys to finish up today once they're done cleaning your bathroom. Hmmm." She tapped a finger on her cheek. "Maybe we can have a little party down by the lake once they're done. It'll certainly be a good incentive for them to finish up. Why don't you join us?"

She blinked. "Me?"

"Yeah, why not? You can meet everyone, including Arlene. She's Bo's old lady, she's a sweetheart."

"I don't know." Her fingers twisted her ring quickly. It

was one thing for them to all come to the cabin because of an emergency, and another for her to voluntarily be around new people.

She wagged a finger at Sabrina. "It'll be fun, I won't take no for an answer." Poking her head through the doorway, she shouted, "Move your asses, ladies! It doesn't take this long to mop up. C'mon, we got a long list of things to do."

As she waved her hand, the four men filed out of the cabin, giving Sabrina some discreet—and not so discreet—glances as they walked by.

Silke rolled her eyes. "I should get started on my list. I'll see you later!"

"But I—" Before she could protest, Silke waved at her and trudged down the porch steps where the guys were waiting. One of the men—a guy with a short mohawk, winked at her, which earned him a playful slap on the head. As Silke herded them away, she wondered if there was any way she could avoid going to this party. She could only hope they wouldn't finish their work on time and there wouldn't be a party at all.

———

It seemed luck was not on her side at all as Silke came by late in the afternoon. "I told you, I'm not taking no for an answer, Sabrina."

She couldn't make up an excuse about not having anything to wear since the other woman had brought her a bathing suit, a sundress, and flip-flops from the resort shop. Sabrina felt embarrassed and promised she would pay her back for the new stuff.

She climbed into the passenger seat of the small utility

truck Silke had driven over. Silke chatted as they drove, pointing out this or that landmarks, and Sabrina actually found herself relaxing in her company.

After a few minutes, the truck slowed down right by the shore of a large lake. Music blared from a speaker, and there was a barbecue grill set up on a large deck built over the water. A couple of people were chatting by a table laden with food, while a few more were scattered about the lake area, drinking beers and talking amiably. They all seemed to be having a good time, and it was the typical barbecue, but the thought of being around all these people was making sweat build on her palms.

"I also asked a couple of the staff to the party." She leaned closer. "They don't know anything about Lycans," she said in a low whisper.

"Oh. Right."

There was a loud whoop followed by a splash, and Silke pursed her lips wryly. "Although they might find out soon if Axle doesn't watch it. I suppose lots of normal people swim in a freezing lake for fun."

She laughed. Although she had worn the bathing suit under the dress, Sabrina had no plans on swimming, seeing as it was still early spring, and up here, it was even colder than it had been in New York. But it seems like the Lycans had no problems with cold temperatures as two more of them dove into the lake.

Silke led them up to the deck and introduced her to a couple of her staff members, then they headed over to the grill where Bo was flipping burgers. He wore an apron that said "Kiss the Chef" as he chatted with a buxom bleach-blonde woman.

"Why, hello, Sabrina," Bo greeted. "Let me introduce you to my old lady, Arlene. Honey, this here's, Sabrina, Silke's guest."

"How's it going, sugar?" Arlene greeted. "Want a beer or something?" She rooted through a cooler by her feet.

Not wanting to be rude, she accepted the cold can from the older woman, as did Silke. "Thank you, Arlene."

"Where're you from, Sabrina?" Arlene asked.

She popped the top open and took a sip. "Uh, New York."

"New York? That's quite a distance, huh?" Arlene chuckled. "How'd you get all the way out here?"

Sabrina cast her eyes downward and took a larger gulp of beer.

"She's actually Cross Jonasson's friend," Silke explained. "You remember him, right? The guy who looks like a Viking and brought Ransom back last year. They're ... visiting."

"Oh. *Him*." Arlene fanned herself. "Woo. That boy ..."

"Arlene," Bo growled.

"I'm kiddin', honey," she soothed, rubbing a hand down Bo's tattooed bicep. "I only got eyes for you."

That seemed to placate the man, and he nodded and took a sip of his beer. Arlene winked at Silke and Sabrina. "And where is that hunk—I mean, boy?" Arlene asked. "I mean, he didn't just drop you off here and leave, did he?"

"Arlene," Silke said in a warning voice.

"Oh. Oh, sugar, I'm sorry." Her gaze turned sympathetic. "Well, he tends to zip in and out of places, right? I remember when he came and brought Ransom back, he'd just pop in and out, checking in on our boy."

"He'll come back," Silke said reassuringly.

She made a non-committal sound.

"Oh, lookie, here they come." Arlene nodded to the four men who rose out of the water and began approaching them.

Bo grumbled. "You know those four. They can smell pus —I mean," he cleared his throat when Arlene and Silke sent him twin glares, "*Girls* a mile away."

"I'll have to apologize in advance," Arlene said. "Those boys are randier than stallions ever since Ransom banned them from taking girls back here."

Silke's nose twitched. "That rule was put into place mostly because Axle was havin' a party at his cabin one night and invited those girls from The Barrel Bottom. Then Sue May came along and snuck into Ransom's bed. Found her laying there, naked as the day she was born." Silke frowned distastefully. "I swear, that ex of his is gonna get him in trouble someday."

"Sue May *wishes* she was an ex," Arlene snorted. "More like, never was. But she's had her eye set on being *his* old lady for years."

"Hey, Silke, Arlene," Blue Eyes—Axle—greeted as he approached. Then his gaze shifted to Sabrina. "Hello again. I don't think we were introduced. I'm Axle." He offered his hand.

"Uh, I'm Sabrina." His hand engulfed hers as they shook hands. Axle was only wearing shorts, and rivulets of water was still dripping down his shoulders, chest, and abs. She couldn't help but stare at the tattoo of a wolf on his right pec.

"Like what you see?" he asked with a grin.

"Ax." Bo sent him a warning look, so the man let go of her hand and backed off.

A guy with the short Mohawk haircut and friendly

brown eyes stepped up to introduce himself. "I'm Hawk." He jerked his thumb to the guy next to him. "This is my brother, Snake." Snake tipped his chin at her. They looked very similar, though Snake was probably a few years younger and had lighter hair.

"Did you meet Ink yet?" Silke asked, motioning to the redheaded young man who had fixed her shower.

"Nice to meet you, ma'am," Ink said with a gulp.

"Thank you for getting my shower fixed," she said. "But I thought your name was Proby?"

"That's his title," Axle explained. "He's a Probate. Means he's not a full member yet. He has to pass the probationary period before he gets a patch."

"That means he's basically our bitch for the next year," Hawk said with a guffaw as he jostled the kid with his elbow. Ink seemed to take the joshing good-naturedly as he laughed along.

"Ink? That's uh, an interesting nickname." Her brows snapped together as her gaze darted back and forth between the men, who were all wearing swim trunks and nothing else. All of them had tattoos all over their bodies, except for the Probate.

"Oh, Proby here's got a tattoo," Hawk said, seemingly reading her mind. "It's just nowhere you want to see it."

Sabrina blushed, and so did Ink.

A voice calling from behind got their attention. "Hey, guys, everything good?" It was the man who answered the door this morning. He walked up to them, though not alone; he was carrying a toddler, maybe two or three years old, whose arms were wrapped around his neck. "Sabrina, right? I'm Hardy. And this is my daughter, Annie."

"Nice to meet you. Hello, Annie. I like your dress," she said, nodding at the girl's bright yellow sundress.

"Hi!" Annie smiled and waved, her curly hair bouncing around her chubby cheeks.

"Burgers are done," Bo declared. "Why don't you all grab some plates and we can start eatin'?"

Sabrina followed Silke's lead and walked over to the table with food and utensils, taking the plate and utensils the other woman offered. "So, everyone here works for you?" she asked.

"For the resort, yes." Silke piled some mashed potatoes on her plate. "Ink and Hawk are our handymen for the lodge and cabins. Axle and Snake do other odd jobs maintaining the property and double as our valet when we have special events. Hardy and Ransom help out, too, but they both work full time with Bucky in town. Arlene mans the front desk when I'm not around and heads up housekeeping, while Bo isn't just the MC's chaplain, but he's also an ordained minister and performs the weddings that take place here." She laughed as she grabbed a hamburger bun and placed one on Sabrina's plate. "I can see by the look on your face that you're surprised."

She glanced over at the man in question, who was kissing Arlene's neck as the woman giggled like a schoolgirl. "He uh, doesn't seem like the preacher type."

"He's more spiritual than religious these days, he says. But he does perform an important job for the MC."

"You said he's a chaplain?"

"*The* chaplain. For the MC. It's kind of a revered position. He's there for anyone who needs counsel or just wants an ear to listen." A sad expression passed briefly across her pretty face. "I know it doesn't seem like it, but they all have their own demons."

Sabrina glanced around. All of the guys did seem like happy, normal people, but then again, that was all surface. People weren't always what they seemed.

When they finished filling up on potato salad, coleslaw, and beans, they walked over to Bo, who served them up some burgers, then walked out by the lake. They sat on one of the lounge chairs on the sandy shore. "So, this is everyone? I mean, all the MC?"

"Hmmm." Silke thought for a moment. "Well, there's Logan, but he doesn't come to these things. Prefers to patrol the territory and stay with the horses. We have a couple around for the tourists, and he does a great job with them. Oh"—she looked around, then grimaced as if she had a bad taste in her mouth—"there's Joanie." She nodded back at the deck, where Ransom was chatting with an older woman who was smoking a cigarette. They stood far away from everyone else, like they were in their own world.

"Joanie?"

"Ransom's mother," she said.

She looked back toward Ransom and the cool-blonde woman. Her head was turned their way, but it was like she was looking right through them. She flicked her cigarette to the ground and smashed it with her heel, then said something to Ransom.

"That's your stepmother?"

That distasteful look come back on Silke's face. "Don't let Joanie hear you say that. To her, Ransom's her only child."

"Oh, I'm sorry. I didn't mean anything by it. You said she married your father."

Silke shrugged. "It's all right. I'm used to it. Joanie wasn't a wicked stepmom or anything, just indifferent. She made sure I was fed and clothed while I was growing up, but Ransom was the apple of her eye. Part of me thinks Pops married her so soon after my mom died because he just didn't know how to take care of a baby. But he loved her in his way, and she cared for Pops. Anyway." She pasted a smile on her face. "Let's not spend the whole time talking about my baggage."

A few more people had joined them on the loungers, and Sabrina actually found herself having a good time, though she mostly listened to everyone else's stories. It was strange, really. A few days ago, the thought of being surrounded by so many strangers would probably have made her anxiety levels shoot up, but now, she actually felt relaxed. Perhaps it was the fresh mountain air and the beautiful scenery. It was inspiring really, and maybe tomorrow she could ask Silke if she could come out here and do some painting. It might be a nice thank you gift, too, after all the other woman had done for her.

The sun was nearly gone by the time everyone decided to start cleaning up and head back. Sabrina volunteered to put the food away, and she chatted with some of the kitchen staff as she helped them place leftovers into containers.

"Hey, you guys seen Annie?" Hardy asked as he jogged up to them, his face a mask of worry. "I swear I just turned around for a second and she was gone."

Sabrina scanned the area and saw a flash of bright yellow by the line of trees on their left before disappearing. "Oh, I think I see her. Over there. Let's go get her before she gets lost." She murmured an apology to the rest of the staff finishing up the work and then signaled to Hardy to follow her.

Together, they jogged toward the direction she saw Annie wander off to, going past the line of trees and walking deeper into the thicket. Bugs chirped around them as they walked along a narrow path covered by a canopy of branches and leaves.

"There you are!" Hardy exclaimed with a relieved sigh when he spotted Annie playing by a large fallen black oak tree. Jogging over, he swooped down and picked her up, sending her into a fit of giggles. "Oh baby, you scared Daddy." He peppered her face with kisses. "Don't you ever do that again."

As he held her tight, Sabrina felt a strange twist in her stomach. *Probably my ovaries exploding*, she thought to herself. It was just so cute watching the big biker go all soft and melty for his daughter. Her fingers were itching to paint them and capture this memory forever. Might make another nice gift too.

"I shoulda kept my eyes on her," Hardy said sheepishly. "Thank you."

"It's nothing, I just spotted her, that's all."

His smile was warm and made him look even more handsome. "Annie's my world, you know? I didn't think I could do this alone. I didn't want to at first. But now I can't imagine life without her."

"Oh, her mom—"

"Isn't in the picture," he said, his tone edgy.

Poor Annie. She reached out and tucked a stray curl from the child's face. "I'm sure you're doing a great job."

"Yeah, well." He shrugged. Annie began to squirm in his

arms, so he set her down, though kept a hand around her tiny wrist to keep her from wandering off. "So are you and Ransom like—"

"Ransom?" She shook her head. Half the time she felt like an annoying gnat he wanted to swat away. "Oh, no." And the other half? Well it felt like he wanted to gobble her up like Little Red Riding Hood.

His face lit up. "That's great. I mean," he laughed nervously. "Just ..." He bit his lower lip. "He's our prez. And I wouldn't poach on his territory."

Oh God, was he flirting with her? Had she drunk some kind of love potion in the last twenty-four hours that made all these hot men start noticing her? "It's not anything like that."

"Sabrina?"

She froze, her body immediately reacting to the sound of that voice. Oh, why was it that faced with two equally attractive men, her damn traitorous body only wanted one, the one who didn't want her back?

"Jonasson." Hardy gave the other man a nod. "Nice of you to finally come back."

The tension in the air became thick as molasses. Cross came up beside her, his shoulders and back stiff. "Hardy," he said curtly. Then he turned to Sabrina. "I went to the cabin and you weren't there. I've been looking all over for you. I didn't think you'd leave."

"Why wouldn't I? Am I some kind of prisoner?" she bit out.

His jaw tightened. "That's not what I meant. I was worried about you."

"If you were worried about her, then you shouldn't have left her alone," Hardy interjected.

Cross's eyes flashed—no, they *glowed*. "Was I talking to you, Lone Wolf?"

"Listen here, Jonasson," Hardy said. "You're on Savage Wolves turf. You don't get to speak to me that way."

"What the hell are you doing out here with her?" Cross growled.

"Oh, for God's sake, Cross! Please, stop," she said. "I—"

She sucked in a breath as Cross looped his arm around her and everything went cold. A shiver ran through her as her surroundings shimmered away, and she found herself inside the cabin. "Damn it, Cross, what did you do that for?" she roared at him.

"Why were you alone with him in the woods?" His hand gripped her arm tight.

She wrenched away from him. "If you stopped and used your head for one second, you would have realized we weren't alone! His kid was there with us. I saw Annie wander off by herself, and so we went after her!"

His face fell. "I didn't mean to be so gruff. I was worried about you."

"Well, you know what? Hardy was right. If you were worried about me, you wouldn't have left."

"That's not ..." He let out a sound of frustration and scrubbed his palm down his beard. "I had to take care of a few things. To find the people trying to hurt you." He reached out to touch her shoulder. "And of course, you're not a prisoner here. I just thought you wouldn't want to leave. With your ... anxiety and all."

How did he know about that? "Well, it was a nice day, and I've been cooped up far too long. And Silke insisted I come to this party, and seeing that she's my host, I couldn't say no. Everyone was nice to me," she said in a soft voice. "We were all having a nice time." *Until you ruined it.*

She didn't have to say that out loud, but it was obvious he understood what she meant from the way his shoulders went taut. "Just say the word, and I'll bring you back to your precious Hardy's company."

"My precious—" Her jaw dropped. There was a small flutter in her belly. *Holy moly, was he jealous?* She observed the way the scowl on his face deepened and how his fingers clenched and unclenched. Then that glow in his eyes came back, and the fluttering intensified. "If you wanted my company, well, here I am. Not like I can go away. But you leave me for a whole day without saying anything. Without telling me about what happened that day in my studio ... what am I supposed to think?"

"It was a kiss, nothing more," he said. "Friends can kiss."

"Not like *that.*" Not in the way that made it difficult to forget or think of anything else.

"Think what you like."

Part of her wanted to shrink back into that frightened, anxiety-ridden, self-conscious shell of a person she'd somehow turned into since the accident. But if she wanted answers—real ones and not the half-truths he'd been supplying her—she would have to take a step forward and take what she needed. "Fine. Kiss me again and tell me it doesn't mean anything."

"You don't know what you're asking."

"Do it, and I'll never bother you again. Kiss me so I can remember that it didn't mean anything." Blood roared in her ears, and her heart thumped loudly against her rib cage. "Unless you're afraid that I'm right."

He growled softly—a sound that sent heat straight to her core—then grasped her by the waist and held her tight. She clung to him, scared that she would melt into a puddle as his lips came down on hers.

Dear Lord, it was better than a memory. Better than any kiss she'd had before and probably any she would have after this. His mouth moved hungrily over hers, making her body ache for more. She felt consumed, and every thought in her brain, and every feeling in her body distilled down to this kiss.

His hands moved to her lower back, pressing her against him, her mouth gasping as she felt his hardness press against her belly. Cross wanted her. *Her.* It sent her mind reeling to know he desired her like this.

His tongue licked against the seam of her lips, plundering her mouth as she opened up to give him access. He practically devoured her, and her overstimulated mind couldn't process if she could smell or taste his chocolatey scent. Fingers thrust into her hair, giving her a gentle tug, and the desire in her core flared.

"Cross," she moaned as his mouth moved lower to kiss her jaw, trailing down to her neck. He nibbled on the skin, his tongue leaving scorch marks in its wake. She wanted to touch him, and so she did. Her hands slipped under his shirt, feeling the warm skin over his taut muscles, kneading them until he moaned aloud.

"I'm sorry," he murmured against her neck.

"For what?" She was dizzy and lightheaded.

"I'm sorry I can't control myself around you. Sorry I couldn't pretend you didn't mean anything to me."

His confession made her chest ache, and she wondered if

it mirrored his feeling. "I knew it," she breathed. It was there. That spark of *something* between them. "But I wish I could remember. Why won't you tell me more about what happened?"

"It's for your own protection, Sabrina," he whispered. "Can you trust me on this? Just this one thing?"

That feeling in her chest was back—the one that told her he wasn't going to hurt her. It was telling her to trust him. Maybe she should listen to it. For now, anyway.

"All right." Pulling away from him, she grabbed his hand and dragged him toward the bed. "Please, Cross."

His eyes turned dark. "Sabrina, you don't know what you're asking."

"I do." She moved back until she felt the bed behind her, then pushed herself up. "I want this."

"You're not ready, Sabrina," he said. "And I'm not a saint, I won't be able to stop."

"I don't want you to stop," she said.

"Sabrina," he said with a sigh as he folded her hands into his. "We haven't ... I mean, before your accident, we didn't get a chance to make love."

A curious feeling bloomed in her chest at those last two words. *Make love.* Not sleep together, not sex, not fuck. *Love.* "You're right." She rubbed her temple. "I do want to remember."

There was a strange look on his face, but it was so fleeting she didn't have time to process it. "And if you don't, that's all right too. You shouldn't feel pressured."

Perhaps the past should stay in the past. And it was time she moved forward and make a new life. And something new with Cross instead of clinging to what they had been, she should look forward to what they could be. "I still want you."

He took in a sharp breath. "Me too."

"Then come here." She pushed herself back farther on top of the mattress. "I just need to touch you." There was an urge driving her to get her hands on him. She desperately wanted to know what his skin tasted like. "And I need you to touch me. We don't have to do ... anything else."

Cross looked like he was battling with himself. And he was slowly losing. Releasing a soft growl, he slipped his shoes off, climbed into bed, and crawled toward her, like a predator approaching its prey.

A thrill of excitement rushed up her spine as she stared into his face, her body going hot all over as she read the expression of pure lust there. He crawled over her, covering her with his big body, making her feel small. She closed her eyes as his head came down, capturing her mouth again in a soft, slow kiss.

His hands moved lower, one cupping her breast through the sundress and the other reaching down, skimming over the soft mound of her belly and lower still to cup her between the legs. She gasped as the heat of his hand seemed to penetrate the layers of clothes. His mouth suckled on hers harder, driving his tongue deeper into her, like he was a man dying of thirst.

"I need to taste you," he growled against her mouth. "Let me taste you."

She nodded, liking the way he seemed both polite and savage at the same time. He didn't waste any time as he moved lower, pushing her dress up to her waist. He frowned as his finger touched the edge of the one-piece swimsuit she wore under the dress. Yikes, she'd forgotten about that.

"I'll take it off." She fumbled for the buttons on the front of the sundress. "I—oh." Suddenly, she couldn't feel the spandex on her skin. Feeling around her torso, she realized that it was gone. "How—" His hands slipped under her ass, and he pulled her forward, sending her body jerking when his mouth touched her damp, naked pussy lips. "Cross!"

Her hands fisted in the sheets as he licked at her, the filthy sounds of his tongue lapping at her setting her cheeks on fire. Looking down and watching his head between her thighs sent her into the stratosphere, and she let out a scream as his tongue thrust into her. That only made him grip her ass tighter and lick at her faster. Her hips bucked up at him, trying to get as much of his tongue inside her, the need clawing at her. Pushing her hips down, he lay a hand on her to keep her still as his mouth found her clit.

"*Nngghh!*" It was unbearable, the pleasure that spread through her as he sucked on her nub. His fingers began to probe at her entrance, and when he thrust one inside her, she couldn't stop the wave of the orgasm that washed over her, sending her body into convulsions. She peaked, then was tumbling over the edge. The edges of her vision seemed to brighten as she fell and finally, her hips settled on the mattress.

She opened her eyes when she fully regained the feeling in her body. To her chagrin, he was still between her legs, looking up at her with those intense blue-green eyes. He wiped his mouth with the back of his hand, and for some reason, that gesture sent a pulse to her pussy. Maybe she should have thought this over. Despite the intense orgasm he just gave her, she still felt hot and needy.

He rolled over behind her and gathered her to his chest, then pushed her hair aside to kiss the back of her neck. "You taste so good."

She turned around to face him and pressed her mouth to his neck, licking at the skin. He tasted so masculine and warm. Her hand moved lower, over the thin fabric of his T-shirt that barely hid the rock-hard muscles of his abs, then down to the buttons on his jeans.

"You don't have to," he whispered. "We can just lay here like this."

"But I want to," she said. "Please, let me touch you."

With a deep sigh, he reached down and unbuttoned his fly. "I might not last ... it's been too long."

"Too long?" The words sent hope fluttering in her chest. "You haven't—"

"Not since I met you," he confessed. "Sabrina!" He moaned as her hand slipped under his briefs and grasped him.

Jesus. He was so large and hard in her palm. Her fingers wrapped around his shaft, holding it firmly. His hips jerked forward, and he shrugged his pants and briefs down lower. She gripped him tighter, moving her hand up and down his cock.

He let out a strangled groan that sounded like her name. A hand thrust into her hair, tangling tight in her locks as he threw his head back. His breath came in short gasps. She looked down, watching with fascination his enormous cock in her hand, the tip purple and angry. A soft cry of surprise escaped her mouth when his hand closed over hers, increasing the rhythm.

"Sabrina," he cried out, then bit his lip as his body spasmed. His hot come spurted from the tip of his cock, painting his stomach. He gave a last shudder before his body relaxed and he closed his eyes.

He released her hand, and she let her arms fall to the sides, unsure what to do next. One eye opened, then the other until he was staring at her with a grin. "Thank you."

"Uh, welcome?" That sounded weird, but from the blissful look on his face, it was probably the right thing to say.

He wiped his hand and stomach on his shirt, then waved his hand over them. She barely blinked when she felt something soft on her skin. Pajamas had appeared on her body; fur lined too, and he had matching bottoms. She snuggled against him, burying her face in his chest.

"We'll make love when you're ready," he said, stroking her hair.

There it was again. Those words. Clearing her throat, she nodded and said, "Are you going to leave tomorrow?"

"Only for a short while." He kissed the top of her head. "I'll be back, I promise."

She believed him. And she supposed that would have to be enough for now.

CHAPTER SEVEN

"WELL, YOU'RE IN A GOOD MOOD," SILKE SAID AS THEY drove in her utility truck. She had come by around noon and invited Sabrina over to lunch at the lodge. Cross had left early in the morning, but he did wake her up with a kiss and a quick goodbye. Seeing as she would be alone anyway, she accepted Silke's invitation.

"Hmmm?" Sabrina turned toward her. "Am I?"

Silke slid her a sly look. "Does it have anything to do with the fact that you disappeared with Cross after the barbecue?"

Warmth crept into her cheeks. "I don't kiss and tell."

"Oh, who said anything about kissing?" Silke laughed. "But seriously, if that smile on your face is any indication, then I'm happy for you."

"Thank you." She released a sigh of relief. "Silke, you and Cross ... there's nothing there, right?" The moment the question came out of her mouth, she regretted it. He told her he hadn't been with anyone since they met, and she should really trust him.

"What?" Silke's mouth opened. "No, there's never been

anything between us. I mean, he's *hot*, c'mon, I'm not blind. But he saved my brother's life, and I'll be grateful to him forever." There was a strained look on her face. "Besides, I'm done with love and men. I'm flying solo from now on."

Though she itched to ask Silke more, she restrained herself. It was obviously a painful subject, so she didn't want to bring it up.

The truck ambled through the hills and valleys, and Sabrina took a long, deep breath. When was the last time she'd been outdoors for an extended period? She couldn't even remember. Definitely more than three years ago, and even then, she'd never really been the outdoors type, except maybe to paint landscapes. But it seemed being out here in the mountains of Kentucky had washed away her anxiety and fears.

"We're here." Silke announced as the vehicle slowed down, and they stopped outside a large, log structure. Though it was very similar to the guest cabin Sabrina was staying at, it was expansive, taking up what was probably the equivalent of half a city block in New York and had multiple stories. There was a beautiful painted wooden sign outside that proudly proclaimed Seven Peaks Mountain Lodge and Cabins.

"It's gorgeous," she said with awe.

"That she is," Silke said as she exited the truck. "The real love of my life."

Sabrina didn't blame her. The lodge was impressive— made of reddish-brown pine logs topped with a green steep-sloped roof, stonework pillars, and surrounded by lush pine trees. She followed Silke inside, and they entered the rustically decorated lobby, waving at Arlene who was waiting behind the front desk. The interior wasn't fancy like the four-star hotels in New York, but it was obviously lovingly done and fit the rustic feel of the place.

"I grew up in the main cabin in the MC part of the land," Silke explained as they walked down the hallway. "Ransom lives in it, and although I still keep a room there, I prefer to stay in the manager's suite upstairs."

They entered the dining room, and there was a table in the corner set up with sandwiches. "It's nothing fancy, but our chef's still prepping for dinner." They sat down and ate their lunch, chatting amiably.

"Thank you for inviting me," she said when they finished.

"No problem. Besides, it's nice having another woman my age around. I'm always surrounded by guys, and it can be tiring. I feel like their mother most of the time." Silke pushed her plate away. "Do you have any more plans for the day? I rarely get any time off, but since we only have one check in today, I thought I'd take advantage. Maybe we could do something fun?"

"I don't have any plans or anything. Cross left, and he says he'll be back, but I'm not sure what time."

Silke's face brightened. "Oh, do you want to see the horses? The stable's just out back."

"Hmmm ... I've never been around horses. Or animals, actually," she admitted sheepishly. "Horses seem so ... intimidating."

"Our horses are very gentle," she said. "I promise. We don't have to go riding or anything."

"All right."

After clearing up their plates, Silke led her outside and to the back part of the property. She pointed out a structure in the distance and the fenced corral around it. "It's right over there."

They walked together, and it didn't take long to reach the small building. "Logan's probably out patrolling still," Silke said as she opened the door. "He's pretty territorial when it comes to the horses. You'd think he owns this place from the way he acts. It's strange, really, how the horses seem to like him. None of the other Lycans can even come near the animals, which is why I tolerate Logan's poor manners."

"They can't come near the horses?" she asked. "Why not?"

"Hmmm, well I'm human, so I don't really know how it works," Silke began. "But see, for Lycans, they share their bodies with their wolves. It's always there, like having another consciousness in their thoughts."

"Huh." She never realized that was the case.

"And, well, Logan says the horses can sense the wolves. It's like, they have a sixth sense that there's an aggressive, dominant animal in all of them. He says they can even sense when there's something bad around. I'm still not sure how Logan manages them, but that's one reason why I can't fire him. No one else would be able to do his job."

They headed inside, and the smell of hay, leather, and animals assaulted her senses. From the entrance, she could see several horses sticking their heads out of their enclosures.

Silke gestured to follow her as they walked along the stalls. "Horses aren't our bread and butter, but it's nice to have that option for the guests. We have twelve horses in total, none of them are from any fancy bloodlines, but we love them just the same." A friendly white horse neighed at Silke, and she caressed its nose. "Hey, Daisy, how's it going? Sorry, no treats today." The mare blew out a breath, making Silke laugh. "I—" A ringing sound interrupted her and she fished out her phone from her pocket. "Hey, Arlene, what's—" Her pretty face drew into a frown. "All right, all right, don't get your panties in a twist. I'll take care of it. Gimme a few minutes, okay?" With a shake of her head, she turned to Sabrina. "Sorry, I need to run up to the lodge. There's a problem with our check-ins."

"Oh, no worries, we can go back."

"No, no," she said, putting her phone back in her pocket. "You stay put, sugar. Won't take me too long. I'll be back in two shakes of a tail feather."

Before she could protest, Silke strode out of the stalls. Sabrina sighed, wondering if she was meant to stay put inside the stables or wait outside. Shrugging, she continued down the walkway, gazing warily at the horses. Their heads turned as she walked by, and a weird feeling crept over her. It was like an energy, as if she could tell the animals seemed ... wary of her. Which was strange because they were huge—much bigger than she'd thought as she'd only seen horses in pictures. But there was something about them ... she couldn't quite put her finger on it.

She neared the end of the stable, and she saw that one of the stalls was empty. *Huh.* Looking back, she counted the stalls. There were exactly twelve, six on each side. Where was the last horse? She jogged over and stuck her head into the enclosure. It wasn't as empty as she first thought; rather, the humongous black horse was inside, backed up toward the rear, whinnying unhappily.

"What's wrong?" she asked. The horse's ears were

flattened back and hooves pawed at the ground. "Are you hurt?"

The horse let out an angry neigh, making her jump in surprise. "Well, I never!" She grumbled. "I'm not doing anything to you, Mr. Horse!" Okay, she was crazy, right, talking to a horse?

All of a sudden, the horse charged forward, its muscled body hitting the metal bars with a loud *clang*. She screamed and leapt back. "Stay away!" She put her hands up in front of her defensively, but that only seemed to make the horse angrier. It reared up and then kicked at the metal gates.

"What the fuck is going on here?"

As her heart beat a tattoo in her chest, she turned her head to the sound of the voice. A very large silhouette engulfed the doorway of the stables. "Who the hell are you?" he shouted.

The horse once again neighed angrily and reared back. This time, the gate flew open, and the animal went charging at her.

"No!" she screamed, raising her arms higher. A strange electricity filled the air, crawling over her skin and making the hair on the back of her neck stand on end. Her vision turned to darkness—or was it that the room turned dark? A ringing sound deafened her, and she slumped on the concrete floor, covering her face with her arms.

It seemed like forever before her hearing returned. She could hear the sounds of soft, nervous hooves stamping and heavy thuds hitting the floor. When she put her arms down and looked up, she saw the man in the doorway, kneeling down next to the black horse, which was now lying on the ground. Horror filled her veins when she saw the animal's glassy, dead eyes staring at her.

"No, no, no." The man cradled the horse's head, rocking it back and forth. "Georgie, no ... no!" He let out a pained growl, then turned to Sabrina. "What did you do?" The man snarled at her, his face twisted into an expression of hate.

She opened her mouth, but nothing came out.

Slowly, he got to his feet. Even if she was standing up, he would have towered over her. His shoulders were massive, and his arms were like tree trunks as he extended them. "I said, what did you do to her?"

"Logan!" They both turned to the sound of the voice. "Logan, what's going on? Sabrina?" Silke's face was drawn into a mask of worry as she helped her up.

"She killed Georgie!" Logan accused. "Look!"

The redhead let out a gasp when her gaze landed on the horse lying on the floor. "Oh, no. Poor Georgie," she choked. "She was pregnant, right?"

Logan let out a snarl and stalked Sabrina. "What are you? A witch or something?"

"What—no!" She pressed herself against the stall behind her. "I'm not!"

"I saw what you did. Your eyes—"

"Logan, stop!" Silke called from where she knelt by the poor horse. "She's not a witch. And there's no way she could have killed Georgie."

He slammed his meaty hand against the metal bars behind her, making them clank loudly. "You're a witch. Don't deny it! Your eyes turned black." he spat. "You raised your hands and everything went dark, then she was dead. What the hell else could it have been?"

"Please, I swear!" Tears pooled in her eyes. "I didn't do anything. The horse—she was aggressive, and all I did was ask her what's wrong." Her chest felt like it was imploding, contracting so hard she couldn't breathe. "I didn't kill her."

"Sabrina? What's going on?"

She sagged against the bars in relief at the sound of Cross's voice. He was standing by the doors, but then his eyes went wide when he saw Logan. In an instant, he appeared behind the other man and grabbed him by the shoulder.

"Get away from her," Cross snarled, as he pulled back Logan then slammed him against the bars. His hand snaked out to Sabrina, tugging her behind him so he was between her and the furious giant.

"Warlock," Logan sneered as he righted himself. "I knew you had something to do with this." His voice dripped with vitriol. "Why Ransom let you stay, I don't know. Your kind ain't welcome here!"

"He's a Lycan," Silke reminded him. "One of your kind."

Cross turned to Sabrina. "Did he hurt you? Are you all right? What happened?"

"Oh, Cross." The last of her strength seemed to crumble, and she collapsed against him, gripping his shirt with her fingers. "I ... I don't know ..." She hiccupped as tears spilled down her cheeks. "I was standing here one minute, then the horse came at me, and I raised my hand, and then there was this darkness."

He stiffened. "Darkness?"

She nodded. "Everything went dark and ... and then it all went back to normal and the horse ... that poor animal." More tears poured down her cheeks. "He said I killed it. But I didn't."

"I saw everything," Logan accused. "Georgie was pregnant, that's why she was so aggressive. And horses can sense evil magic." He pointed a finger at Sabrina. "Were you planning on using her for a ritual or potion or something?"

"Put that fucking finger away if you want to keep it," Cross warned.

"I didn't do it, I swear," she cried. "I'm human. I'm not a witch." She looked up at him, wanting to find comfort. Wanting to find something in them that confirmed her innocence. But that wasn't what she found in their stormy, ocean-colored depths. A pit in her stomach formed, and she dropped her arms to the sides. "You think I did this."

"Sabrina—"

He didn't have to say it; she saw it in his eyes. "How could you think that?" She pushed him away and wrapped her arms around herself as a shiver went through her. "I would never kill an innocent creature."

"I know, Sabrina." A hand came down on her shoulder, and it took all her might not to shrug it away. "I know you didn't mean to."

"What?" Her head snapped up to meet his gaze.

"Sabrina ... you didn't mean to kill the horse. And you can still reverse this."

Her eyes widened. "Reverse? What are you saying?" Her hands, her voice, her whole body shook as a pounding began in the base of her skull.

"You just have to remember, Sabrina." He took a step forward and placed his hands on her shoulders. "Remember, Sabrina, you can do it. You did it before."

The thumping on her nape spread, becoming a full-blown headache that made her vision blur.

And she began to remember.

———

Three years ago ...

Dinner went much better than Sabrina had imagined. Cross picked her up at home, and then they made their way to The Metro Union, a private club she and her father belonged to located on the Upper East Side. She had always loved coming here, because since she became a member herself, they would always dine here once a month, no matter how busy he was. It was their special father–daughter time, and for him to invite Cross was a big thing. Though he'd met most of her previous boyfriends, he'd never invited any of them here. Jonathan always said he had a good instinct when it came to people, so she hoped he could tell that Cross was a wonderful person.

They all met up at the reception area and then headed to the dining room, where they were led to their usual table. During the dinner, Jonathan had been amiable and inquisitive, asking Cross questions about himself, normal things one would ask if they were trying to get to know someone. Sabrina had to admit there were some things about Cross even she didn't know, but then again, they'd hadn't known each other very long or spent a lot of time talking about themselves.

Cross was polite and answered all his questions, and the rest of their conversational topics ranged from sports, to art, and world news. Her father would catch her eye sometimes and give her a knowing smile and wink. Cross, too, would look at her warmly and squeeze her hand under the table. All in all, the evening was a success, and suffice to say, she was on a happiness high by the time they all walked out of the restaurant.

"How about a nightcap?" Jonathan offered. "I have a seventeen-year-old whiskey from Japan that I've been saving up for a special occasion. It just so happens I have it in my limo. Maybe we can have it at your place, sweetheart?"

Sabrina suppressed the urge to roll her eyes. This was obviously a ploy to prevent them from being alone. "Dad, it's getting late. Maybe we should call it a night."

"Are you sure you don't want any whiskey, Cross?" Jonathan asked. "Just one drink."

He glanced at Sabrina, who shrugged. "Sure. One drink would be good."

"Excellent. Let me call my driver, and I'll meet you outside." Jonathan took his phone out of his pocket and began to walk toward the door.

"You don't have to have that drink, you know," Sabrina said. "I think he's trying to prevent us from being alone. So, you know ... we won't ..."

"Won't, what?" he asked, but the corners of his mouth were curling up. "It's all right, Sabrina. I enjoyed talking to your dad."

She sighed. "He still thinks that I'm a kid." *Or a virgin,* she added silently. "I want to be alone with you," she confessed in a low voice.

His eyes darkened, and he placed a hand on her shoulder. "Me too."

"But my dad ..." She blew out an impatient breath. "I hate to say it, but he's kind of a cockblock."

He laughed. "You're his daughter. In his mind, you'll always be his baby girl. It's just one drink. If it makes you feel better, I can follow him out and then I can come back after he leaves." A thumb brushed her collarbone, and she shivered. "We'll have all the time then."

"Let's play it by ear, okay?" She'd waited this long, she figured she could wait another couple of hours.

They walked out of the club, and Jonathan's driver was already waiting there, so they climbed into the vehicle. The limo drove them back downtown and dropped them outside Sabrina's building, and they took the elevator to her top floor loft.

"I'll get the glasses," she said as they entered. "Go ahead and get comfy."

Her father and Cross walked toward the couches as she went to the kitchen area. She was about to reach for the glasses in her cupboard when her phone rang. *Huh.* It was late for anyone to be calling. Who could it be? Grabbing her purse, she fished her phone out and read the name on the screen. "Barbara?" she read aloud. With a shrug, she picked up the call. "Hey, Barbara, what's up?"

"Sabrina, doll!" Barbara's nasal Brooklyn accent burst through the speaker, making her wince. The agent was boisterous and loud, but still, she loved the woman's sass and confidence. "Are you sitting down?"

"What?"

"I said, are you sitting down?"

There wasn't really anywhere to sit in her kitchen, so she leaned against the island. "Uh, sit down? Why?"

"Doll! I have the best news. I'm here in LA, right? And I'm talking to this gallery owner friend of mine. Well, he's not really a friend, friend, more like a friend, *friend*. Ya know what I mean?"

Not really, but sometimes she didn't know half the things the other woman said. "Yeah, sure."

"*Anyway*, this guy knows everyone who's anyone in LA. We were having dinner at the Beverly Hills Hotel and we run into these friends of his. We invite them to hang out with us, and I'm talking about what I do, and one of these guys asks me if I know any up-and-coming artists, and I say, 'sure I do,' and I whip out my phone and show him your paintings. And guess what?"

Frankly, she had only been half listening to what Barbara was saying because she kept one eye on her father and Cross in the living room. But wanting to get on with her night, she answered, "What, Barbara?"

"He wants to exhibit your paintings. At the Magnussen Gallery in Malibu!"

She sat straight up. "E-exhibit them? Wait, hold on." Clutching the phone with both hands, she made a dash for her studio but stopped by the living area. "Sorry, I have to take this," she said apologetically to the two men. "This might be a while. Glasses are in the open cupboard." She rushed into her studio and closed the door behind her.

"Is this a bad time, doll?" Barbara asked.

"No, no." She sat down at the small desk by the window. "So, this guy really wants to do a show of my paintings?"

"Oh, yeah. He was blown away," Barbara exclaimed. "As in, blown. A. *Way*."

Her heart thumped in her chest. Someone liked her

work! And she was going to have her own show. "Barbara ... this is fantastic. I don't know what to say."

"Doll, I haven't told you the best part."

"There's more?" She slumped back on her chair and kicked off her heels.

"Oh, yeah. Get ready for this." Barbara paused for dramatic effect. "He thinks he can sell your paintings to his best clients. You'll never guess how much he estimated. No wait, lemme tell you ..."

When she heard the figure, Sabrina thought she would have a heart attack. "R-r-really? *That* much?"

"This is it, doll, this is it! Now, I need you to take down a couple things for me, okay?"

She scrambled for a pencil and her notepad. "Okay, go ahead."

Barbara gave her a few more details, so she scrawled them down. Her hand was still shaking when she put the phone down on her desk. *This is it.* Her big break. And she couldn't wait to tell her father and Cross the good news. But she didn't want to get too excited. Nothing was set in stone. So, she took a few, deep calming breaths and tiptoed toward the living room.

"... and I've never met a man who didn't have a price. Name it."

She stopped short. Was her father conducting business over the phone?

"Sir." Cross's voice sounded strained. "Please reconsider. I don't want Sabrina to be hurt by this."

Her stomach flip-flipped. What was going on?

"She'll only be hurt if you continue to pursue her." That was definitely her father's voice. "Now, I have my checkbook here, my pen's ready to sign. Name. Your. Price."

"No."

"I have to hand it to you, Jonasson, you're a hard negotiator. Not nearly as easy as the others."

Others?

Jonathan snorted. "You're shocked. Yes, I paid off every man who came close to my daughter. Don't you give me that look," he said in a warning tone.

A pain stabbed right through her chest, and it felt like her heart was breaking into a million pieces. She'd never heard her father speak this way to anyone. *Dad* ...

"Someday, when you have children of your own, you'll understand. Now, give me a number. There's no number too big. If you tell me now, you can walk out of here a rich man. But you have to leave *now*."

"Stop!" It was like an outside force was driving her forward, and she couldn't stop it. "You ... you ..." She was shaking so hard she couldn't articulate any words.

Jonathan had gone pale. "Sabrina. Sweetheart." He cleared his throat. "Don't jump to any conclusions. Let me explain."

She marched toward him and yanked the pen and checkbook out if his hands. "Don't jump to any conclusions? And what conclusions could those be?" Tears burned her throat. "I can't believe you would do this!" The realization that every man in her life had been bought off by her father suddenly hit her. "How *could* you?"

"Sabrina!" Jonathan pleaded, his hands reaching out to her. "It was for your own good. For your own protection."

"Why then? Why would you do this?"

"Because ... because ... I couldn't let any of them get too close." Jonathan got on his knees. "Please, Sabrina. Trust me. This was for the best."

Bile was rising in her throat. "Go to hell!" she screamed, and when he reached out to her, she pushed his hands away, her arms stretching out to keep him as far away as possible. "Don't touch me! I hate you, and I never want to see you again."

Jonathan wouldn't stop and kept advancing. "Sabrina—"

"I said *don't touch me!*"

It was like the atmosphere was lit up with electricity. The air crackled with it, making the hairs on her arms and neck stand on end. She heard Cross shout 'no!' then tackle Jonathan before they both disappeared into thin air. She screamed as her vision turned dark, like someone had turned out the lights in her apartment. There was no illumination anywhere, not even through the large windows facing the street.

The ringing in her ears made her head ache, and she crumpled to the floor, hands covering her head. How long she'd been curled up into a ball, she didn't know, but when the ringing stopped, her body relaxed. The light returned as she slowly opened her eyes.

"Dad?" she croaked. "Cross?"

Carefully, she got to her feet, rubbing her eyes. There was a lingering throbbing in her temples. "Hello?"

"Sabrina."

She whirled around. Cross and her father were just behind her. Had they been there the whole time? Did she imagine it when she saw them disappear into thin air? "D-D-Dad? Cross? What happened?"

"Oh, sweetheart," Jonathan cried. "My Sabrina."

"Dad, why are you crying?" Twin tracks of tears ran down his cheeks. "What's wrong?" She followed her father's gaze, realizing why he was pale as a ghost. Blood drained from her own face when she saw it—all the plants along the one wall in her apartment were withered and dead. They had been healthy and thriving, but now they looked like they hadn't been watered in weeks. Her prized orchids, too, were wilted and dead. "No!" Oh God, what happened? Did she do this? A small voice in her head said, *yes*. "What did I do? What did I *do*?"

"I'm sorry, Sabrina," Jonathan choked. "It's my fault."

"Sabrina." A warm hand landed on her shoulder. Cross's voice and his presence were like a soothing balm, and she instinctively leaned into the touch. "Sabrina ... do you trust me?"

"Yes." God, she didn't know why, but she did. Maybe because it felt like the way she knew the world to be was a lie, and Cross was like a steady beacon.

"Sabrina, you can undo this."

Her head snapped up. "This?"

He nodded at the plants. "Bring them back."

"Bring them back? You mean, the plants ..." What was he saying? Did he believe all this?

"I believe in you, Sabrina." His hands cupped her face. "Just ... think of the plants. Think of life. Life that flows through you. Close your eyes."

She didn't know why, but she did. "Okay."

"Imagine the life from your own body, flowing out ... flowing out of you ..." Cross's voice was mesmerizing, making her feel all warm inside. Unlike the earlier sensation of cold and darkness, she now felt warmth. Brightness.

She opened her eyes, her entire apartment had filled with a bright, white light. And it was so warm. Like the roof had opened up and the sun shone down on them. "It's so ..."

She sucked in a breath as the light dissipated and her vision went back to normal. A sharp cry left her mouth. "Oh God."

All her plants—every single one—were back to life, as if nothing had ever happened to them. She looked at her father, who had gone ashen, then back to Cross. His blue-green eyes turned dark and stormy, like a sudden storm appearing out of nowhere over the ocean. "How did you know I could do that?"

———

The events of that night were so clear in Sabrina's mind. She didn't know how, but she just knew it happened, even though she had no recollection of it until this moment.

Her plants ... her father said he got rid of them because they all died while she was recuperating from the accident. But they were alive ... she brought them back. Did he take them away for another reason? A thought entered her head when she thought about that accident. An ache bloomed in her chest, and a suspicion was beginning to nag her brain.

"Do you remember?" Cross's voice was gentle as a breeze. "The plants."

"Yes." *Oh God.* "But they're plants." Her gaze turned to the poor horse and to Logan, who was kneeling down next to it, stroking its neck. "She's an animal. Surely it's different."

And frankly, she couldn't bear the thought of failing if she attempted it.

"Life is life." Cross placed a hand on the small of her back and led her toward Georgie. "You can do it, Sabrina. Just like you did before."

"Get the fuck away," Logan growled, as he stood up to full height. While not as tall as Cross, he was easily wider, and the veins popping in his neck made him look even more fierce. "You've done enough, witch."

"Let her try," Cross urged.

"There's no harm in letting her try to fix it," Silke said. "Please, Logan."

With a gruff snort, Logan took a step back. Though her hands were shaking and doubt filled every nook in her mind, Sabrina knew she had to try and make this right.

I'm sorry for what I did, she said to the horse silently. *I'll do my best to make it right.* Holding her hands over the animal, she tried to recall what happened that night in her apartment. She imagined the life flowing from her, out of her and into Georgie. Warmth moved over her skin, and the edges of her vision became fuzzy until the entire room was filled with a white light and everything went quiet. A comforting, snug feeling flowed over her, like a cashmere blanket being wrapped around her body.

A soft nicker made her jolt, and she scrambled back and tripped over her feet. Hands caught her before she landed on the ground, then hauled her upright.

"Mother of mercy." Silke took in a sharp breath before covering her mouth. "She's ..."

Georgie had rolled up to her feet and was now standing on all fours.

"What. The. Fuck." Logan stared at the horse, wide-eyed and wary. Georgie snorted at him, taking a careful step forward. Her nose nudged at his shoulder, but he seemed frozen. Finally, he blinked and rubbed the horse's nose.

"See, I told you." Silke sniffed and rubbed the tears from her eyes with the back of her hand. "Sabrina did it."

"She still killed her first," Logan growled. "Georgie would never have attacked her in the first place. These horses ... they can smell evil a mile away."

God, was he right? Was she evil? She stared down at her hands. But how could she have done all that?

"Logan, please," Silke said. "Stop it. Everything's all right."

"Nothing is all right!" Logan squared his shoulders and glared at Sabrina. "Not until *she* leaves. What if she does it again? What if she can't bring them back?" He turned to Silke. "What if it was you? Or Ransom? Or little Annie or one of the staff?"

"She won't." Cross stood in front of her protectively. "I'll make sure of it."

"The only way you can be sure of anything is if she gets outta here." Logan's eyes flashed with rage. "And if you don't do anything about it—"

Cross's entire body tensed. "Don't come any closer. Or—"

Logan stretched to full height and stood toe-to-toe with him. "Or what, warlock?" he growled.

"Cross, no!" She grabbed at his bicep. "Please, let's talk this out."

A rumble came from deep within his chest. She seriously thought he was going to lunge at Logan, but when she felt the coldness gripping her and the stables shimmering away from her vision, she realized Cross was transporting them. Seconds later, the interior of the cabin appeared around them.

He turned around. "Are you all right?"

"Why did you bring us back here?" She glanced around the cabin. "You should have brought us somewhere else." Pulling away from him, she turned away and wrapped her arms around herself. "Logan's right. What if I kill something—someone—else? And I couldn't bring them back?"

"Sabrina ... don't worry, I'll take care of everything. We can't go anywhere else. There's nowhere safe."

"Why not?" She whirled around to face him. "You can go anywhere in the world! Why is this the only safe place?" Her anger and frustration were bubbling to the surface. "Why can't I remember anything else? Why won't you tell me what happened and what I really am?" He didn't say anything, but she could see the war he was fighting inside. "Why won't you just tell me the truth?"

"Because I promised!" His eyes grew wide, and he ran his fingers through his hair. "I promised someone ... someone important that I would never tell you."

A pain pinched at her chest, and though she really wanted to ask him who was this person more important than her, she stopped herself. "Leave," she whispered.

"Sabrina—"

"I said *leave*!" she hissed. "Get out! I can't ... I can't look at you right now."

His face went stony and his jaw hardened.

She huffed and crossed her arms over her chest. Though she didn't have to say it, the message was clear. *Go.*

He let out a breath. "All right. I need to check on a few

things anyway." Then in an instant, he was gone. She collapsed on the bed and curled into a ball. God, the sheets still held a faint trace of his scent, and she buried her nose in a pillow, trying to get as much of it as she could.

Minutes ticked by before she sat up. Cross told her that this was the only safe place for them. But surely that wasn't true.

She stood up. "I'm done." Though no one was around to hear it, she said the words with conviction. There was no way she was staying here and waiting for Cross to feed her scraps of information. Not when she could find out on her own. In her memory, her father had been there. He was the one who did this to her, so he had all the answers. She had to get to him.

What to do? What to do? She paced back and forth, twisting the silver ring out of habit. There really was nothing keeping her here, only her own ignorance of where they were exactly. There had to be a way she could leave here. During the barbecue, one of the housekeepers said she drove an hour to the town and back the other day.

Hmmm. She could try to go on foot, but it might take her hours to reach town, and that was assuming she walked in the right direction. The thought of stumbling in the dark in the wilderness wasn't appealing. If only someone could help her, but Silke would never agree because she was so kind-hearted, and Ransom wouldn't do it because he wouldn't want to make Cross mad. If only—

"That's it!" She snapped her fingers. There was one person here who would be happy for her to leave.

Logan.

She rushed out the door, trying to figure out the direction

of the main lodge. Silke had driven them in her truck, but they followed some unpaved trails that had obviously been made by constant traffic. She walked around and found it, then began to walk forward with determination, following the path.

The trail had branched out in some places, and several times she had to backtrack when a path she took ended. She grew frustrated, but forged on. When she finally spied the lodge in the distance, the sun was low behind the mountains. With one last burst of energy, she stomped toward the stables. It was a gamble because Logan might not be there, but she had to try. Relief washed over her when she saw the giant at the end of the stables, patting Georgie on the nose.

"Logan," she gasped as she toddled forward.

"You." His mouth twisted, and his eyes narrowed. "What are you doing here? I told Silke—"

"Shut. Up." She caught her breath. "I know how you feel about me. So"—she took a step forward—"why don't we help each other out?"

"Help you?" he sneered. "Why would I help you?"

"Because we want the same thing."

He crossed his massive, tattooed arms over his chest. "And what's that?"

"For me to leave."

He stared at her, slack-jawed. "Silke said you had to stay here. And that you had nowhere else to go."

"Are you going to argue with me or h-h-help me?" It was a miracle she'd lasted this long before breaking. God, she'd never thought she'd be able to talk to anyone that way before. Desperation was helping her grow a spine, it seemed.

"Whaddaya want, then?"

"A ride to the nearest bus station. A-a-and bus fare to New York. And some cash." On the long walk here, she had thought of asking to use his phone to call her father but then came to the conclusion that Jonathan had to be in on this deception. He was probably the "someone important" who had made Cross promise to never tell her the truth.

Cross was probably on his way to New York to warn her father at this moment. No, she would have to confront her father without tipping him off that she was coming. "If you leave me your account information, I'll send you—"

"No need." He pushed himself off the metal bars of Georgie's stall. "The nearest bus station's in town. You'll probably have to connect through Louisville to New York. I'll give you enough to get there, plus extra for whatever else you need."

She stared at him as he walked past her, all the way to the doorway. "You probably won't want to ride with me, but I can borrow one of the lodge's trucks and drive you to the station." He stopped before he exited and said to her without turning his head, "You comin' or not?"

Despite her heart thumping wildly in her chest, she marched after him.

CHAPTER EIGHT

CROSS KICKED ONE OF THE OVERTURNED BOXES IN frustration. "Goddammit!" Another hard punt sent it flying toward the wall and smashing into pieces. *This was all my fault.*

With a sigh, he sat down on the last remaining box—the only one he hadn't overturned or smashed yet—and buried his face in his hands. His inner wolf cried woefully.

The last three years of his life had been spent in deception, and it was finally catching up with him. He'd been lying to his father, to his mother, his colleagues, his Alpha, and everyone else. He knew exactly where the ring was, but he didn't tell them. Sabrina's life was more important than anything in the world, and he'd sacrificed everything so she would remain safe.

All this time, he thought he was doing the right thing. As long as he kept this secret, then Gunnar's vision would never come true. He'd asked his brother several times, but so far, Gunnar had yet to see the premonition again, and so he kept up the lies. He and Jonathan had been so careful. Thought of any eventuality. Made sure there were no holes in their stories.

But what they didn't expect was for Sabrina's memory to return. That wasn't supposed to happen. He and Jonathan made sure of it. The mages had no idea that Cross knew about her, and they checked in with her father several times. Of course, Jonathan couldn't remember any of those times. Another part of their plan.

After bringing Sabrina to Kentucky, Cross had spent the last two days going back to every single mage hideout, stronghold, and sanctuary he and the rest of the Guardian Initiative had raided and destroyed, trying to find a clue or any indication on how they could have found out about her and what else they knew. Now, here he was, in the outskirts of Moscow, ransacking the last mage headquarters he and his father had succeeded in raiding for any clue as to what the mages knew and what their plans were. He'd combed through the entire place, but found absolutely nothing.

Give us the dagger. Or your mate dies.

The mages somehow discovered that Sabrina was his mate. He'd thought of all the terrible things they could do if they did get to her, but he didn't even *think* they would bribe him so he could steal the dagger. *Two birds with one stone, indeed.*

Daric was confident the Lycans would prevail because they had defeated the mages thirty years ago. But Cross wasn't feeling so optimistic now. Was Gunnar's vision inevitable?

He pushed himself up to his feet and wrung his hands together. *No.* They could still change the future. He had to believe that, and he wouldn't give up now, not after last night. There had to be a way.

Focusing his thoughts, he reappeared seconds later inside the cabin. The empty cabin, it seemed. It was dark outside, so maybe she had gone to the lodge to have dinner with Silke, since he had not provided her with any food.

After a brief check outside to make sure she wasn't there, he transported himself to the main lodge, in the hallway outside the manager's suite.

He knocked on Silke's door and heard her call out, "Just a minute." A few seconds later, she poked her head through the open door.

"Cross?" A frown marred her face. "What's wrong?"

"Is Sabrina here?" he asked. "I should explain a couple of things to her."

"No, why would she be here?" Silke crossed her arms over her chest. "You were the one who brought her back to the cabin."

"Yeah, but I left for a couple of hours and I just came back. Cabin's empty. Figured you might have invited her here for dinner."

She shrugged. "Well, I haven't seen her since this afternoon at the stables."

A pit began to form in his stomach and his inner wolf's ears tipped forward. "Where could she have gone to? She doesn't know the area. Where has she been in the past two days?"

Silke thought for a second. "Only the lake and Ransom's. She went over there when the pipes broke."

He didn't waste any more time and headed to Ransom's cabin, not even bothering to appear outside. Ransom, Hardy, and Bo all jumped to their feet and let out defensive snarls when he appeared in the living room.

"What the fuck!" Ransom cursed. "Never fucking do that, man."

"Where's Sabrina?" he asked.

"How the fuck should I know?" Ransom growled. "You said you'd take care of her."

Ransom's words made his chest tighten. Yes, that's what he was supposed to do. Take care of her. Of his mate. "She's not in the cabin or at Silke's."

"Well, she ain't here either." Hardy took a menacing step forward.

If Cross had the time to spare, he would deck the other Lycan just for being alone in the woods with his mate. Or bring him to Timbuktu and leave him there. His wolf very much liked all those ideas, but that wouldn't help him find Sabrina, so he told it to quiet down. "Did Silke tell you what happened this afternoon with Logan?"

"No." Ransom gritted his teeth. "But you're gonna tell me now."

He relayed a quick version to them of the events at the stables. "... and now I can't find her."

"Shit, how come you never told me your girl could do that?" Ransom scrubbed a hand down his face. "Logan *hates* witches."

A cold chill ran down his spine, and the pit in his stomach grew. "Would he harm her?"

"What the fuck are you saying, Jonasson?" This time, it was Ransom who took an aggressive step forward. "You think my wolves would harm a female?"

Bo cleared his throat and placed a gentle hand on

Ransom's shoulder. "I don't think he would hurt the girl, even if she was a witch. Logan's hate for anything magical runs deep, but he would never lash out at any innocent."

"Let's put an end to this now." Ransom pulled out his phone and tapped on the screen, then put the receiver to his ear. The furrow between his brows deepened as seconds ticked by, and there was obviously no answer. With a frustrated growl, he put the phone down. "Voicemail."

Hardy scratched his chin. "Could be busy."

"Is his cabin far?" Cross asked.

"Won't be in it, I guarantee," Bo said. "He rarely spends time indoors. Only goes to his cabin to change clothes and do his business. If he's not with the horses, then he's patrolling around the territory."

"I'll check the stables; you check his cabin." Cross didn't bother to wait for the other Lycan's confirmation, but instead, transported himself to the stables. A quick check in the stalls and around the perimeter told him that neither Logan nor Sabrina were there, but he could definitely detect their faint scents in the air, which meant both of them had been here recently.

His wolf growled; it hated the other Lycan. More than that, it could sense Logan's beast. To his wolf, that's what the other man's animal felt like—a caged monstrosity, waiting to get out.

His hands curled into his fists, and though he seriously wanted to tear the entire building apart, that wouldn't help, so he popped back to Ransom's cabin.

"—Snake or Hawk haven't seen him either, but someone from housekeeping saw—" Hardy stopped short when Cross reappeared.

"What did housekeeping see?" Cross asked, his voice tight.

Hardy's lips pulled back into a grim line. "Someone from housekeeping said she saw one of the trucks driving away. Couldn't see the driver, but said the passenger had white-blonde hair."

"Goddammit!" Cross wanted to rip something up. Preferably Logan's entrails out of his stomach. His inner wolf agreed as it bared its teeth. "I'm going to kill—"

"Cross, don't," Ransom warned. "Calm the fuck down."

"Calm down?" he groused. "How the fuck can I calm the fuck down when he's taken her—"

"Logan did not fucking take her!" Hardy shouted.

"Then explain how she's gone and how—"

"Every truck has a GPS tracker," Ransom said calmly, though the dominant authority in his voice was unmistakable. "We can find out where they are. Silke has them at the lodge. She'll pull up—"

He didn't even bother waiting for him, but instead, grabbed both men and transported them to the main lodge, outside Silke's suite. Ignoring Hardy's colorful curses as he staggered back from their landing, he banged on Silke's door. When she came out, he quickly explained to her what was happening. She led them down to her office so they could track the missing truck.

Her dark red brows snapped together as she squinted at her computer monitor. "Where are you ... where are you ... ah!" She slapped her palm on top of the desk in triumph. "There you are! Damn it, Logan!"

"Where are they?" Cross asked.

"Looks like they're in town. Just pulling into the credit union's parking lot."

"Credit union?" Hardy asked. "What the hell are they doing there?"

Cross could only guess, but he had a pretty good idea. "Sabrina has probably convinced Logan to give her money, maybe to take a bus out of town." He pulled the monitor around to face him, focusing on the location and the address on the map.

While both he and Daric had the ability to transport to places they hadn't been to, as long as they had a map and clear view, his father was much better at it. That was why whenever they needed to go somewhere, Daric would lead, and he would follow. But he had to try. If he didn't get to Sabrina now, he'd have to chase her halfway across the country.

"You going to them?" Ransom asked.

He snorted.

"Take us with you."

"What?" Hardy waved his hands and shook his head. "No way. I ain't travelin' via magic airlines. Gives me the creeps."

"Well, I ain't letting lover boy deal with Logan alone," Ransom said. "You'd probably send him to Antarctica just for being alone with your girl."

Hardy waved his hands. "No way. You—"

Silke grabbed onto his arm. "I'm coming too."

Ransom glared at his sister. "No, you stay—"

"Sabrina's obviously in distress." Her nails dug half-crescents into his skin. "Please. If she was upset enough to ask

Logan to help her, then she'll need someone there she can trust."

His wolf growled angrily at him. She was supposed to trust *them*, not that other beast. "Fine. Hold on."

Hardy's face turned red. "Goddamn motherfu—"

Adrenaline, desperation, or maybe it was the thought of Sabrina, but somehow, he was able to safely bring them to their destination in one piece. He had chosen the rear of the building, just to be sure no one saw them appear out of thin air.

Not bothering to wait for the others, he quickly sprinted toward the front and spied the truck at the end of the parking lot. He hurried over to the vehicle, but saw it was locked and empty. Muttering a curse, he turned around and began to walk toward the bank. He was only halfway across when he saw the glass doors open, and Logan and Sabrina came out. Instantly, her gaze connected with Cross's.

Before he could say a word, the hairs on the back of his neck stood on end. His wolf was on alert, as if warning him of something. He should have acted on his animal's warning because a split second later, his body hurtled backwards as a loud explosive sound nearly shattered his eardrums. The world was silent for a moment, like his ears were stuffed with cotton, before the ringing sound began. Staggering to his feet, he managed to regain his balance. Heat rushed around him, and he realized that the parked truck was now on its side, the entire body aflame.

The ringing in his ears subsided, and he thought he heard someone calling him. Turning, he saw Sabrina by herself, standing on the curb, screaming his name. So, he ran towards her, his heart pounding as he reached her. But before he could grab her, a force pushed him forward and slammed him against the side of the building, his head hitting the concrete so hard he saw stars.

"Cross Jonasson." The voice made his skin crawl. It was familiar; he'd definitely heard it before. But where?

He tried to move but found that he couldn't. It was like he was restrained by invisible chains. As his vision returned to normal, his stomach twisted in knots. A bald man in a red robe stood in front of him, his mouth curled up into an evil grin. When Cross struggled against his magical bonds, the mage tutted.

"Uh-uh-uh." A bony pale finger wagged in his face. "Don't even try it, you abomination. Selyse has got you, and you can't escape."

There were two people behind him, one man in the same mage robe, but his eyes were a cold icy blue. The other was a woman who also wore a red robe and had her hair shaved down. She held a hand up at him, and he could feel the power coming from her. Though he'd never encountered this particular mage before, he knew what she was. A blessed witch turned mage, one who had the power of telepathy. The evil nature of her corrupted power crawled over his skin as it held him against the wall.

Behind the three were another six mages. It wasn't unusual for mages to travel in groups; in fact, it was necessary because they'd somehow found a spell that allowed them to teleport short distances, but it required at least three people.

"Didn't you get my message?" The mage asked. "I told you to bring me the dagger. Or your mate dies."

That's why his voice sounded familiar. He followed his red gaze and saw another mage with his arms around Sabrina, one hand over her mouth. Her eyes were wide with terror as she struggled against her captor.

His wolf pushed to the surface, wanting to get at them. He reined it in, because shifting now and losing control wouldn't do any good. "How did you find us?"

"Did you think you could hide from us forever? Our reach is far. Farther and deeper than you think." The mage cackled. "Now, I'm going to take your mate, and you will get me the dagger. When you have it, you can have her back."

"And the ring?"

His nostrils flared. "I have to admit, I underestimated you. I didn't think you'd figure it out," he sneered. "We'll keep the ring, of course. In fact, we'll be taking it away from her now for safekeeping." He nodded to the man holding Sabrina. "Take it off her!"

The man released Sabrina for a second, only to grasp her right wrist. With his other hand, he grabbed the ring and attempted to pull it off. She let out a pained cry, and Cross's wolf came so close to coming out that he knew his eyes were probably glowing.

"Goddammit, Godfrey!" The man holding Sabrina shouted at them. "It's stuck! I can't get it off!"

"Then cut it off, I don't give a damn," Godfrey shouted back.

Cross let out a savage roar as the man took a knife out. However, when he tried to put it to Sabrina's hand, he let out a pained scream and then dropped to the ground.

Godfrey opened his mouth, but the sound of growls and a long howl made him clamp his mouth shut.

Two large blurs leapt out from behind the building. *Ransom and Hardy.* He'd almost forgotten about them. When they realized the mages had arrived, they must have stayed out of sight until they saw an opening. One of them, a large brown wolf with black streaks, leapt toward Godfrey. Unfortunately, Selyse saw the wolf and flicked it away, sending it flying into the air. However, that meant the female mage lost her hold on Cross, and he was free.

Anger raged through his veins as he stretched his arms forward. His wolf could no longer be held back, and so he let it take over. The transformation was fast; he'd learned the skill from fighting the mages in the last three years. While his magic was pretty effective, in combat against mages, his wolf always did best. Fur exploded from his skin, and his limbs stretched, and his animal burst from his human form. The great white wolf lunged forward, taking down both Godfrey and Selyse. They struggled, and Cross reached for the female first, his giant, claw-tipped paw raking down her face and front. She screamed in agony as blood gushed from her wounds.

"Impudent dog!" Godfrey screamed. Somehow, he'd managed to crawl out from underneath the white wolf while it had been busy with Selyse. "Take the girl and go!"

No! Cross screamed internally. The wolf got to its feet and scrambled toward the last place he saw Sabrina. Two mages were there, but to his relief, a dark gray wolf leapt in front of them and let out a growl. Its glowing gold-green eyes told him who it was.

Cross saw Silke creeping in from behind the building, ready to grab Sabrina, so he sprinted forward to take one of the robed figures down. However, the mage turned around and raised his hand. Something long and sharp formed in his hand. Cross attempted to pull back but it was too late.

As his wolf came down, the spear pierced the wolf's left hind leg.

The white wolf howled as icy pain spread up its leg, and it fell to the ground. Cross realized it wasn't a normal weapon. No, it was wet. A spear made of ice was sticking out from the wolf's thigh, its blood blooming out from the wound, staining the snowy white fur.

The mage raised his hand as another icicle began to form in his hand. The wolf struggled to get to its feet. *Get up,* he urged. He braced himself mentally as the mage raised his arm, weapon in hand, but before he could do anything else, a large black shadowy figure took the ice mage down. Though he couldn't see it, the sickening sounds of teeth tearing through flesh and bone told him what was happening.

A dizzy feeling washed over him. He thought he heard a scream. *Sabrina.* But he was feeling faint from the blood loss. His wolf lolled its head back, trying to make sense of what was happening. There was more screaming and shouting, but it wasn't Sabrina anymore.

"What in God's name is—"

"An abomination!"

"The beast is—"

"Monster!"

Cross directed his wolf to lift their head, and he saw what the mages were screaming about. It was the black wolf—or something like a wolf. It looked like any other Lycan in wolf form but two giant incisors speared out of its mouth, like a saber-tooth tiger's, and its back had a large hump that was lined with bony spikes, and its jet-black fur was mottled in places.

What the hell is that?

The animal let out a roar and leapt toward the group of mages forming a circle.

A throbbing pain made him wince. He had to get the icicle out so his wounds could heal, so he quickly shifted back to human form. Unfortunately, he couldn't focus and get his brain to think of what he could transform it to. Ice was just frozen water. Heat would melt it. Gathering up as much as he could of his strength and willpower, he concentrated and created heat from the molecules of air around the icicle. He gritted his teeth as the pain and scorching heat made his skin burn, but he knew he had to get rid of this thing so he could protect Sabrina.

The icicle spear melted quickly, but he was exhausted. *I'm sorry, Sabrina*, he thought as his body lay limp on the ground, unable to move.

"Cross!"

Sabrina. Her voice sounded so sweet. His vision was starting to blur at the edges, but he could make out her blonde hair around her pretty face, encircling it like a halo. God, she was so beautiful and wonderful. Talented. Kind-hearted and trusting. He didn't deserve her. "Sab—" he reached out to her, but his wound was making it impossible to move without sending shooting pain down his leg.

"Don't move. Oh, Cross. Cross, I'm sorry for leaving," she sobbed. "I swear—"

"Shh ... Angel. So—" He coughed, and she cried out. "Don't be sorry, I should be sorry. It was all my fault. Shouldn't have. Shouldn't have ..."

"Shouldn't have what?" Delicate hands took his. "Cross?"

"The forgetting potion," he choked. "Shouldn't have given it to you. Shouldn't have made you forget—"

And he rolled his head back, closed his eyes, and let the darkness take him.

———

A throbbing headache greeted Cross the moment he woke up. Scrubbing his hand down his face, he looked around, trying to figure out where he was. It was a bedroom, sparsely decorated, though the bed was comfortable. He guessed he was inside one of the cabins, but not the one Sabrina was staying at. A cursory sniff in the air caught a lingering hint of Ransom's scent, though there was no sign of the Lone Wolf. There was also a stronger scent in the air—apples and fresh snow—and his head snapped toward the source—sprawled on the lounge chair in the corner, eyes closed in slumber, her long blonde locks like a beacon in the dark room. The tightness in his chest eased. Sabrina was safe. The mages hadn't gotten to her.

Looking out the window, he saw the sun was already high up in the sky, bathing the mountains in late morning light. He sat up gingerly. His leg was throbbing, but the flesh was done knitting itself back together, so he had no worries about getting up. Despite his clumsiness, Sabrina didn't stir; thank God she was a heavy sleeper.

He waved his hand over his body and clothed himself, then limped out the door. The stairs gave him trouble, but eventually, he got to the ground floor. It was empty, too, though he noticed the pillows and blanket on the couch. He smiled to himself and walked out onto the porch, producing two cups of hot coffee in his hands.

Ransom was sitting on one of the chairs, gaze focused

ahead. When Cross came to him and offered one cup, he accepted it. "Thanks."

Cross sat down next to him. "Thank *you*. For last night."

The other man said nothing as he took a sip and continued to stare ahead.

"What happened after I passed out?" he asked. "Did they get away?"

Ransom cupped the mug with both hands. "No. Logan killed them all. We'll get rid of the bodies tonight. Or what's left of the bodies."

Damn. He was hoping at least one of them was alive so he could question them. But Logan ... "What the hell is he?"

Slowly, Ransom turned his head and fixed that green-amber gaze on him. "You don't want to know."

Something he'd learned the past few days about Ransom was that he was highly protective of his family and his wolves. If Lone Wolves had such a thing, Cross would have thought it to be very Alpha-like of him.

Ransom stared down into cup. "The others ... they're not happy about what happened last night. They're all out here tryin' to live like normal people. Spent enough of their lives runnin' away from shit like this, ya know what I'm sayin'?"

Cross rubbed his jaw. Staying with Ransom was a temporary solution. He had always hoped to recruit Ransom and his crew into the fight with the mages, but it was obvious they didn't want any part of this. "It's all right. I'll think of something else."

"What about your clan?" He took another sip of his coffee and leaned an elbow on his knee. "Your Alpha's pretty powerful." There was a hint of bitterness in his tone, though where it came from, Cross didn't know. "Can't anyone help you there?"

He owed Ransom the truth. At least some of it. "If it's not obvious by now, I'm not on good terms with them. They don't know about Sabrina." He swallowed the lump in his throat. "And I've spent the last three years making sure they didn't know about her existence."

"Why the fuck would you do that?"

"Because she's my True Mate." The admission made his wolf yowl, and strangely enough, made the heaviness in his chest lighten, like he'd let go of a big weight he'd been carrying around all this time.

"I'm your *what*?"

Cross stiffened at the sound of Sabrina's voice. She stood at the doorway, wrapped up in a blanket, pale hair in waves down her shoulders, her face a mask of confusion.

"Sabrina." He got up and took a careful step toward her. "How much did you hear?"

"What does it mean, I'm your True Mate?"

"It's not what it sounds like—"

"Damn you and your half-truths and explanations!" Her amethyst eyes flashed with anger. "Tell me the truth *now*. If you don't want to tell me what a True Mate is, at least tell me about this forgetting potion." Then she held up her hand. "And why those men want this ring."

Dread filled his stomach. "I can explain."

"I don't want an explanation, Cross. I want the *truth*." She crossed her arms over her chest and gave him a freezing stare. "Or so help me, I'll walk out right now, and you won't be able to stop me. I'll go back to New York on foot if I have to."

Cross stared at her, weighing his options. He closed his eyes. Three years ago, he thought he'd done the right thing, that this moment was something he wouldn't have to worry about because it would never come.

But no, the truth was like the rising tide; no matter how you tried to stop the waves, they would always come. It was time to come clean.

"All right."

She seemed taken aback by his lack of resistance. "Y-y-you'll tell me the whole truth?"

"You'll have to hear it from someone you'll believe." And when she did find out, he only hoped she could cope with what they had done.

"Who?"

He couldn't tell her. Not yet. So, he took her hand. "We should go see your father."

CHAPTER NINE

Truth be told, Sabrina was getting used to Cross's power. The coldness wrapping around her was almost comforting. When her feet landed on solid ground, she immediately knew where they were. "The penthouse," she said.

Her father's penthouse on the Upper East Side, to be precise. They were outside on the large terrace that had an amazing view of Central Park. She'd grown up in this apartment, played out here, and had numerous breakfasts and parties on this expansive outdoor space.

Before she could take her hand out of his, he pulled her to him, wrapping his arms around her and tucking her under his chin. She didn't protest, and instead, sank against him. "What is it?" she asked, sensing his apprehension.

"Sabrina, what if ... what if I took you away now? To anywhere else in the world. We can live anywhere you want, and you can be whoever you want. With my powers, I could even build us a cottage in a little village in Norway I know that overlooks the fjords. You could paint all day."

She smiled against his shirt. "And what would you do?"

"I could learn to farm. Remember what you said about painting me as a farmer? Or I could fish. I don't have to do anything really. I could stay home and ... watch the kids."

Her chest tightened, and she closed her eyes. She imagined a little boy and girl. Both with eyes the color of the sea.

"We could leave all this behind."

Her body tensed. Pulling away from him, she turned her head up to meet his gaze. "If we live in this little cottage by the fjords, will you tell me what really happened three years ago?"

"We ... we'll start afresh," he said. "We don't need the past."

It was oh so tempting. And for just a second, she wanted it. All of it. The cottage, the painting, the children. But she knew that if she were ever going to live a peaceful life and become the person she wanted to be, she had to know the truth. So, though it took all her strength, she took a step back. "I'm sorry. I can't, Cross."

He gave a solemn nod. "All right. We should go inside."

They walked toward the glass door that led into the apartment. Sabrina slid the door aside and walked inside.

"What the—Sabrina?" Jonathan sat at the breakfast nook, body frozen, his cup of coffee halfway to his lips. "Sweetheart, is that really you?"

Despite everything she had learned about her father, his possible involvement in all these lies, the sight of him made her break down. She ran into his arms, embracing him and breathing in the familiar scent of his old-fashioned aftershave and enjoying the feel of his freshly-shaven cheek against hers. "Yes, Dad, it's me."

"I ... I went to your apartment, and you were gone. I called the police." He released her, then cupped her face in his hands. "Sweetheart, I—" His face switched expressions. "*You*." Letting go of her, he marched toward Cross. "What are you doing here? I *knew* you were involved in her disappearance! We had an agreement!" he hissed. "What if they find out?"

"They already know, Jonathan," Cross said. "I think we should sit down."

His gaze moved from him to Sabrina, then back to Cross. "Does she know? Did you tell her?"

"I didn't. She figured it out. I'm afraid she's remembering."

"You said she wouldn't! She couldn't!" He exploded and grabbed Cross by the collar. "It was supposed to be effective."

"The potion was powerful but untested. I told you that."

"But—"

"Can someone *please* explain this all to me?" she cried. "Please, just tell me the truth."

"What the hell happened?" her father asked Cross.

Cross relayed all the events of the last few days to him, from the time the mages had come to her apartment, until she remembered the night she'd killed all the plants in her apartment, then he stopped. "You should tell her again, Jonathan. What you said the night she brought them back."

Jonathan went pale. "I did it for you, Sabrina. I promised your mother. I promised her I would do anything to keep you alive."

"Even make me forget about what happened? Forget about Cross?" she said through gritted teeth. "Was it because he wouldn't accept your bribe?" She was shouting now, and her body shook with each breath. "Why did you do this to me? Did you force me to take that potion?" Her skin crawled at the thought. She suddenly felt violated. "There was no accident, was there?" He shook his head. "Why did you do that? How—how could you take my memories away without my consent?"

Jonathan and Cross looked at each other, not saying anything.

"What is it?" A strange pit in her stomach began to form.

More looks passed between them, until finally, Jonathan spoke. "It wasn't our idea, sweetheart."

"No?" she spat. "Then whose idea was it?"

Jonathan turned on his heel and walked over to one of the paintings on the wall. He took it off from where it hung and placed it on the floor, revealing a hidden safe, then unlocked it. Reaching inside, he took out something rectangular and flat.

"Here," he said quietly, handing the object to her. It was a small tablet PC. "You should watch this."

Her hands were shaking as she took the device from him. She tapped on the screen but nothing happened.

"Put your thumbprint on the sensor," Jonathan said.

She did, and to her surprise, the black screen lit up. "But how?"

"It's programmed for your biometrics," Cross explained. "Only you can open it."

Slowly, she turned back to the screen. There was only one icon on the desktop, so she tapped on it. The file expanded, and she felt her heart jump to her throat when she saw what was on the screen. Or rather, *who*.

"If you're watching this, Sabrina, that means that somehow, despite all our efforts, you remembered everything."

Horror. Surprise. Anxiety. Distress. Her emotions swung back and forth like a wild pendulum. "That's ..." She covered her mouth. "That's *me*."

The woman in the screen was definitely her. The video was taken on her sofa, and she was wearing her favorite purple sweatshirt. "... but before I explain everything," Sabrina in the video continued. "Don't blame Dad. And definitely don't blame Cross." The light in video Sabrina's eyes seemed to die when she said his name. "This was my idea. I made him promise never to reveal it to you ... me. I wanted ... needed to forget. The fact that you're watching this means you know why."

"I ... I remember," she gasped. The pounding at the base of her skull came back. "I asked how you knew I could do that to the plants ..."

———

Three years ago ...

"How did you know I could do that?" Her voice trembled so violently she hardly recognized her own voice. Cross remained silent, but his gaze flickered to Jonathan. "Dad? What's going on? Do you know anything about this?"

"Sabrina ..." He took a cautious step toward her, then

took her hands in his. "Sabrina, do you remember what I told you about this?" Lifting her hand up, his gaze fixed on the ring on her finger.

She nodded. "Y-y-es. You said it was Mom's." She'd had it since she was a baby and had worn it around her neck as a necklace until she was grown up enough to put it on her finger.

"What else did I say, sweetheart?"

"You said that ... that I should never lose it or give it away. That no matter what, I needed to keep it forever."

His Adam's apple bobbed visibly. "Melanie ... your mother ... she was healthy throughout the pregnancy. There was no indication at all ... but she went into labor earlier than expected." He became even paler, and his eyes glazed over. "She knew something was wrong, so she made me promise. Made me promise that whatever happened, I would choose your life over hers. And that I would do anything to make sure you lived. She died giving birth to you, but the doctor said you weren't going to make it. And you didn't. You died right after your mother did."

Her lungs squeezed painfully, and she couldn't make a sound, no matter how hard she tried.

"I held you, alone, in the operating room. The doctors and nurses left to give me some privacy. And then ... and then I can't explain it to you now, but they appeared. These men. They were wearing red robes, and they said they could bring you back. I was delirious with grief, and I said yes, even before they told me what they wanted in return. And they did. I cried when you started breathing again, right there, in my arms."

"Who?" she gasped. "Who were they? And what did they do?"

"The ring, Sabrina." His face was stricken with horror. "They said that you needed to keep the ring close and never lose it or destroy it. It was what brought you back to life."

"No. That's not true!"

"I'm sorry, sweetheart." He shook his head. "I'm so sorry."

"What did they want in return?"

Her head whipped toward Cross. She'd almost forgotten that he was still here. Oh God, now he was going to get mixed up in this mess!

"Those bastards," Jonathan spat. "What else would they want from me? Money, of course. From that moment on, they had me by the balls. I've poured an unspeakable amount of money into their coffers, and who knows what they're doing with it?" He gritted his teeth. "But you were worth it, darling girl. Every single moment with you is worth it."

"Why did you try to bribe Cross?" she asked. "And all my other boyfriends?"

"Because they told me no one could ever know the truth," Jonathan admitted. "That's why I kept you isolated. A boyfriend or husband might have questions. And if you had children ... who knows what they would do? They said that if anyone ever found out about the ring, they would kill you in front of me. Sweetheart, these are powerful men. They could do things ..." He shuddered. "Things you could only dream about."

"I'm going to throw this away." She grasped the ring with her thumb and forefinger. "I don't want it. I don't want this!"

His expression turned to horror. "Don't, Sabrina."

"I'm ... I'm going to destroy it." She grabbed at the ring

and tugged. "I'll toss it down the disposal or ... or ... Damn it!" Why couldn't she take it off? The silver band seemed soldered onto her skin. She'd worn it for years, never really thinking about it. When was the last time she had taken if off? It had been her mother's—or so she'd thought—which was why she never thought to remove it, not even while she was working or washing her hands. "It won't come off!"

"I don't think you can take it off, Sabrina," Cross said.

She whirled toward him. "How do you know?" A shudder went through her. "Who the hell are you? Is your name even Cross?"

"It is. I don't know how to explain this." He raked his fingers through his hair. "Sabrina, those men your father are talking about, they're called mages. They're the enemy of my kind. Bad people."

"Your kind?"

"I can't tell you any more, not without putting you in more danger."

"If they're bad, why did they bring me back to life with this ring?"

His eyes turned dark. "That I'm not sure of yet. But you see, the mages want only one thing: to rule the world and enslave everyone in it. And that ring is part of their plan."

"How?"

"I don't know yet, but ..." he hesitated. "My brother can see visions of the future and he saw them win. The mages will rule over the world. Then they're going to kill my family and the rest of my kind."

"It can't be ... no, it's impossible. Magic doesn't exist, right?" She turned to her father, hoping to get some confirmation from him. But his expression told her that this was all happening.

"The ring," Cross continued, "the ring they gave you is one of the tools they will use to do this."

"Wait, did you bump into me because you wanted the ring?" Hurt and betrayal made her chest ache.

"No!" he said quickly. "That was coincidence." He shook his head. "No, my brother predicted it too. And I tried to stay away, but I couldn't."

"The world's going to end?" she asked. "You'll die? And my father? And everyone?"

"Those left will become slaves of the mages."

This was all crazy, but something inside her was telling her it was all true. After tonight, after everything she'd seen, it became more and more obvious that he was telling the truth. How could she even deny it after what she'd seen; after what she'd *done*?

She stared down at the ring on her hand. God, she hated it! Wished she could cut if off. Wished there was some way to stop that future he was talking about.

"God." Jonathan buried his face in his hands. "I wish ... but even if I could go back in time, I would have done everything to save you, Sabrina."

"Dad ..."

"Isn't there any way to stop it?" Jonathan grabbed Cross's arm. "If you care about my daughter, you'll find a way. Please. I'll do anything."

Cross's jaw hardened. "I've been trying to find a solution. But my brother's premonitions have always come true."

"And there is no way to change the future?" she asked. "Something we can do now?

"My brother's visions aren't set in stone, he says. But he doesn't know what we can do now to change it."

A dread filled her. "You said that in his vision ... this ring is one of the things that they need to bring about the destruction of the world?"

"Yes."

"And because I can't take the ring off, what he really means is me and the ring, right?" He didn't answer, but he didn't have to. "It's me, isn't it? *I'm* the reason that vision will come true. It's because of me."

Cross swallowed. "You were in the vision. Right before my family dies and the mages take over."

"Then you have to ... you have to do something. Make sure I don't cause that." She took a deep breath. "Maybe I wasn't supposed to live," she concluded. "Maybe I need to die—"

"Sabrina, no," Jonathan embraced her tight. "No!"

"Dad, there's no other way."

"No! I will not allow this to happen!" He turned to Cross. "If you care for her one bit, you won't stop trying. You'll find a way to save Sabrina. There has to be a way. You said you've thought on this for a long time. You must have some ideas. Please," he cried. "Please save my daughter."

She looked at him, at his face. There was an inner battle she could sense he was fighting. "You've already thought of a solution."

"One *possible* solution," he said after much hesitation. "But we can't—"

"What is it, Cross? Tell me," she pleaded.

He took a deep breath, and his hands clenched at his

sides. "I should have walked away from you that day I saw you."

"At Wicked Brew? When you bumped into me?"

"I saw you earlier than that, Sabrina. A few days before that. I saw you across the street and followed you to Wicked Brew. Then I came back every day to try and see you. Then we bumped into each other accidentally, and that was when I realized who you were. When I saw you and your ring."

He'd known about her even before that day? "Why didn't you leave me alone?"

"I couldn't."

Those two words made her ache. She knew how it felt. How it felt to be pulled toward someone like a magnet, unable to stop. Because that was how she felt the moment they met. "You said there was a way? What if we just stay away from each other?"

"It's not that simple," he said. "In my brother's vision, he says you're there because of me. He was specific about that."

"So, what do we do? We can't reverse time. We can't make it so you and I never met." The serious expression on his face made her heart stop. "Is there?"

———

Sabrina sucked in a breath as the memories flooded back into her head. It was a strange sensation, like she was empty and then suddenly filled. She remembered all of it. Well, most of it anyway. Not the exact events, but she could already guess at this point. "The forgetting potion."

"Yes," Cross confirmed. "It wasn't just any forgetting potion. While most forgetting potions only erase recent memories, this potion could make you forget one significant aspect in your life. My grandmother knew how to make it. She never told anyone. But I was learning potion and spell craft from her, and she told me how and made me promise to never tell anyone."

There might be one way. You could forget about me. Forget you ever met me. Forget I ever existed.

The words echoed in her head, but it wasn't her voice. It was Cross's.

Then we need to do it. If that's the only way.

It was strange hearing her own voice saying something she didn't recall. But there it was, clear as a bell.

We don't have a choice, Cross. If we don't ever meet, then Gunnar's vision will never come true. He said it. I'm there because of you.

But Sabrina ... this potion ... it will mean that it's as if you and I never met.

I know ... but do we have a choice? We're talking about the fate of the world. Promise me, Cross. Promise me.

Tears burned at her throat. "Oh God ... it was all ... the accident ... Dad?"

"You came up with it, and we concocted the cover story together," Jonathan said. "I had a whole wing of that hospital blocked out just for you. You took the potion there and woke up a few hours later with no memory of the last twenty-four hours or of Cross."

"I created the potion so that you would forget we ever met, while preserving everything else," Cross explained.

She swallowed and closed her eyes. A searing pain knifed through her chest as she recalled that moment, when she was in that room and took the vial from him. There were words that had been stuck in her throat. Words she wanted to say, but couldn't.

Goodbye, Cross.

"Aside from getting their regular payout from me, those men asked about you on a regular basis," Jonathan explained. "They would check on you, to see if you still had the ring and who you'd been involved with. That's why I kept bribing your boyfriends away. I didn't want them hurt."

"Why didn't we all three take the potion?" she asked.

"It's difficult to make. I could only make enough for one person at a time," Cross said. "And we needed to remember in case there was a problem."

"And my poker face has gotten me far in business," Jonathan said, amused. "It was easy enough to lie to them and tell them half-truths about you."

"But I remembered anyway," she said. "I—I don't think I truly forgot. Those paintings in my studio ... they were all of you, Cross. Somehow, I could still remember you."

He shook his head. "Maybe I made a mistake with the formula. I'm not sure."

"Couldn't you give her a stronger dose?" Jonathan asked. "We could try again."

Fear rose up in her chest. "No! You can't make me forget again!" She clutched Cross's arm. "Please don't make me do it. I don't want to forget you. Besides, it didn't work the first time. We tried to stop it by making me forget, but I still remembered. We'll always find each other, I know it. Please, Cross," she begged.

"I won't," he said solemnly. "I don't want you to forget either."

"Thank you."

"Then what should we do now?" Jonathan asked. "How can we protect Sabrina?"

"Can't we fight them?" she asked. "Erasing my memory obviously didn't help. You're so powerful, and you have others of your kind, right?"

His eyes darkened. "You're right. But we can't do it alone," he admitted. "We will need help." He stretched out his hand. "You should come with us, too, Jonathan. For your own protection."

Sabrina tucked herself against Cross's side. "Please, Dad?"

He hesitated but nodded anyway. "All right. We'll try this your way."

As she felt the comforting coldness wrap around her, she breathed in his scent and whispered something that she hoped he would hear. Words she had been wanting to say for a very long time.

CHAPTER TEN

CROSS STAGGERED FORWARD AS THEY LANDED RATHER ungracefully at their destination. Though he heard the words coming from her lips, he wasn't sure if he understood them correctly. He looked down at her, cuddled up to his side. The smile on her lips, and the sparkle in her amethyst eyes told him he hadn't imagined it. "Sabrina? You—"

She nodded. "And I meant it."

He knew he had made the right decision. *Never again.* He would never lose her again. It had torn him apart having to stay away from her. "I—"

"Well, now," a seemingly disembodied voice said. "I was wondering what time you'd drop in."

He froze at the sound of the familiar voice. "Mom?"

Meredith Jonasson stood up from behind the sectional couch in the living room, hands on her hips. "Hello, Cross," she said, a smirk on her face.

"Cross?" Sabrina looked up at him, confused. "Where are we?"

"At my parents' loft in Tribeca," he explained, then turned to Meredith. "How did you know I was coming?"

Meredith was unusually calm as she rounded the couch and headed toward them. Cross had honestly expected hysterics. But knowing his mother, she was probably ready to explode at him.

"Who do you think?" she asked as she stood toe-to-toe with him.

Who else? "Gunnar."

"We went to see him tonight, but when we arrived, he said I had to come back here to wait for you. Care to explain a few things? Like where the hell you've been the past couple of days and *why* you've been lying to us?" Her whiskey-brown gaze landed on Sabrina, then Jonathan, and then Sabrina again. "Cross?"

"Mom, this is Sabrina Strohen, and her father, Jonathan," he said. "Sabrina is—"

"Your True Mate," Meredith said, eyes going wide.

Sabrina stiffened beside him, and he gave her shoulder a reassuring squeeze. There had been so many explanations that had to be made that he hadn't yet gotten to that particular one. "Yes," he confirmed.

"Oh." Her face turned from simmering anger, to surprise, to pure joy. "Oh. She's the reason. Oh, honey." She embraced them both. "Oh God. I knew there was a reason you would do that." Releasing them, she wiped her eyes with the back of her hand. "Sorry, I'm not usually like this. It's just ... things have been crazy around here, ya know? We've been trying to reach Cross, but at the same time, make sure the Alpha doesn't find him first. Lucas—he's in a rage, and we don't know what kind of punishment he has in mind for what you did."

"Punished?" Sabrina asked. "What do you mean, punished?"

"We should sit down and talk," Meredith said. "Oh, sorry. Haven't introduced myself." She wiped her hand down her jeans. "I'm Meredith." She glanced down at Sabrina's stomach. "Or should you be calling me Mom, too?"

"*Mom,*" Cross said in a warning tone. He knew what Meredith was thinking, of course. One way to determine if someone was a True Mate—precognitive family members aside —was that during the first coupling, the couple always produced a pup. It didn't matter if one of them was human either, as long as they were True Mates. "We should get to the task at hand."

"All right," she said wryly. "Let's head to Gunnar's cabin and we can all talk." She held onto his forearm, and once Jonathan took his other hand again, he focused his thoughts on where they needed to be.

"That's rather ... disconcerting," Jonathan mumbled as he tugged on his suit jacket and buttoned it up. "I'll stick to airplane travel. Where are we anyway?"

"West Virginia. Shenandoah Valley, to be precise."

Cross's stomach clenched tight at the sound of Daric's voice. "Dad, I'm sorry," he said to the older warlock. "I can explain everything."

Daric's blond brow lifted, then he glanced at Sabrina and Jonathan. "It seems explanations are in order. Come," he gestured to the living area, where a large pot of tea sat on the table. "Have a drink first. I shall call Gunnar."

"I'm already here." His brother stood in the doorway

leading to his bedroom. "Let's all sit down and have some tea." He walked past them, smiling at Sabrina as he made his way across the living room.

They all sat down, Gunnar on the leather recliner, his father and mother on the small love seat, and him, Sabrina, and Jonathan on the couch.

"Tell us what happened." Daric's blue-green gaze briefly went to Gunnar, then landed on Cross. "From the beginning."

Cross took a deep breath, and began to tell them everything that happened, from the day Gunnar had his premonition and told him that Sabrina was his True Mate, up until this morning when Sabrina finally realized the truth. Beside him, she remained quiet, though her hand gripped his tight. He didn't even realize he'd been holding and squeezing hers when he'd told the most painful part of the story—her saying goodbye to him before she took the potion. It was a day he would never forget, after all—the day it seemed like his heart and soul were being ripped apart.

"Your instinct was to protect her." Meredith looked at Daric. "That's what it's like when your mate is in danger. We'd do anything for them."

"W-w-what does it mean, True Mates?" Sabrina said, finally speaking up.

"It means you were fated to be together," Daric said.

"Among other things," Meredith said with a small smile curving her lips. "Nothing can keep you apart."

"This potion," Daric began. "Signe never told me about it."

"She said not to tell you or Mom," Cross explained. "She

showed me the recipe, made me memorize it, and told me to never give it to anyone."

"But why?"

"Isn't it obvious?" Gunnar interjected. "Grandma knew he would need it. She probably didn't know how and when, but she just knew."

"It's incredible," Daric said. "So, it completely erased all her knowledge of you? How does it work?"

"I'm sorry, but I promised her never to tell anyone how to make it or how it works." He glanced at Sabrina, realizing there was something else he hadn't mentioned. Something he should tell her. "It also has another side effect—slight paranoia. That's why you had a hard time leaving the house."

"And I knew this side effect?" she asked.

He nodded. "You thought it was a good thing, to further prevent you from knowing the truth. If you interacted with too many people, they might start asking questions. I didn't want that for you ... I mean, if you found someone else, I would have understood." Actually, he would probably have gone insane, but he didn't want to say it out loud. "But you were too good. You wanted to save us so bad."

"I ..." Her eyes closed briefly. "I remember. It made sense, right? It was a small sacrifice on my part, to prevent the end of the world as we knew it."

"Oh, sweetie," Meredith had a sad smile on her face. "My son is lucky to have a mate like you."

"What do we do now?" Jonathan asked.

"The ring ... I can't remove it," Sabrina said. "I tried. One of the mages did, too, but when he tried to forcibly cut it off, it was like the ring hurt him and knocked him to the ground."

"Probably a type of safeguard. Son," Daric began, "what else have you learned about the ring?"

"Nothing much more than what we already know," he said. "Although, I can confirm now that it does have the power of death and life. But I don't know why she can't take it off."

"Some magical objects are known to bond with whoever possesses them," Daric explained. "We didn't have that problem with the dagger because it's only used whenever there was an ascension ceremony. We don't know about the necklace since the mages have that."

"But why would they give it to Sabrina?" Meredith asked. "If it was so powerful, why hand it over to someone who wasn't one of them?"

"Do you think they need Sabrina as a host for the ring?" Cross asked. He'd thought about it for a while, because he, too, had the same thoughts as his mother.

Daric paused for a moment. "Could be. But sometimes, the simplest explanations are the most likely."

"That still doesn't solve how we're going to fix all this," Cross said. "Should we go to Lucas?"

"Yes. But before that, you should know the reason we called you here." Daric turned to Gunnar. "Will you tell them?"

Gunnar straightened his posture, then leaned forward, his fingers steepling together. "My vision has changed."

Cross stared at his brother, dumbfounded. "What do you mean, changed? Did we stop it from happening?"

"Not quite," he said. "Everything still happens as I told you. Up to a point." His whiskey-brown eyes glazed over, and he stared forward blankly. "That ceremony ... the necklace, the dagger, and Sabrina. She touches the two objects. She falls, and you catch her. You hold her, and she whispers something and then ..."

"And then?" Cross asked.

"And that's it."

"That's it?" he echoed.

"There was nothing after it," he said. "I didn't see the other events. Didn't see or feel anyone dying. It didn't end, you see. I think ... I think it may mean the future changed. Or is still changing, I'm not sure."

"But the rest didn't change," Cross said, frowning. "You still see the mages capture Sabrina and the other two artifacts."

Gunnar had a strange look on his face. "I still see Sabrina and the artifacts."

Sabrina's grip on him tightened again. "We'll find a way to stop them."

"First, you must come clean to the Alpha," Daric said. "Lucas is tough, but he will listen to you and your reasons."

"And we'll be there with you." Meredith said, sending him a reassuring look.

Lucas Anderson wouldn't be happy about this, but like his father said, he was a reasonable man. If his Alpha meted out any punishment, it would be well worth it if it meant keeping Sabrina safe *and* defeating the mages. "You're right."

"I'll call the office and check where he is, then explain the situation." Meredith reached for the mobile phone on the couch. "Then we can arrange to meet him." As she dialed on her phone, she strode away from them, heading for the privacy of the kitchen.

"Your Alpha ... he's like your leader?" Sabrina asked.

"Yes. He's the leader of the entire New York clan."

Her brows wrinkled. "He's mad at you for what you did. For helping me forget. And because you didn't hand me or the ring over to him."

"Yes," he admitted. "But I don't regret protecting you, Sabrina. I would do it over and over again. You're my priority."

"We're ... mates," she said. "We were meant to be together." Her head snapped up. "Maybe that's why I couldn't forget you."

He smiled. "Yes, that's probably why." Her words earlier still shook him to the core. Three little words that turned his world upside-down. "When you took that potion and forgot about me, I felt like half a person. Which is strange, because I never felt like that before I met you." He'd often wondered if the potion dulled the bond between them as well. He wanted to tell her how he felt, too, but not now, when he was surrounded by his family. Later, when they were alone, he would tell her.

"Cross, I—"

"He's at Muccino's," Meredith said as she strode back into the living room. "He's not alone. But he says we should come anyway."

"Will you be all right, son?" Daric asked Gunnar.

"Yes, you should go now," Gunnar said. "There's no time to waste."

"We can use the alley in the back." Meredith looped her arm through Daric's. "Lucas should be done clearing it by now."

Cross turned to his brother. "Gunnar ... thank you so much."

"You're thanking me?" Gunnar offered him a rare smile, his face looking much younger and less burdened than it usually did. "I'd thought you'd be cursing me by now."

"I could never do that," Cross said. Gunnar's gifts were a part of him, and he loved his brother.

His smile didn't fade as he turned to Sabrina. "It's lovely to meet you. I hope it won't be a while until we meet again."

"You're the one who can see the future, why don't you tell me?" she asked.

"I like her," Gunnar chuckled. "In case it's longer than we expect ..." He leaned down and brushed his cheek to hers as he put an arm around her.

Cross thought he heard his brother murmur something to Sabrina, but even his sensitive ears couldn't pick it up. When she pulled away, there was a quizzical look on her face, but she nodded.

"What—"

She grabbed his hand and wrapped it around her waist. "We should go," she said.

It gnawed at him, but he knew there were more important things right now. He offered his hand to Jonathan. "Let's go. The Alpha will need to talk to you too."

A few seconds later, they arrived in the alley behind Muccino's. Cross had expected the Alpha to be there, and although Meredith had mentioned he wasn't alone, he didn't think there'd be this many people.

Aside from Lucas, his wife and the Lupa of New York, Sofia was there, as was the Beta of New York, who happened to be Cross's sister, Astrid, and her husband Zac Vrost. Behind them were two more couples—Julianna and Duncan MacDougal, and Elise and Reed Wakefield. The latter's presence was an even bigger surprise as they were based in San Francisco. All of them, however, were on alert, as if they were preparing for something. The tension in the alley was palpable, and it seemed everyone's wolves were on the edge.

"Welcome back, Cross." Though he looked the picture of calm, there was no doubt of Lucas Anderson's power and position as Alpha. His dominant vibe radiated off him, making Cross's inner wolf shrink back. "Though your mother assured me that you won't try to run away again, you'll have to understand that I'm skeptical." He nodded at Astrid.

His sister stepped forward, a serious expression on her face. She held up a shiny, circular object in her hand. "I'm sorry, Cross. You know I have to do this."

He recognized the object, of course. The bracelet that dampened powers.

Astrid continued, "You'll have to put this on. I—" Her eyes darted to Sabrina, to the arm wrapped around her waist. "Who are—" She looked up at Cross, blonde brow lifted. "Anything you care to tell us?"

"I'd be happy to explain everything and to wear the bracelet." He held his hand out and Astrid cuffed the bangle around his wrist. It was a weird sensation, the moment he put it on. He felt normal, except that he just didn't *feel* right.

"Let's all go inside." Lucas led them into the door that led to the restaurant, where they all gathered around the chef's private dining table just behind the kitchen.

Cross had been here several times, as they tended to celebrate many family occasions here. Lucas's parents were part owners of the restaurant, and currently, his Uncle Dante was the head chef.

"Sorry it's a bit cramped," Sofia said. "We were in the middle of lunch when you called."

"Since we had everyone here, we thought we'd include them," Lucas added. "Now, Cross. Why don't you tell us what's really going on?"

Taking a deep breath, he repeated the entire story again, for the second time that day. It was obvious everyone was shocked by his story, but he didn't have time to process all their reactions. His focus was on Sabrina. She remained quiet, but he kept glancing at her, making sure she was all right. Her face was a serene mask, but from the way the knuckles on her hands turned white as they gripped his, he could tell a lot was going through her head.

"... which brings us here," Cross concluded. "I'm sorry, Alpha," he said to Lucas, "for deceiving you. All of you. I was trying to find another way to defeat the mages while protecting Sabrina."

"You should have told us from the beginning," Lucas admonished. "You know we would have understood." He looked around the room. Every single Lycan there was part of a True Mate pairing. "I'm your Alpha. I would have helped you."

"I realize that now. And if you must punish me, I'll accept any penalty. Just let me make sure Sabrina is safe."

She stiffened beside him. "I think this is way beyond protecting me, Cross. You already tried to protect me."

"The real issue here is the mages," Lucas said. "We need to strike first and soon, even before Gunnar's vision comes true."

"I'll do whatever I can, Alpha," Cross said. "And you're

right. Perhaps the only way to stop the premonition is to defeat them once and for all."

"Jonathan," Lucas began. "You're the only person here who's dealt directly with the mages. Would you be willing to help us?"

"Of course," he answered. "Anything to finally get rid of those bastards. But I don't know how to fight or do any magic, how can I help you?"

"You said that you've been funneling money into their operations for years. There's someone on my team who might be interested in knowing the details. She actually was able to trace some of the funds back to you and a few others, but so far, her investigation hasn't yielded anything solid."

"Anything you need, you can have it," Jonathan said. "I want those guys gone as much as you do."

"Excellent. Now"—the Alpha turned to the rest of the people in the room—"we should begin preparations and make some plans. Let's all head to the Guardian Initiative headquarters downtown. We should get Alynna and her team up to speed too. Jonathan, you should come with us so you can have a chat with Lizzie."

"Lupa," Cross said. "Will you keep Sabrina safe, please? At The Enclave?"

"Of course," Sofia answered. "I was on my way home anyway to check on Alessandro."

"What?" Sabrina's grip on his hand tightened. "No, Cross! I want to be with you. You can't leave me—"

"I'm not leaving you," he said. "But I'm afraid that because of the ring, we can't have you out in the open." His chest tightened at the thought of being apart from her, but he knew he had to keep her safe. "I can't help but wonder if somehow they knew you were at the bank last night because of the ring. If that were the case, The Enclave is the safest place in the world for you. There are magical protections there that the mages can't penetrate, old magic that's been there for decades, plus new ones that have made it difficult to breach. But the Guardian Initiative's offices aren't as well-protected. You could inadvertently lead the mages there."

He hated having to appeal to her altruistic nature, but from the look on her face, he knew he had succeeded.

"All right. But promise me you won't do anything stupid to protect me. Don't even think of leaving and fighting them off without coming to see me."

While he knew there was no way he could keep the first one because he would always protect her, he could, at least, promise her that second one. "I promise I'll come to see you. Tonight."

That seemed to mollify her. "I didn't go through all this to not be with you."

"Cross!" A hand slapped him playfully on the head. "That's for being an idiot and scaring me half to death." Astrid exclaimed before she enveloped him in a hug. "And that's because I missed you, and I'm so glad to see you." Grabbing his wrist, she removed the bracelet. "Boy, am I glad to be taking this off you." Her whiskey-brown eyes sparkled when they landed on Sabrina. "Hello! I'm Astrid, Cross's favorite sister."

"You're my only sister," he reminded her, but laughed anyway.

"I'm Sab—oh!" She had reached out her hand to Astrid, but his sister pulled her into a tight hug. "Uh, nice to meet you."

"I'm so glad to meet you. You don't know how happy I am to meet his mate." She flashed him a dirty look as she released Sabrina from the bear hug. "I'm just so relieved I didn't have to kick his ass for being on the mage's side."

Sabrina chuckled. "Me too."

"We should get going, Cross," Astrid said. "Lucas will want to get started as soon as possible."

"I'll follow along."

"I can take her back," Sofia said. "The driver's outside, and we have two bodyguards."

"I feel a lot better knowing she's in your hands, Lupa," Cross said.

"I'll be right outside, Sabrina." She turned and walked toward Lucas, who was chatting with Reed, Julianna, Duncan, and Elise.

"Cross—"

Unsure what else to say or do, he snaked a hand around her waist and pulled her close, as if trying to memorize the feel of her curves against him. "I'll see you tonight," he said before he lowered his head and kissed her, not caring they were surrounded by his family, the Alpha and Lupa, and everyone else. It had felt like a million years since he had tasted her lips, and he was reluctant to let her go.

When he finally released her, she sank against him, her hands gripping his shirt. "I swear, if I don't see you tonight, I'm going to ... to ..."

"I know." He kissed her forehead. "I promise, I'll come to you tonight." Those words made her shiver. And if he were honest, his heart raced with excitement. Hopefully, he could get through the day before he went crazy with thinking about her all day.

CHAPTER ELEVEN

SABRINA COULDN'T QUITE BELIEVE SHE WAS BACK IN New York, even as she watched the throng of tourists in Rockefeller Center as their town car crawled down Fifth Avenue.

Of course, she'd traveled to three states in the span of a morning, so it was understandable that her mind had not caught up with her body yet. *Like jet lag.*

So much had happened in the span of such a short time. She'd remembered so much, not to mention, heard it from Cross. It was a strange feeling, like being disembodied. Her brain remembered it all, but the information had come in at the same time, so it was still parsing through all the data.

"This must be such a shock to you," Sofia said, reaching out to pat her knee. "I know it was for me, learning all about Lycans."

She couldn't help the shocked gasp that came out of her mouth. "You ... you didn't always know about Lycans?"

The other woman shook her head. "Not initially. I'm human, just like you."

"But, you're the Lupa." Her driver and two bodyguards all acted in deference to Sofia and she heard them call her that more than once. "Like the leader, right?"

"Technically, I'm the mate of the Alpha, which is why I have that title," Sofia explained. "But I didn't know about Lycans until Lucas shifted in front of me to save my life. It turns out, we're True Mates."

"I still don't know what that means, really," Sabrina said. "It seems like an abstract concept right now."

"I know what you mean. But, well, you see—oh, we're here," she announced as the vehicle stopped. "C'mon, let's go up to our place. I'll get you some food, and maybe some comfy clothes? You look like you've had a day."

Running her hands through her ratty hair, she laughed. "That I have. After Cross got hurt last night, I didn't want to leave him alone, so I slept in a chair next to his bed while he was recovering." With a frown she sniffed at her shirt. "Ugh, sorry. There wasn't any time for a shower or change of clothes."

"Don't worry about it." Sofia exited as the driver opened the door, then led her through the elevator lobby of a large, stylish apartment building. "My sister-in-law might have something you can borrow. She lives right below us, though she should be in our apartment. She's watching the kids today because it's her day off from the restaurant."

They took the elevator up to the top floor. When the doors opened, she followed Sofia into a luxurious and beautifully designed apartment. "Wow."

"It's one of the perks of being married to the Alpha," Sofia said. "We have three spare bedrooms. I can show them to you, and you can choose whichever one you want; don't think you're a bother," she added, as if sensing Sabrina's hesitation. "Trust me, we have so much space, we might lose you in here. But before that, I hope you don't mind, there's someone I really need to see."

Sabrina followed Sofia down a long hallway, then stopped outside the second to last door. Knocking softly, the other woman opened the door and stepped inside. "Isabelle?" She called. "Are you—oh you're awake!"

The room they had entered was a spacious nursery, based on the pastel animal theme it was decorated in. There was a row of shelves filled with books and toys on one side, a changing station on the other, and on the far side was a crib and a rocking chair, both occupied. A dark-haired toddler was standing up in the crib, his chubby arms reaching out to Sofia, who picked him up. Meanwhile, a beautiful young woman was sitting on the rocking chair, holding another child in her arms. She smiled warmly at Sabrina.

"Hello, my boy," Sofia greeted, peppering the boy's face with kisses. "Did you miss Mommy? I missed you." She perched him on her hip and turned to Sabrina. "Sabrina, this is my son, Alessandro."

"Hello, Alessandro," she greeted. The boy who, curiously, had one green eye and one blue eye, stared at her for a few seconds before his face broke into a smile.

"And this," Sofia gestured to the woman in the rocking chair, "is my sister-in-law, Isabelle."

"How do you do?" Sabrina asked in a soft voice, not wanting to wake up the sleeping child in Isabelle's arms.

The petite, curvy woman in the rocking chair stood up, keeping the child in her arms close as his head rested on her shoulder. "Hi, Sabrina. Are you a friend of Sofia's?"

"Er ..."

"Actually," the Lupa began, "Sabrina is Cross Jonasson's mate."

"Oh, wow." Her eyes widened, and Sabrina realized Isabelle, too, had mismatched eyes like Alessandro. *Must be a family trait.* "Really?"

Sofia gave her the short version of what happened, which, to Sabrina's surprise was still surprisingly detailed despite the other woman having only heard the story once. "And so now, she's going to stay here."

"There's no place safer, or so we're told," Isabelle said. "The Enclave is where most of our kind live, that includes all the children and elderly, so the clan ensures that it's locked up tighter than Fort Knox."

Sabrina frowned. "But aren't you afraid then, they might come for me—I mean, the ring, now that I'm here? Aren't I putting you guys and everyone in danger?"

"We have spells to keep everyone out of The Enclave, and those get updated and strengthened every now and then too," Isabelle explained. "We recently added new allies to our cause, and they're adding their magic to safeguard us. If Lucas and Daric said you can stay here, then they know you're not putting anyone in danger."

Sofia continued. "Besides, the mages want more than the ring. They've been trying to kidnap Lucas and Alessandro for some time now, though they haven't succeeded. They want their blood for some ritual or something."

"That's horrible."

"Yeah," Sofia said. "I haven't been able to take Alessandro out without an army of bodyguards. But hopefully, we can get it all resolved soon."

"My dad, the former Alpha, fought them before and won," Isabelle explained. "I'm sure we can do it again." Her expression changed as the child she was holding began to wake up. "Oh, hey, Evan," she cooed as she lifted the child and turned him around, tucking her arms under his knees. "Awake already, huh? That wasn't a long nap." Evan smiled as his mother ruffled his light brown hair. When he saw Sabrina, his mouth shaped into a perfect O. "Evan, did you notice someone new? That's Sabrina. Say hi to Sabrina."

The child giggled as he lifted a hand and opened and closed his fingers. Like his mother, he too had mismatched eyes.

"He's beautiful," Sabrina proclaimed. "They both are."

"Do you know when you're due yet?" Sofia asked.

The question caught her off-guard. "D-d-due?"

"Your baby." When Sabrina didn't answer, she clasped a hand to her mouth. "Oh, my God, I'm sorry! I just assumed, being True Mates and all ..."

Why would she assume she was pregnant? "No ... um, Cross and I haven't ... uh, we haven't, you know ..."

Both women looked at her, jaws dropped. "You haven't?" Sofia shook her head. "I'm sorry, of course that's none of our business. I mean, it's been three years since you've seen each other, *and* you've only just regained your memory. Now that you know you're True Mates and it's not a surprise, you might want to wait until—" A sharp ringing sound cut her off, and she fished a phone from her pocket. "Sorry, this is important—I need to take this. Would you mind?" She handed Alessandro over.

Dumbfounded, Sabrina accepted the boy.

"Thanks!" Sofia said with a wave and then strode out of the nursery.

"Uh ..." Alessandro looked at her curiously, then little by little, his tiny chin began to quiver. Before she knew it, he was all-out bawling, and tears flowed down his rosy cheeks. Panic crept into her brain, and she scrambled to think of what to do with a crying child.

"Tsk, tsk, Alessandro," Isabelle said with a shake of her head. "Here, let's switch." She handed Sabrina her son as she took Alessandro. "He's at that age where he only wants to be held by people he knows. There, there, now, Aunty Isabelle is here." That seemed to quiet the child down as his cries slowed to hiccups.

Evan, on the other hand, didn't seem to mind being handed off to a virtual stranger. In fact, his mismatched eyes lit up with curiosity, and his little fingers reached out to grab a strand of Sabrina's hair. As she stared at the baby's face, she couldn't help but think that Evan looked eerily familiar. As an artist, she tended to study people's features closely, and there was something about his that told her she'd seen it before.

However, glancing over at Isabelle, it was obvious that except for the eyes, he had gotten none of his mother's features. Isabelle had an exotic feminine prettiness, with her dark hair, olive skin, and slightly upturned eyes. Though Evan's features were still developing, he would not be taking after his mother. She wondered if any of the Lycans she had met earlier was his father, but they all seemed like matched pairs, and none of the men looked remotely like Evan.

Sofia re-entered the nursery just as she was tucking her phone back into her pocket. "Sorry about that. Ugh, so it looks like I need to head into the station. A beat cop hauled in one of the suspects from a current investigation, and they need me to question him."

"Suspects?" Sabrina asked.

Sofia pushed her jacket aside, flashing her a shiny police badge strapped to her waist. "Yeah. I'm a detective with the NYPD."

"Really?" Sabrina couldn't believe it. From what she could tell, based on the luxurious apartments and the chauffeur and bodyguards, Lucas Anderson was a wealthy man. Sofia obviously did not need to work.

"Yeah," she chuckled. "Lucas isn't crazy about it, but he knows my career means a lot to me." She turned to Isabelle. "Do you mind keeping watch? I'll try to wrap up by six."

"No worries, Sofia, take as long as you need," Isabelle said as she struggled with a wiggling Alessandro, who clamored for his mother now that she was in the room. "I can stay until you come back."

"Thanks, sis," Sofia took the squirming child out of her arms. "Also, if you wouldn't mind, could you help Sabrina get settled in? She can stay in whichever room she wants. And she could use an extra set of clothes."

"Gotcha," Isabelle said.

"This is the hardest part," Sofia said sadly. "I know it's only a couple of hours, but I do miss him so much whenever I'm away."

Though it took a while to say goodbye, as Alessandro started crying when Sofia was trying to leave, eventually, Isabelle was able to calm the boy with a toy, then put both children down for a nap in the nursery. Afterward, Isabelle showed her to a luxurious guest bedroom, which she immediately took a liking to.

"This will be great. Thanks Isabelle."

"I'll run down to my apartment and grab you some sweats and a shirt while you shower," Isabelle said. "My top should fit, but I think the sweats might be a little short."

"Thank you, I'm sure it'll be better than what I'm wearing now," she said with a self-deprecating laugh.

The bathroom was just as luxurious as the rest of the apartment, and Sabrina took her time washing up and getting clean with all the fancy toiletries.

When she was done, she felt a whole lot better. Walking out to the bedroom as she toweled off, she spotted the folded clothes at the foot of the bed. She put them on, though as Isabelle had warned, the pants came down mid-calf. She blew out a breath. The first thing she was going to do when this was all over was to wear her own clothes again.

"Hey," Isabelle greeted as she walked out into the living room. The two boys were now playing on the plush carpet while Isabelle sat on the couch, magazine in her hand. "I made you a sandwich," she said, nodding at the tray on the coffee table. "Nothing fancy, but if there's anything else you want or if you have any allergies, you can help yourself to whatever's in the kitchen."

"No allergies, and I'm sure it's fine." She sat down on the couch and grabbed the plate, taking a bite of the sandwich, then swallowed it down. "Thank you so much, Isabelle. This is delicious. And thanks for everything as well."

"I'm happy to help. I can't believe that after all you've been through ..." There was a wistful look on her face. "I mean, three years ...."

"I'm still unclear on the whole True Mates thing, but I think I'm starting to understand a little." It was still processing in her mind, but she was beginning to realize a few things, especially now that her head was clearer after that long, hot shower.

"You do?"

"I don't remember him, but I do," Sabrina continued. "About a year ago, I started painting Cross, even though the potion made me forget I ever met him." Isabelle looked stunned at her revelation. "I mean, unconsciously, I was drawing and painting him. And it's like ... though I don't remember we were True Mates, I knew there was something not complete. It's not like I feel empty or unfulfilled or anything. But ... it's as if there was something *not there* and when he came back, it was there again. Though I still can't explain what *it* is."

Isabelle didn't say anything, though her lips tightened and pursed together.

A cry made them both look toward the carpet. Evan looked unhappy, as Alessandro held up a teddy bear in triumph, giggling naughtily.

"Oh, Alessandro," Isabelle tsked. "Give that back."

Sabrina couldn't help but get that gnawing feeling again that Evan's face was so familiar, especially now that he was frowning. It was something about that furrow between his brows and his lips turning down in a pout ...

"That's not yours, Alessandro."

Evan let out an indignant sound and snatched the toy back, making Alessandro cry.

"C'mon now, you two," Isabelle warned. "Evan, you can share Teddy for a bit, can't you?" After a second or two, Evan gave the stuffed bear to Alessandro, mollifying him. "Kids," she shrugged. "So, Sabrina, you said you paint? You're an artist?"

She nodded. "I've always loved painting. I did my BA at the Rhode Island School of Design and then came back here."

"I wish I had some kind of talent," she said. "I mean, I used to like fashion a lot. Thought about becoming a social media model of some kind. But when Evan was born, I kind of gave all that up."

"When all this is over, maybe I can paint Evan," Sabrina offered. "It could be a family portrait. You, Evan, and his dad?"

Isabelle visibly paled. "He doesn't ..." She swallowed hard. "Evan's dad isn't in the picture."

Sabrina winced. "Sorry. I didn't mean to bring it up if it's a tough subject."

"It's not. I mean, it is." Isabelle worried her lower lip. "But I don't like to talk about it."

She reached over and covered the other woman's hand. "Then we won't."

For the rest of the afternoon, Sabrina helped Isabelle watch over the two boys. Just as she promised, Sofia arrived before six, ecstatic because she was able to close the case she was working on. There was still no word from Lucas or Cross, so they all decided to stay at the penthouse, with Sofia cooking them some Greek food she had learned to make while working at her grandfather's restaurant in Queens.

After dinner, Isabelle announced it was time to say goodnight and put Evan to bed. After their goodbyes, Sofia turned to Sabrina.

"I should get Alessandro ready for bed too, then I need to lie down after this long day," she said. "I'm sorry, I'm not much of a host. But you can watch TV or borrow a book if you want."

"I'm fine," she said. "But ... do you have any news about Cross and everyone else?"

"Lucas is keeping me updated, yes," Sofia said. "But nothing significant. They're still planning. They said it might last through the night, but he'll let me know when they're done."

"Oh."

Sofia squeezed her shoulder reassuringly. "Everything will be all right, you'll see. I'll knock on your door if I hear anything else. I'll remind Lucas that you're staying with us and to make sure he and Cross come back here as soon as they can." She leaned closer. "And just so you know ... all the rooms in here are soundproofed. His parents thought it was a prudent move since all their kids had sensitive hearing."

A blush heated her cheeks. "I'll, uh, keep that in mind."

"I'll see you in the morning then," Sofia said with a wink before she took Alessandro with her to her room.

Not sure what to do with herself, Sabrina headed back to her room. Even though it was early for her, the weight of the entire day pressed on her, and so she lay down on the soft, comfortable bed. Fatigue crept up on her, and she let out a yawn. Maybe a few hours of sleep would help. Besides, there was nothing else to do.

Before sleep took over, though, the words Gunnar whispered in her ear came back to her.

"Sometimes the only way to change the future is to follow its path," Gunnar had said cryptically.

———

Sabrina was having a dreamless sleep when she felt the sudden urge to wake up. As her eyes fluttered open, she saw the figure standing by the bathroom door. The light filtering from behind obscured the identity of the figure, but she didn't need to see his face to know who it was.

"Cross," she whispered.

"I didn't want to wake you." He stepped forward as she sat up and reached for the lamp on the bedside table. "Not that I could ever wake you. You were always a heavy sleeper. You never woke up, all the times I came to visit you."

When the light came on, she realized that he was only wearing a towel around his waist. Her mouth went dry as light and shadow played over his magnificent torso, showing off the hard muscles and ink covering his bronzed skin. Droplets of water dripped from the ends of his hair and down his shoulders, tracing a tantalizing path down his broad chest. She licked her lips, a move that made his nostrils flare, and she cast her eyes downward in embarrassment.

He continued moving toward her, then sat on the edge of the bed. A finger tipped up her chin, urging her to look up and meet his ocean-colored gaze. "Did you mean it?" he asked in a low, velvety voice. "What you said before we went back to New York."

Her cheeks burned as she was reminded of that impulsive confession. But it wasn't impulsive, not the emotion anyway. She had always known it, even though he made her forget. "Y-yes." Her breath caught in her throat, but she managed to speak. "I love you, Cross. I don't care if it's too soon or if you think that it's the danger or because we're True Mates. I think ... I think I've loved you for a long time."

His eyes shone with emotion as he cupped her cheek.

Shyly, she asked, "Do you feel the same way?"

"Are you asking me if I love you?"

She nodded.

"Sabrina ..." He caressed her cheek with his thumb. "I never stopped loving you."

"Cross."

There were no more words to say after that as he lowered his lips to hers. Electricity awakened every nerve ending in her body, making her feel alive; like she'd been dormant her entire life and was now only existing.

He moved closer, his lips never leaving hers as he pushed her onto her back on the mattress. Her hands clasped at his shoulders, moving lower down his back, feeling the clean damp skin over the hard muscles. Her fingers tugged urgently at the towel around his waist, and he whipped it aside, spreading her knees apart so he could settle between her thighs.

She rocked her hips up against him feeling his hardness press into her. He groaned against her mouth, then moved lower to kiss her jaw and neck before lifting her shirt over her head to bare her body to his sultry, heat-filled gaze. When he popped a nipple into his mouth, she groaned and dug her hands into his hair. His tongue lashed at the bud, biting gently and making her moan out loud. She could feel the dampness between her thighs and pushed up harder against him.

After giving the other nipple the same attention—and driving her insane in the process—he moved his head lower, kissing a path down to the waistband of her sweats. Disposing of the piece of clothing, he dove between her thighs, licking and sucking at her wet lips hungrily.

"Oh. God!"

Her body twisted as pleasure coursed through her. "Too ... much ..." But Cross didn't hear her, or maybe he did and didn't care. His mouth was relentless as it explored and feasted on her. When he moved to suck on her clit, she bucked her hips off the mattress. His tongue speared into her and his thumb replaced it, plucking and teasing the bud until she was shaking with an orgasm.

"Cross, please," she sighed when feeling returned to her body. "I need you, now."

He looked up at her. "Sabrina ... before we go on, there's something I need to explain to you."

"Huh?"

Sitting up, he took her hands and tugged her so she was facing him. "There's something you should know about being True Mates. About what it means."

"What is it?"

"I know it's been somewhat explained to you, about being fated to be together, but there's more." He paused and kissed each of her palms. "The first time True Mates make love without any protection, they always conceive."

It took a second, but it dawned on her. Actually, it all made sense now, at least the part where Sofia asked her when she was due. "All the time?"

He nodded. "Yes. I can use protection, if—"

"No," she said without hesitation. Oh God, a child with Cross? It seemed impulsive, but deep in her heart, she knew that was what she wanted. To hold a tiny little baby that was half him. To treasure and love and cherish. To be a family.

He sucked in a deep breath. "Are you sure?"

"Yes, I am," she rasped.

A look of relief crossed his face. "I needed to make sure. Needed to ask you first. See, one of the side effects of carrying a True Mate baby is invulnerability."

"I ... what?"

"You won't be hurt. From the moment the baby is conceived, nothing can hurt or kill the female carrying the child. It's the magic of our child, shielding you from harm."

The words sank into her. She wouldn't be hurt. She wouldn't die. And maybe his brother's vision wouldn't come true. "Why didn't you tell me before? You said he saw me fall and die. We could have prevented it."

"I ... I wanted you to have that choice," he said. "I wanted to make sure—"

"That I loved you before agreeing? But we could have changed everything."

"That wasn't a guarantee, even now we know the vision hasn't completely changed," he said. "And it wasn't that I wanted to make sure you loved me. It was that I wanted to make sure this was what you really wanted."

"Oh, Cross," she cried, her heart soaring. "I've never wanted anything so much in my entire life." She drew him closer for a soft, slow kiss. He responded by urging her mouth open and deepening the kiss. His delicious scent tickled her nose, and his mouth tasted so warm and masculine.

His knees nudged hers apart, and he pulled her to his lap. "I've been waiting for this forever," he moaned against her mouth.

She rose up onto her knees, straddling him. "Me too." Reaching down, she guided his cock to her entrance. When she felt the tip nudge at her, she sank down slowly, taking him inside her inch by inch until she sank down on his lap.

"God, you feel incredible," he said through gritted teeth. His hands came down to her hips, guiding her as she moved experimentally back and forth.

Pleasure curled up in her core and she wanted more. She wanted all of it. Planting her hands on his broad shoulders, she moved faster, rising up and down on him, loving the feel of him sliding in and out of her.

A guttural growl escaped his lips, and his hand snaked into her hair, tugging her forward. His mouth slanted over hers in an urgent, consuming kiss. She opened up to him as his tongue snaked inside her mouth, devouring her. She ground her hips down harder, picking up the pace as her body tightened and coiled.

"Cross!" she cried when he suddenly lifted her up and planted her on her back. He hooked an arm under one leg, making her squeal in delight as he pushed deeper into her.

When she squeezed her thighs around his hips, he began to thrust with long, deep penetrative strokes that she met with eagerness. He drove into her, harder and faster until she was clawing her nails down his arms. He changed the angle, his strokes becoming shorter and teasing, drawing her out to the edge, but not pushing her over yet.

They rocked together, and she felt the peak about to overcome her. When his hand thrust between their gyrating bodies to where they connected and plucked at her clit, she let out a sharp cry as her orgasm crashed into her without warning. It sent her body shuddering against him so hard she thought she'd buck him off. His other hand slipped under her, cupping her ass firmly against him as he gave a few hard thrusts and then a long groan. She felt his cock twitch and pulse inside her, flooding her with his warm seed. Her eyes shut tight, her body tensing, then relaxing as he slowed down and fell on top of her. Her heart thudded wildly against her chest, knowing it was done. Or was it his heart she felt? With a soft sigh, she cradled him closer, rubbing his scalp with her fingers as they lay in silence.

When their heartbeats finally returned to normal, Cross rolled away from her, landing on the mattress beside her with a heavy thud. Curling up toward him, she rested her head on his chest.

He pressed a kiss to her forehead and slipped an arm around her to pull her closer. "I love you, Sabrina," he said.

"I love you too," she murmured. It seemed like it was all a dream, but her sated body was telling her it was not.

"Are you sleepy?" he asked.

"Not at all," she said, smiling against his damp skin. Looking up to meet his gaze, she asked, "Are you?"

His mouth turned up into a lazy smile. "No."

She let out a small shriek when he covered her body and pinned her to the mattress with his hips. She took a sharp intake of breath when she felt his hard cock press against her. "Again?"

"I've waited a long time for you," he said. As the head of his cock brushed against her slick entrance, she sighed. "And I want to make up for it."

"Ohhhh." She closed her eyes and threw her head back as he plunged into her again. "Cross!"

CHAPTER TWELVE

CROSS WAS SURE IT WAS NEARLY DAWN WHEN HE finally let Sabrina sleep. Having waited three years before making love to her, he was determined to make their first night together pleasurable, his goal being to give her as many mindless orgasms as he could manage.

After the first two rounds, he let her doze off, but the sight of her gorgeous body in bed when he came back from a trip to the bathroom aroused him so much, he had to have her again. So, he woke her up by tasting her again, the look on her face of surprise turning to pleasure would be burned in his mind forever. He couldn't resist her and was determined to make up for lost time.

Carefully, he slipped a hand to her middle. It seemed impossible, but he knew that a new life was taking root in her womb. This was meant to be, he knew it in his heart. He had no doubt she would be a good mother to their pup. His wolf agreed with a knowing snort, and he laughed inwardly, letting his animal gloat about being right this time.

A buzzing sound invaded his thoughts, and he realized

his phone was ringing. Hopefully, it would be Lizzie or Jacob or someone from the Guardian Initiative Headquarters. They had spent the whole day planning, yesterday, though they still hadn't found the mage headquarters. Lizzie said that Jonathan's information definitely helped narrow it down, but it would take some time to untangle the web the mages had weaved. Meanwhile, he, Lucas, Daric, and Alynna Westbrooke, the co-leader of the Guardian Initiative, had taken stock of their assets and fighters and tried to put into place a plan of action that they could immediately deploy once the location was found. They would have very little time to strike, so all the preparations now would save them time later.

The buzz from the vibrations didn't stop, so he got up and padded quietly over to the chair where he had hung his jeans before going into the shower. "Hello?"

"Cross, its me."

"Gunnar?" he whispered. "What is it?"

"I need to talk to you," he said. "Can you come here?"

"Of course." Glancing over at Sabrina, he could see that she was still fast asleep. "Give me a minute."

His inner wolf wasn't happy to be away from their pregnant mate, but this was his brother. He slipped his shirt on, hopped into his jeans, then in a split second, he transported himself to the cabin. Gunnar was already seated on the couch. "What is it?" he asked as he strode over and sat next to him. "Did you have more visions?"

He nodded. "It's a different one. I think this one's about the artifacts."

"The artifacts?"

"Yes. I don't think this was the future either," he said. "It's from the past. Everyone's wearing strange clothes."

"The past?" Gunnar had never had visions from the past before. "What was it about?"

"In the vision, there was a mage. He was wearing the usual red robe, but everyone around him was wearing strange clothes and speaking a foreign language, though I can understand them for some reason. The ring is on his finger."

"Magus Aurelius's ring?"

He nodded. "Anyway ... he had this other man hanging upside down, his blood dripping down into a gold cup. The man was still alive. The mage dipped the ring into blood. Then turns around and there's a woman. She's pregnant and she's crying ... begging for her mate's life. The mage touches her and then ... she falls over dead. The man hanging upside down is screaming ..." He grabbed handfuls of his hair. "Oh God, oh God!"

Cross slipped a hand around his shoulders and pulled him close. "It's okay. Gunnar ... shh." He ran a soothing hand down his brother's back. "Are you sure it wasn't just a dream?"

Gunnar shook his head. "It couldn't have been. I've never told anyone this ... but I don't dream. Not anymore."

"But what does your vision mean?"

His brother stared up at him, his brown eyes glassy. "Don't you see, Cross? The ring ... it has the power of death and life, right? I think ... I think when the ring is dipped in double Alpha blood, it can kill anything. Even a True Mate."

His heart stopped in his chest. "It can't—Are you sure?"

"I can't be one hundred percent sure, but what else could

it be?" he said. "We already know what the dagger can do when infused with double Alpha blood."

Indeed, they did. "What if you're wrong? What if it was only a dream? Is there a way to be certain?"

"You know I can't be certain," Gunnar said. "But that's the only logical explanation."

If that was the case, then that meant no one was safe. Not even Sabrina. "What do we do?"

"I don't know." Gunnar buried his face in his hands. "But you can't let them win."

"We're going to strike first," he said. "We spent the whole day yesterday putting a plan together. The only thing we have left to do is to find out where the mages are hiding out. Then, we're going to put an end to all this."

He waited for Gunnar to say something about the plan. When he remained silent, Cross asked the question he'd been dreading to ask. "Has your premonition changed at all?"

"I haven't had it again, but as soon as I get one, I'll call you or Dad."

"All right." He got up, then stopped. "Gunnar, why did you call me just now and not Dad?"

"I don't know." Gunnar lifted his head. "I just felt like ... like you needed to know it."

Cross searched his brother's face, trying to see if he was telling the truth. There was something about this whole thing ... maybe he should trust Gunnar. He hadn't led them astray yet. "All right. Is there anything else?"

"Yes." Gunnar stood up. "After you do what you need to do, go see your friend."

"Which friend?"

"The Lone Wolf, the one with the wolf tattoo on his hip."

Gunnar said. "Ask him for his help. You'll need it. And he needs to come back to New York. Do whatever it takes."

There was only one Lone Wolf he knew with that kind of tattoo—he'd seen it when he fished the man out of the Hudson. "You mean—" He stopped short. No one in New York knew about Ransom. "How do you know him?" But his brother ignored him and walked toward the bedroom, shutting the door behind him.

A cold feeling crawled over his skin. Hours ago, he had felt so confident that they would get to the mages first. That Sabrina would be protected, if temporarily, by making her invulnerable. But now, even that wasn't 100 percent certain. He would have to find another way to protect her and make sure no one could get to her. To take her somewhere the mages could never find her.

An idea popped into his head. He knew of one place far enough away, and the mages would never be able to reach her. Of someone who could keep her safe.

Of course, Cross felt like a piece of shit asking her for this favor now after avoiding her for over a year, but what choice did he have?

Mind made up, he transported back to The Alpha's guest room. Sabrina was still in bed, and hadn't even moved an inch. Thank goodness she was a really heavy sleeper, and after their exhausting evening, she was surely out like a light. He slid into the bed behind her and embraced her, then waved his hands to create pajamas over her naked body. She stirred and twisted around to face him, nuzzling at his neck before relaxing in his arms again. After a minute or two when her breathing evened, he closed his eyes and concentrated.

The bed they reappeared in was still made, and his

enhanced senses told him this entire wing was empty. Carefully, he slid away from her, placing a pillow in his stead.

As he moved away from the bed, he wondered about the long explanation he was about to make. *Honesty*, he said to himself. *She's always appreciated honesty.*

Closing his eyes, he transported himself again, though this time, not very far away, only to the next wing in the Royal Palace of Zhobghadi. He found himself in the spacious living room of the king and queen's private apartments. His enhanced hearing picked up sounds from a room off to the side, and he carefully walked toward it, peeking inside the open door.

A woman dressed in a green tunic had her back to him as she hummed softly, cradling a child to her chest as she swayed back and forth. He'd only taken one step inside the room when she froze, her entire body tensing. He stopped in his tracks as she slowly turned around.

"Cross," Deedee whispered, her light green eyes shifting colors as a myriad of emotions flashed on her face. "I was told ... I spoke to my dad, and he told me you left ... but then you came back again."

"Deedee, I'm sorry to drop in like this," he said sheepishly, scratching at his head as he approached her. His wolf recognized hers instantly, yipping happily as he drew closer to his best friend. At one point, he had thought there could have been something between them, at least until he met Sabrina. That maybe Deedee could have meant something more than a friend to him, but by then she had met her True Mate, King Karim of Zhobghadi.

Her mouth was still open with shock. "You came here, didn't you?" she asked. "A few days ago."

"How did you know?"

She reached into her pocket and pulled out something gold and shiny—his GI medallion. "I found this on the balcony. I still have the one you gave me. I keep it in my dresser. I had hoped it was you ... You haven't visited or called all this time."

"I know, and I'm sorry. I thought it best to stay away. Your husband isn't too happy with me."

"But I'm not too happy with you being away," she said with a pout. "You didn't come for the wedding or when Caspar was born."

He glanced down at the sleeping child in her arms. "He's beautiful."

"I know." Her mouth turned up into a smile as a wistful look passed on her face. "He's everything to me." She kissed the top of the child's forehead.

"You look happy, Dee." A total understatement. She was *glowing*. "Really happy." He couldn't help but see the remarkable difference in her as she fussed over her son as she placed him back in his crib.

"Of course," she replied. "I—"

"What in *An's* name is going on here?"

Deedee started at the sound of her husband's voice, but she recovered in a split second. "Darling, look who's come for a visit."

His Majesty, King Karim of Zhobghadi strode into the room, his cerulean blue eyes trained like daggers on Cross. Dressed in a dark gray tunic with a dozen or so shiny medals on his chest, he looked every bit the imposing royal he was. There was also a great power he kept wrapped up inside him that Cross's wolf couldn't ignore—a mighty dragon that could raze lands with its fiery breath.

"What are you doing here?" The king asked. "Do you think you can just come here anytime—"

"Karim!" Deedee admonished as she marched toward him. "Stop it. Please don't be angry."

He glared at Cross, then looked down at his wife, his expression softening. "I could never be angry at you, *habibti*." Then he turned back to Cross. "But you still need to explain your presence. You have avoided my wife for more than a year. She sent you an invitation to our wedding, to Caspar's welcoming ceremony, her birthday, and yet, you ignored her. What kind of best friend does that?"

"Karim please—"

"*Habibti*, I know how much it hurt you, could always see the disappointment in your face when he failed to turn up each time," he said. "And now he thinks he can just come back—"

"Don't be jealous, darling," she cooed. "I love only you; you know that."

That seemed to mollify him, at least, a little bit. "This ... *friend* of yours still needs to explain and apologize to you."

Cross hated to admit it, but the king was correct. *Honesty*, he reminded himself. "I was ashamed, Deedee."

"Ashamed?" she asked.

"That night I came back ... your father told me you had been held against your will here. I was so angry. I blamed myself that I was the reason you left."

"I told you, you weren't," she reminded him.

"I know that," he said. "But I'm still ashamed. About what I did—tried to do—that night. I told you I would have used you to forget." That earned him another heat-filled glare from Karim, but he continued. "I'm truly sorry."

Her brows drew together. "You never did tell me what you found."

"I found her, Dee. My True Mate."

She sucked in a quick breath and then let out an excited gasp. "You have?" Using her free arm, she grasped him in a side-hug. "I'm so happy for you. When do we get to meet her?"

"Er, that's the thing. She's already here. In the guest bedroom where I stayed that day we defeated the mages here."

"You brought her *here*?" Deedee exclaimed incredulously. "Does she even know where she is?"

"I'll explain it to her, but I might have to leave right away. When she finds out, she won't want to stay here. But she has to."

"So, you have spirited a girl into my palace without her knowledge, possibly against her will, and expect us to deal with it?" Karim asked, a dark brow raised.

"Well that wouldn't be the first time for you, would it now?" he retorted, unable to resist the jab.

Karim's nostrils flared with anger. "You watch what you—"

"Karim, please!" Deedee put a soothing hand on her husband's chest. "Cross and his mate obviously need us. Need our protection. It's why you brought her here, right?"

"Yes," Cross said. "The mages, they're coming for her."

"Then we will protect her." The firm determination on Deedee's face was enough to quell her husband's anger. "Right, darling?"

"Fine," Karim relented. "Since the mages' infiltration last year, I've shored up our magical defenses. Your father was able to connect me with some witch covens nearby, and thanks to them, we've had protection spells placed around the palace."

"I know," Cross answered. Several times, Daric had asked him if he wanted to come to Zhobghadi, but he declined. He felt like a bastard, only coming now when he needed something, but he had no choice. If he survived what was coming, he vowed he would be a better friend to Deedee. "Thank you, Your Majesty."

"I'm not doing this for you," he growled back. "You best remember that."

"I will, Your Majesty," he said with a nod. Karim didn't have to say it, but Cross knew what he was trying to say: *If you ever make my wife unhappy again, I will burn you and gobble up your ashes.*

"Do you really have to go soon?" Deedee asked.

"Yes, I'm afraid so," Cross said. "So much has happened. You should talk to your father or mother so they can get you up to speed." He turned to Karim. "You should prepare for the worst, Your Majesty."

"What do you mean—" A sharp cry made Deedee start. "Sorry, Caspar's woken up." She hurriedly stalked back to the crib and lifted the child, cooing and soothing him.

"You don't deserve her," Cross muttered so only Karim could hear him. Maybe he was a little jealous that the other man had his best friend all to himself now and kept her from living her old life back in New York.

To his surprise, Karim merely smirked. "Someone once told me, none of us deserve the women who love us," he said.

"And that we can only hope they stick around long enough so we can prove ourselves worthy someday."

Cross smirked, guessing it was probably Karim's father-in-law, Sebastian Creed, who said that. "Sounds like good advice from a wise old man."

The king snorted. "Old, yes."

Deedee walked toward them, Caspar in her arms. She handed him to Karim. "Come, darling, I want to meet Cross's mate."

They all walked together toward the guest wing of the palace, until they reached the room he had transported into. He crossed the room and kneeled by the bed, shaking Sabrina gently awake.

"Cross?" Light blonde lashes fluttered open. "Hmmm ... good morning. What time is it?" She yawned and stretched her arms out. "Hey, did you make me pajamas again, I don't remember putting any clothes on—" Her amethyst eyes widened when she looked behind him and realized they weren't alone. "Cross?" She quickly sat up and glanced around, also now fully aware they were not in the Alpha's guest bedroom. "Where did you take us?"

"Sabrina," he began, taking her hand in his. "I transported us to a safe place. With some friends of mine." He glanced up at Deedee, who had walked up behind him. "This is Deedee, she's my best friend. And she'll take care of you. Dee, this is Sabrina Strohen."

"Hello, Sabrina," Deedee greeted. "I'm so happy to finally meet you. And you're very welcome here."

"I—wait." She scratched at her head. "What do you mean she'll take care of me?"

Silence passed for a few seconds. "I'm sorry, Sabrina. But I need to know you're safe."

"Safe?" Her voice turned panicked. "What do you mean, safe? You said I'd be safe anywhere!" Her hand slid down to her stomach. "You said our—our baby would protect me." Her hands gripped at his shoulders. "Cross, whatever you're planning, please—"

"I love you, Sabrina," he said, leaning down to kiss her mouth and silence her protest. Arms slipped around him, embracing him tighter as if she could stop him. For a brief second, he considered not leaving her, but he had no choice. He concentrated on where he needed to go, ignoring her protesting cry as she and the rest of Zhobghadi disappeared around him.

Moments later, his feet landed on solid ground. The first thing that hit him was the fresh, mountain breeze tinged with the scent of pines. Glancing around the porch of Ransom's cabin, he realized that it was still early morning in Kentucky, being a few hours behind Zhobghadi. He took a step forward and then knocked on the door.

Heavy footsteps thudded closer and the door swung open. "Who the hell—Cross?" Ransom looked up at him, the ever-present scowl on his face deepening. "What're you doing here?"

He didn't quite know how to put it. Gunnar was insistent that he needed Ransom's help, but for what, he couldn't explain. "I don't have much time," he said. "But I was wondering ... if I could ask a favor."

A brow shot up as he crossed his arms over his chest. "A favor, huh?"

"Yeah. I've got a situation back home. Could use some helping hands."

"Me and my guys aren't goons for hire," he groused. "Go find someone else to help you with your war. We don't want any part of it."

The door was about to close in his face, but he braced himself against it. "Please. I need your help."

"And why should I help you?"

"I'll owe you." He hoped he wouldn't regret this. "Anything that's within my power, I'll give you. You know what I can do. Please. Everyone in my clan ... they could die."

There was a flash of emotion on his face, but he must have imagined it. Because it almost looked like Ransom was worried when he said everyone back in New York was in danger.

"Well?" Cross asked.

The other man growled softly. "Fine. But I'm only taking Snake and Hawk."

"That's fine," he said. "How soon can we leave?"

Ransom was already fishing for his phone in his pocket. "Within the hour."

CHAPTER THIRTEEN

"CROSS, NO!" SABRINA CRIED WHEN SHE FOUND HERSELF embracing only air. "Please ... you said everything would be okay ..."

The woman Cross had introduced as his best friend—Deedee—sat on the mattress next to her and placed a comforting hand on her shoulder. "It will be all right, Sabrina. Everything will be all right. You have to trust Cross."

"Trust him?" she said incredulously. "How can I trust him again after what he did? After everything he did?"

"I'm sorry, you must be so distressed." She shook her head, a sympathetic look on her face. "Why don't you come with me, and we can have some tea? Then maybe we can talk and you can tell me everything that's happened."

"I ..." Glancing around, she didn't recognize anything in this bedroom. The bed was humungous, much bigger than the one in Sofia and Lucas's guest room. The pillows were square and made of fine silk, the covers a riot of jewel colors. The walls were decorated in mosaic tiles and swathes of colorful fabric hung from intricately carved wooden lattice arches overhead.

"Where am I?" Her eyes narrowed at Deedee as she studied her pretty features—delicate and feminine, but there was an inner strength that shone through, especially in her unusually colored eyes—light green, almost yellow. There was something else familiar about her, but Sabrina couldn't quite put her finger on it.

"Oh, you poor dear." Deedee cleared her throat. "Um, like I said, my name is Deedee and that," she nodded to the tall, imposing man behind her holding a baby. "That's ... my husband and son." Her eyes darted around nervously. "Darling, maybe you can take Caspar back to the nursery, and I can talk to Sabrina alone?"

Why did Deedee look so familiar? That face ... she'd seen it before, but where? "Wait." Her hand gripped Deedee's arm as it came to her. "It's you." The name was there on the tip of her tongue. "Am I in ..." Oh dear, she was tripping up over the name of that foreign country ... Z something? "I mean, I know you!"

Deedee's cheeks reddened. "From where?"

"It was a trial, wasn't it?" she said. "I watched it on the news. You testified and put that guy away, and you had these escorts while you came out of the courthouse and the reporters said you were ..." Her jaw dropped. "You're the American who became a queen, right?" Her eyes darted to the man she introduced as her husband. "Desiree. *Queen* Desiree. And he's ... he's ..."

"Yes." Deedee took her hand reassuringly. "I'm Queen Desiree of Zhobghadi, and that's my husband, King Karim and our son, Prince Caspar. No, don't get up," she said with a laugh.

"Zhobghadi." Yes, that was the name of the country. She'd researched it and recalled the picture of the handsome prince that came up on her screen. That was definitely him. Her nerves and anxiety made her fidget. "Um, aren't I supposed to-to curtsey or something?"

"It's fine, don't worry. Darling," she called to the man—the king! "Would you mind taking Caspar back to the nursery?"

"Not at all, *habibti*." With a quick nod to Sabrina, the king pivoted and left the room.

"He can be intimidating," Deedee said. "But I promise you, he's a good man. That's why he's agreed to keep you safe."

"Keep me safe? I don't understand." Her hand came down to her stomach. "He said ... did Cross lie to me? He said I was supposed to be pregnant and then I'd be invulnerable."

"It's all true," Deedee said. "Trust me, I know. But he must have a good reason to bring you here. Look, I know you're confused, Sabrina. Do you want to rest? Or maybe have some food? You must be starving."

"I'm not." However, her stomach chose that time to growl loudly. "Uh, sorry."

Deedee smiled. "I totally understand. The hunger is something you'll have to get used to, being pregnant with your True Mate's baby. Now, why don't you come with me, and I can have someone bring us up some food? Do you want a change of clothes and maybe freshen up?"

"Uh, sure." What else could she do? Apparently, she had been spirited away to a remote country and now had no choice in the matter. So, she got up and followed the queen out of the bedroom. As they walked down the richly-decorated halls of what she guessed was the royal palace of Zhobghadi, she felt underdressed in her pajamas.

After a few turns, they reached a large door covered in gold tiles. Deedee pushed the door open, and they entered a large, spacious living area with high ceilings that was even more luxurious than the room she had appeared in. She followed the queen to a bedroom off to the side and headed to a smaller room that looked to be a walk-in closet.

Deedee grabbed some clothes hanging from a rack. "These should fit. Bathroom's over there. Come out to the living room when you're done."

"Thank you, Your Majesty."

"Please, just call me Deedee."

As soon as the other woman left, she headed to the bathroom. Though she was tempted to take a long, hot shower, she didn't want to keep Deedee waiting. So, after doing her business and a quick wash up, she donned the clothes—black leggings and a matching white tunic with beautiful red embroidery. There wasn't much she could do with her hair, so she combed it with her fingers as best she could and then walked out into the living room. Deedee was already waiting by the couch, as was the king, who stretched his long legs out and had an arm around his wife. A tray of tea and a pile of delicious-smelling bread was on the low table in front of them.

"Have a seat, Sabrina," Deedee instructed as she poured tea into cups, then pushed one toward her. "And help yourself to some bread."

Unable to curb her hunger, she tore off a piece of the

bread and dunked it in some golden-brown liquid she guessed was honey. "Hmmm ... this is delicious," she said as she swallowed and washed it down with some tea. "Thank you so much."

"You're welcome," Deedee said. "I hope you're feeling better. And if you don't mind, perhaps you could share with us what happened and how you met Cross?" she asked. "I hope you don't mind if Karim listens as well. We're both curious."

She took one more bite and then cleared her throat. "Not at all." Being her hosts, she supposed she owed them an explanation, especially since Cross had dumped her here without any warning. She took a deep breath, wondering where to begin. From the beginning, she supposed. "I met Cross at a coffee shop in New York. He bumped into me and spilled all my painting supplies."

"Painting." Deedee's jaw dropped. "Wait ... you're an artist?"

"Yes."

"Sabrina Strohen, as in S. *Strohen*?"

She nodded.

"Oh my." Deedee's face lit up. "She's S. Strohen!"

The king spoke, his cerulean blue gaze setting its sight on her. "I tried to buy a painting of yours, Ms. Strohen." His accent wasn't as thick as she'd expected, and there was even a hint of boarding school poshness in it. "But your agent was insistent that you wouldn't sell it, not at any price."

"I know," she said sadly. "When she told me who you were and that you desperately wanted it as a present for your wife, I looked you up. And then months later, I saw her on the news." She gave a small laugh. "I admired her for standing up to that man and putting him away, I almost called Barbara to tell her you could have it."

Deedee looked up to her husband, a knowing smile on her face. The king, on the other hand, merely rolled his eyes. She nudged him with her elbow, then turned back to her. "Sorry, please continue."

And so, she did, detailing everything that happened, from the time they discovered the ring's abilities and how she took the forgetting potion but remembered him anyway, all the way until he came back and ended up here. Honestly, she felt exhausted after all of it, and she took a gulp of the now-cold tea.

"That's some story," Deedee said. "I'm so sorry for everything you've been through. But don't worry, you'll be safe here."

The king put a hand over his wife's and nodded. "You will be well protected here, Ms. Strohen. And welcome to stay as long as you like."

"But I don't want to stay here," she said. "I mean ... I'm sorry, I don't mean to sound ungrateful. But this wasn't part of the plan. Cross brought me here without warning. I thought everything was fine. I should be safe from harm. Gunnar's vision changed. The end isn't written yet." *Gunnar.* He told her something before he left. *Sometimes the only way to change the future is to follow its path.* It must have been important enough for him to mention it to her.

"Sabrina? Are you okay?"

Sometimes the only way to change the future is to follow its path.

... change the future ...

... follow its path ...

"Holy moly!" She shot to her feet. "I have to get back to New York."

The queen got up and took her hands. "Sabrina, you're obviously not safe there. Cross wouldn't have brought you here otherwise."

"I have this feeling ... this intuition." She took a few deep breaths. "I think I can save them. Save everyone."

"Save everyone?" Deedee asked.

"Gunnar's vision." That was the answer. Her instincts were screaming at her. "I need to be there. Please," she cried. "Deedee, if you want Cross and everyone to live, you need to send me back to New York. Something's going to happen. I think Gunnar's vision is going to come true, and I need to be there."

"Do you think you can stop it?"

"No, I'm not going to stop it," she said. "He said there's no end. Or the end can be changed, but not by trying to stop it. We have to let it happen. Let fate take its course. We cannot stop it."

Deedee looked confused and met her husband's gaze.

It was the king who finally spoke. "I do not know anything about fate, except that it has brought me my mate." Rising from the couch, he stood behind his wife, cutting an imposing figure as he crossed his arms over his chest and towered over Sabrina. "Do you really think that is what needs to happen?"

Her throat went dry, but she managed to say, "I know it."

His shoulders relaxed. "Then perhaps we should let it happen."

"Karim?" Deedee asked. "What are you saying?"

"*Habibti*, I have spoken to your brother, Wyatt," Karim said. "Things are being set in motion as we speak."

"I need to go back." She didn't know how, but she just knew it. "I have to be there when it all happens."

"I cannot go with you or allow my wife to go," Karim said. "But I will have my plane prepared and have two of my own personal guards to go with you."

The knot in her chest loosened with relief. "Thank you, Your Majesty."

"Don't thank me yet," the king said, a dark brow raised. "Now, I must make preparations." He tilted his head at the two women and pivoted on his heel, then left the room.

"Do you really think you can save them?" Deedee asked, a worried look on her face.

"I ... yes." She bit her lip. At least, she hoped so.

CHAPTER FOURTEEN

THE MOMENT THEY TOUCHED DOWN IN NEW YORK, Cross knew something was up. He could feel it in the air, a charged electricity that made his wolf stand at attention, its ears flattening forward and twitching its muzzle and lips.

Before they left Kentucky, he had called his father and Lucas to get permission for the three Lone Wolves to accompany them and bring them to the secret Guardian Initiative Headquarters hidden inside one of the pillars of the Brooklyn Bridge. Though the Alpha was hesitant, Cross vouched for Ransom and his wolves, telling them that Gunnar insisted they needed to be there.

"I don't think I'll ever get used to that," Snake said as he waved his hands to steady himself as they arrived in at the GI headquarters. Cross had chosen to transport them to the basement garage, away from the flurry of activity happening upstairs.

"I think I'm gonna throw up," Hawk moaned and heaved. Ransom, on the other hand, snorted impatiently.

"Welcome back." Daric stood a few feet away, the Alpha

standing next to him, feet planted shoulder width apart and shoulders held back stiff.

"Dad, Alpha," Cross greeted, then gestured to the three men behind him. "This is Ransom, Snake, and Hawk."

"Welcome to New York." Lucas's tone was not welcoming or warm, but there were formalities to follow whenever a visiting Lycan from another clan or Lone Wolf came into a territory. Usually, Lycans would need permission to enter a territory, unless they had a formal alliance. Lone Wolves, having no territory, occupied a gray zone that didn't require them prior authorization to go to any clan's domain, provided they acknowledge the Alpha.

Hawk and Snake, perhaps sensing the Alpha's dominant nature, immediately bowed their heads and showed their tattoos that signified their Lone Wolf status. "Thank you for welcoming us, Alpha," Snake said in a deferential tone.

Ransom, on the other hand, took his time pulling his shirt from his waistband to show Lucas his tattoo. He muttered something under his breath, and for a moment, Cross thought he saw contempt in his eyes, which was strange because as far as he knew, the two men had never met before.

If Lucas thought Ransom's greeting wasn't sufficient, he didn't say anything. "Let's go upstairs," the Alpha said. "We have a lot to discuss." His gaze briefly drifted back to Ransom before he turned around and headed to the elevators. Daric, Cross, and the three Lone Wolves followed him, and soon they were on their way to the central operations room.

A flurry of activity greeted them as they stepped out of the elevators. It had been this way since yesterday, when Lucas had decided they were no longer waiting for the mages to attack them.

Waiting by the elevator was Wyatt Creed, who managed their operations. "Alpha," he greeted, before his light green gaze flickered to the newcomers, but he made no comment about them. A few years younger than him, Cross had known Wyatt since he was a child, as he was Deedee's younger brother, and they had all been neighbors. The younger Creed had always been kind of stuck up, though that had gotten worse after his grandmother had convinced him to attend a fancy boarding school in England.

Cross quickly introduced the Lone Wolves, then asked Wyatt, "What's our current status?"

"Mika's upstairs with Cliff, Killian, and Arch," Wyatt explained. "They're mobilizing all the forces we have, plus additional support from our allies. Your father is ready to transport them if we need backup."

"How are we on finding their location?" Cross asked. When he left last night, there was still no news, but Lizzie assured him she would find them.

"Lizzie's close," the Alpha answered. "But nothing solid yet. Let's go check in with her." Lucas crossed the room, and they followed him to one of the enclosed offices at the back of the room. The Alpha opened the door and gestured for them to follow him inside.

His cousin, Lizzie Martin, was seated behind her desk, tapping furiously on a keyboard. As the head of tech for GI, anything technology related was under her jurisdiction. She was a genius hacker, not to mention, a hybrid who had the power to control and communicate with computers—a technopath. Usually, Lizzie had a smart retort or quip when people came into her office. That, or she was playing pranks on the phone. But he knew she must really be working hard as she barely looked up at them as she continued to tap furiously on the keyboard.

"Any luck, Lizzie?" Lucas asked.

She sighed dramatically then leaned back into her beat-up leather chair. "Strohen's information was solid and helped me find the right path, but I'm still untangling this web. The transfers and records go back years and years, and the money hopped from country to country, under at least a hundred shell companies. There's just so much to go through, and I can't get the info I need fast enough."

"Have you thought of using CDNs?"

All eyes turned to the source of the voice—Snake.

Lizzie flicked an annoyed glance at him. "Does a bear shit in the woods? Of course I used CDNs."

"Ah." Snake dashed behind the desk to stand over Lizzie. He peered down at her screen. "Let me see."

The female let out an exasperated sighed and tapped on the keyboard. "Go ahead."

The Lone Wolf tapped his chin and narrowed his eyes. "Hmmm. You don't have enough servers. And the networks are too far apart, thus the latency in your data. Here, let me—"

"Hey!" Lizzie protested when he grabbed her keyboard. "Do you even know what you're doing, you caveman?"

"Lucky for you, I can access a couple more CDNs run by friends of mine." Ignoring her protests, he tapped on the keyboards for several seconds. "Aha! Yes!" He fist-pumped in the air and then handed her back the keyboard. "See what you can do with that."

She sent him dagger eyes but grabbed the keyboard anyway, then went back to typing. "Oh!" she exclaimed excitedly. "Holy guacamole, you did it!" Lizzie hopped to her feet and kissed him on the cheek. "Now we're cooking! Pull up a chair and help me with this. We can get through this quicker together." Snake grabbed a stool and positioned himself on the PC behind Lizzie as her fingers moved like lightning across the keyboard.

Cross picked up a soft growl behind him. Wyatt bared his teeth for a second before he cleared his throat and tugged at the knot on his tie. "I should go check on what's happening upstairs," Wyatt mumbled.

"Good idea," Lucas said. "We should all go. Lizzie, call us as soon as you get anything."

But Lizzie was too busy and simply waved them away. Everyone else proceeded to go up to the top floor where the main command center was located.

If it was busy downstairs, then it was even more hectic up here. Cross saw that the conference room was turned into some kind of war room. It was crowded too, as several people sat on the chairs or simply propped themselves up against the corners as they listened to the woman speaking at the front of the room.

"... and so, if we need San Francisco, they're our closest—Alpha!" Mika Westbrooke greeted, but she frowned once she saw Ransom and Hawk. "What's going on?"

"I brought help," Cross said and quickly introduced them to everyone. "Looks like we've got a full house."

All the members of GI were there—Mika, her mate Delacroix, Killian Jones, his son, Arch, Cliff Forrest, and Jacob Martin, but so were Julianna, Duncan, Elise, and Reed. Plus, there were two more people he didn't know—a woman who looked to be in her mid-forties and a young girl who looked to be about thirteen or fourteen—though he did recognize them from a few days ago when he appeared in the Alpha's office and his association with the ring had been outed.

"You weren't formally introduced," Mika began. "But this is Delacroix's aunt and cousin, Gabrielle Beaumont, and her daughter, Marina. They also happen to be powerful witches, and they're here to help too."

The young girl looked at him, and her face lit up. "You fixed your glow!" she said happily.

Cross eyed her curiously. "What do you mean, glow?"

Lucas cleared his throat. "Can we do this later? We do have more important things to take care of right now."

"Of course, Alpha," he said.

"Now," Lucas began. "Mika, let us know what your team's been up to."

"Right," she said. "Let me continue. Now this...."

Cross, Ransom, and Hawk each found an empty spot in the back of the conference room. As they settled in, however, Cross only half listened to what Mika was explaining. Worry was beginning to nag at his brain. There was something wrong. He didn't know why, but he could feel it.

What disturbed him was the presence of two people in particular: Was it a coincidence that two of the people in Gunnar's vision—Julianna and Elise—were here in New York while they were about to launch a full-scale attack on the mages?

Over a year ago, he and the two females had accidentally traveled back in time when they all touched the dagger dipped in Lucas's blood and powered by Elise's electricity-generating abilities. Though they were lost in time, it was

Gunnar's vision that told him that eventually all three of them would find their way back to the present, and so they did. But did that mean that Gunnar's vision was about to come true?

It was a good thing Sabrina was safe back in Zhobghadi. She would be annoyed at him—maybe even hate him, but there was no way he was going to just let the mages take her. If they got ahold of her and the ring, then that would mean the premonition really would happen.

But, no one could get to her in Zhobghadi. Despite that pit forming in his stomach, he told himself that everything would be all right.

Beside him, Ransom shifted his weight from one foot to the other but didn't say a word. The Lone Wolf had been quiet the entire time, acting like his usual aloof self. However, Cross did notice him glancing at Lucas every now and then, and when he did, that look came back on his face. Was it loathing? Hatred? It seemed strange. Ransom surely had many enemies, but there was something visceral about the way he looked at the Alpha. Cross only hoped Gunnar was correct in insisting he be brought back here. He didn't have the time or the energy to watch over Ransom while fighting the mages.

———

The rest of the day was spent planning and rounding up their resources, creating several plans of action to cover any kind of eventuality, as well as making sure their most vulnerable clan members would be taken care of. Lucas insisted they all take a break in the afternoon, and try to relax and rest or take care of any personal business.

While Cross was too agitated to relax, he did show Ransom and Hawk to spare rooms in the GI dormitories where they could have some privacy and get cleaned up. Cross was tempted to go back to Zhobghadi to check on Sabrina, but he knew that would be a bad idea. Instead, he decided to go with his father as they did some checks of the spells and defenses around The Enclave and their loft. Later, after dinner in the cafeteria, everyone gathered in the conference room again.

"Welcome back," Mika greeted. "Since this afternoon, we've managed to contact more—"

The door to the conference room flew open, and Lizzie burst in, Snake right behind her. "I found them!" she exclaimed.

"You mean we found 'em," Snake said.

"Yeah, yeah, whatever, Worm," she snorted.

"It's Snake," he reminded her.

Lizzie ignored him and waved the tablet PC in her hand triumphantly "I—we have a location on the mages."

"Where are they?" Lucas asked.

"You won't believe this, but"—she flipped the tablet toward them—"they're right here. In New York. Headquartered in a building on Fifth Avenue, a couple blocks down the road from The Plaza Hotel. They're hiding under a company called Sur Elian Corporation."

"What?" Lucas roared, his eyes glowing with his wolf. The dominant vibes emanating from him made almost everyone visibly uncomfortable. "Those bastards! Right here in my city? How dare they." His voice was edgy as a well-honed blade. "We need to get them, right now. Get our forces together—"

"Alpha," Mika began. "We can't possibly attack them right this moment."

"I don't care!" Lucas growled. "I want them exterminated from my city."

"Please, Alpha." Daric's said. "Use reason. Fifth Avenue is teeming with tourists right now. There would be too many casualties and witnesses."

"I—" Lucas raked his fingers though his hair in frustration. "I know you're right. I just want those bastards out of here." He blew out a breath. "Let's sit and prepare a game plan."

"We'll need all the help we can get," Mika said, massaging her temple. "I guess we always thought we'd meet the mages somewhere remote, like in the battle of Norway. A fight right here in New York wasn't something we prepared for, but I'm sure if we all put our heads together, we can think of a way to contain it."

"My people can help," Gabrielle said. "The shadows can help conceal many things."

"And we have our guys ready," Cliff added. "We've all trained for this."

"You know you have our help," Elise said.

"Aye, as you do ours," Duncan said.

"Thank you." Lucas looked around him. "Today might be the day we end this war. So." He clasped his hands together. "Let's get to work. Now—"

A knife-like pain suddenly sliced into Cross head. "Argh!" The world began to spin and he had to brace himself against the wall to keep from falling over.

"Cross?" Ransom asked. "What the hell is the matter?"

"Son!" Daric rushed over to him. "What's happening?"

"I don't—" Air rushed out of his lungs as his vision went black.

Central Park. The Obelisk. Midnight. The voice in his head said.

Not again.

Bring the girl and the dagger.

"No!" he screamed. "You'll never have her."

Bring them or her father dies.

Jonathan. But the thing was, what he was hearing in his head was *Jonathan*'s voice.

Everyone dies.

When the pain receded, Cross took in gasps of air and sat up. He didn't even realize that he had fallen down.

"What happened, son?" Daric looked visibly pale as he knelt down beside him.

"Dad," he gasped. "The mages ... where's Jonathan?"

"He went home," Lucas said, his brows knitting together. "He gave us all of the information he had and then asked to be brought home. I sent two Lycan guards with him, though."

"The mages have him," Cross said. "And they're going to kill him, possibly others." He blinked. "The rest of the clan ... where are they? Are they safe?"

Lucas's face suddenly became a mask of rage, then he turned to everyone. "I need an accounting of all clan members," he ordered. "Make sure your family and loved ones are secured. If they're not at The Enclave, make sure they get there ASAP!" He ran his hands through his hair.

"The Lupa?" Cross asked.

"She's at home with Alessandro. I just got off the phone

with her after dinner, thank God," he said. "What happened? Did you get a vision?"

He shook his head. "No. But the mages, they found a way to send me messages. Just like Stefan did with you, Dad," he said to Daric.

"What did they want?" his father asked.

"They want me to go to Central Park at midnight. And … to bring the dagger and Sabrina."

Lucas's mismatched eyes glowed with anger. "Over my dead body. I'm not handing over anything or anyone to them!"

Cross breathed a sigh of relief. "She's safe and far away from here. I had to make sure to keep her away." He paused and realized he hadn't had time to tell the Alpha what Gunnar had discovered. "Alpha, there's something you should know. Something Gunnar found out."

"What?"

"Remember how your blood could make the power of the dagger stronger? Well, I think … I mean, Gunnar had a vision, and he saw that dipping the ring in double Alpha blood could kill a pregnant True Mate."

His normally unflappable father seemed to falter. "That's disturbing news."

"Well, then," Lucas cracked his knuckles. "I want this to end tonight. Mika," he called. "Let's put all this preparation to good use. We need a plan."

CHAPTER FIFTEEN

As the jet touched down on the private airstrip in New Jersey, Sabrina felt her anxiety—real this time, not a magical side effect—shoot up. Her palms were sweaty, her mouth was as dry as a desert, and her hands couldn't stop fidgeting. Despite the luxuriousness of King Karim's private plane, she still couldn't relax. Exhaustion had knocked her out enough so that she slept for two or three hours, maybe. On the other hand, her seemingly never-ending hunger had her eating through most of the ten-hour flight. But when she wasn't stuffing her face with food, she was either nervously tapping her fingers or fidgeting on the plush leather seats.

The jet slowed down, and a few minutes later, the polite young steward came out of the galley. "Is there anything else I can get you or assist you with before you deplane, Ms. Strohen?"

"No, Makir, I'm good. Everything was great. Thank you so much."

He bowed his head. "I'm at your service. The captain is just going through some formalities, and then you may go."

Not long after, Makir opened the doors and motioned for her to exit. As she headed toward the stairs, the two hulking members of the *Almoravid*, the royal family's personal guard, followed behind her. King Karim had insisted she take them with her for protection and said they were well-trained in combat, and just as formidable as any Lycan.

There were two black SUVs waiting at the foot of the stairs. She was halfway down when the passenger-side door of the first one opened, and Astrid practically flew out and met her halfway. The younger woman enveloped her in a tight hug before her feet had even touched the ground.

"Oh, my God, Sabrina." Astrid tugged her toward the vehicle. "I didn't get Deedee's message until about an hour ago and by then ..."

"What's happening?" she asked as she sidled into the car after Astrid.

"I should have checked my phone, but everything happened so fast." She worried her lip. "I'm doing a terrible job of being Beta."

"Stop saying that, sweetheart." The man in the driver's seat looked back at them, his hand reaching out to touch Astrid's knee. "You're doing a great job."

"Sabrina, this is my husband, Zac Vrost."

"Nice to meet you."

Zac turned to her, ice blue eyes twinkling. "Nice to finally meet you too, Sabrina. You're all Astrid's been talking about for the past twenty-four hours."

"Zac, we should get going," Astrid said. "Your bodyguards are in the car behind us, Sabrina. They'll follow along."

As Zac turned back and started the engine, Astrid

enveloped Sabrina's hands in hers. "Deedee said you could help. That you can stop all this from happening."

She swallowed hard. "What's happening?"

Astrid took a deep breath. "Originally, we were going to find the mage hideout and attack them there. However, it turns out they've been here in New York City all along. Then, one of them sends a message to Cross, telling him to meet them at Central Park at midnight, with you and the dagger or else." She gripped Sabrina's hand tighter. "I'm sorry ... they ... they have your dad and two of our guys. The mages are probably controlling him with their necklace."

Sabrina gasped as dread wrapped around her like a vice. "No!"

"I'm sorry. We tried to protect him, and we failed."

Now panic was starting to overwhelm her. "We need to go. I have to go save my father," she cried. "They'll kill him if I'm not there!"

"That's why I came all the way here when Deedee said you were on your way," Astrid said. "Lucas and Cross, they came up with this plan." She let out a frustrated sound. "I told them it was a terrible one, but they wouldn't listen!"

"What plan?"

"They're going to meet the mages with the dagger and someone ... someone glamoured to look like you."

"Glamoured?"

"It's a type of magic that can make you look like anyone," Astrid explained. "Usually, it would be easy for any other magical being to see through a glamour potion, but we have these new allies, the Beaumont witches, who can perform a different type of magic. One of them has the power of shadow glamour or something like that, I'm not entirely sure how it works. But anyway, she's going in to look like you to fool the mages."

"But what use would that be?"

"Once they're within the vicinity, Cross plans to transport your father out to safety, and then our forces will attack. We're going all out, apparently, just in case. A couple of people are staying behind, including me since I'm Beta and my job is to protect the clan and I'm not involved with GI stuff. But Lucas wants this done now."

A terrible feeling made Sabrina's stomach turn in knots. "If the mages find out it's not me—"

"They'll be furious. Who knows what they'll do?"

She had a suspicion, but didn't want to vocalize it. "We need to get to Central Park."

"Are you sure you want to go there, Sabrina?" Astrid asked. "Really sure? I mean, I could take you away and keep you safe. Or send you back to Zhobghadi."

"No." She squared her shoulders, mind made up. No, she'd made up her mind even before she got here. Gunnar's words were the key. How it was going to work out, she didn't know, but she had to trust her instinct. "Let's go, please."

"All right."

The rest of the ride was mercifully silent, and Sabrina stared out the window, her heart pounding as they drew closer to the city. Finally, they arrived on the east side of the park, right by the Metropolitan Museum.

"We're here," Zac announced as he cut the engine. "Let's go. We'll head 'round the building."

"They're supposed to meet at The Obelisk behind the museum," Astrid explained as they got out of the car. "Our guys are hiding in there," she pointed with her chin at the museum building. "Lizzie's keeping the alarm and surveillance system busy, and a majority of our forces are waiting inside, and they'll sneak out the back once it's time. 'You'"—she did air quotes to signify she meant the glamoured witch—"and Cross are going to walk up to The Obelisk while a small backup force is coming in from the other side."

"It's just after midnight," Sabrina said woefully. "Are we too late?"

"We can't give up yet." Astrid grabbed her hand, and they hurried to the back of the Met Museum.

Up ahead, Sabrina saw the massive Egyptian artifact, rising up ominously above them. Growing up, she'd always loved going to the Met, yet she'd only seen The Obelisk, or Cleopatra's Needle, a few times. It was supposedly made in 1460 BC in Egypt and then transported to New York in the 1800s. Lights blazed around the impressive granite structure, making it look ominous, though right now, her focus was on the people at the foot of the monument. Her heart stopped as she recognized Cross's form among the hooded figures.

"... impostor!" someone shouted, followed by a scream. "Where is she?"

Fear for her father's and Cross's life made adrenaline pump into her veins, and Sabrina ran as fast as her legs could carry her, up the set of stairs that led to the base of The Obelisk.

"If you don't tell me where she is, I'm going to kill Strohen!"

"No!" she screamed as soon as she reached the top. "Please! Don't!"

Cross, who was bent down next to the figure crumpled

on the ground, turned toward her. "Sabrina?" His face turned visibly pale. "Sabrina, no—"

"Woman. Come closer," said one of the men in the hooded robes.

"You can't have her!" Cross got to his feet and took a step forward. "I—"

"Move an inch and they die." The mage gestured to his right. Jonathan stood, unmoving, his eyes were open but looked straight ahead, like he didn't see or hear what was happening around him. Beside him were two men wearing dark suits, also frozen and glassy-eyed.

She sent Cross a pleading look, then turned to the mages. Slowly, she approached them, her heart hammering wildly in her chest. She noticed there were a dozen red-robed figures standing around a white marble table, while three more mages stood off to the side.

"Finally," the mage in the middle of the trio said. He was tall, and unlike the other mages, he had long, straight gray hair that fell down to his shoulders. "Welcome, dear Sabrina. Those dogs might have fooled everyone else, but I could see through their tricks."

Sabrina's eyes immediately went to the necklace around the mage's neck. It was silver with a blue jewel in the middle. She didn't know why, but it was like it was calling to her ...

The mage smiled. "You can sense it too. Sense the power of Magus Aurelius's necklace." He glared at the unconscious figure by Cross's feet. "That's how I knew she was a fake. I couldn't sense the ring. But you," his gaze dropped to her right hand, "you're the real deal."

The ring seemed to get warmer around her finger and

sent a shock of electricity up her arm. "What do you want? Please, I'll do anything. Just let them go."

"Oh, you will, my dear," he said. "But—" The mage gasped as several figures began to materialize behind Cross. "You damned dirty dogs!"

"You're surrounded," Daric said. "You won't leave this place alive." Sabrina recognized most of the people who had transported in with the warlock from that day they came to New York and met the Alpha—Cross's mother, Meredith, Julianna, Duncan, Elise, and—Ransom? *What was he doing here?*

"You traitor," he hissed at Daric. "You think I don't know how your feeble little minds work? I know you'd come prepared, and so did we." He turned his head toward the mages around the table. "Now."

Three of the mages linked their hands together and began to chant, then something began to rise from the circle they formed—like a red energy beam that rose to the sky, reaching the top of The Obelisk, then trickled down and formed around them, like some kind of red glass dome. Once the area was fully enclosed, they stopped chanting.

"Now you're all trapped in here," the mage cackled. "No one can get in or out," he glared at Daric. "And if you try anything, remember that I can end Strohen and your cohorts' lives with a snap of my finger. Now," he turned to Sabrina. "*Come here.*"

"This is what you want, right?" She lifted her hand, showing him the ring. "Why did you give this to me in the first place? Why didn't you just let me die? Why come for it now?"

The mage's face twisted in hate, and red bloomed under his ashen complexion.

"Krogan," one of the mages said impatiently. "We told you to move on from the errors of your past. There's no need to rehash things. Just get the ceremony done. We've already wasted so much time."

Krogan let out an indignant growl. "May I remind you, if we had not given Strohen the ring, then we would never have been able to get the funds to build our army and contacts." He turned to Sabrina. "I *should* have left you dead," he said. "But that wasn't part of the plan."

"The plan to get my father's money, you mean? In exchange for saving my life?"

The mage let out an evil laugh. "Saving your life? My dear, we were the ones who took it."

Her throat went dry as the knot in her stomach grew. "What?"

"After our master Stefan's defeat in Norway, those of us who were left banded together and gathered everything that the master had left in the various strongholds around the world. During our search, we found the manuscripts of Magus Aurelius. Also among the master's things were priceless magical artifacts, including the necklace. We worked out how to use the necklace eventually, but the manuscripts were in an ancient language no one spoke anymore, so it's taken us years to translate everything. Volumes and volumes of spells and instructions that we could only dream of.

"However, that ring"—his gaze turned to hate as he looked down at her hand—"was the most useless piece of junk we recovered. It had the power of death and life—in the most literal sense. It could only kill a living being and then bring it back to life. That's it." His yellowed teeth ground together. "That's when I came up with the brilliant plan, one that would help fill our coffers and help our cause. And you and your mother were the perfect candidates."

"No ..."

"Yes, my dear. I glamoured myself to look like one of the hospital nurses and then poisoned your mother while she was giving birth to you. As soon as you were born, I used the ring to kill you. Once your father was alone, I reappeared as myself and revived you, then told him it was the only thing keeping you alive.

"We've kept your father under our thumb all these years by threatening to take the ring away from you, which we falsely told him would kill you again. It was a small sacrifice, but it was worth it, considering the staggering amount of money he's funneled to us over the years." His eyes darkened. "But it was only recently we discovered in the later volumes of the manuscripts what the ring *really* was. What Magus Aurelius's intentions were for the artifacts and his final instructions for his followers. By then it was too late, and that *abomination*," he sneered at Cross, "had already gotten to you first."

Sabrina felt her knees wobble. All this time ... they had killed her mother! A burning rage began to bubble inside her. *They couldn't get away with this!* No, she had to make sure they paid for taking Melanie away from her and her father. "Even if I wanted to give you the ring, you bastard, I can't get it off. Your colleagues already tried."

"I know. And poor Azael and Selyse, along with the rest of our colleagues paid for their mistakes," Krogan said. "But how were we supposed to know that the ring had bonded with you? You've become its host, its conduit for the power contained in it." His hand clasped around the necklace. "That's the reason we don't let anyone use the necklace for too long. But, that's why we've called you here." He walked over to the white marble table, took off the necklace, and placed it on the table. "Get the dagger from your mate," he ordered. "And don't try anything funny or your dear father dies."

Hands clenched at her sides, she slowly walked over to Cross.

"Sabrina, why?" he asked softly. "I sent you away so you could be safe. So this wouldn't happen."

"I know," she said. "But that's why I had to come back."

Blue-green eyes searched hers. "What do you mean?"

"Do you trust me, Cross?"

"Yes."

"Then you have to give me the dagger," she whispered. "Please."

Though he hesitated for a few seconds, he reached into the small satchel at his side and then took out something long wrapped in cloth. "Sabrina ... I love you."

She took the dagger from him. "I love you too."

"What's taking so long?" Krogan barked. "Stop dawdling, and come back here."

After one last glance at him, she turned on her heel and walked back. She wished she could reach out and touch and kiss Cross, but she knew what had to be done. *Sometimes the only way to change the future is to follow its path.* She could only hope she understood the meaning correctly.

"Put it on the altar," Krogan instructed.

Her hands shook as she unwrapped the dagger. It was much longer than what she'd imagined a dagger to be, but not as long as a sword. On the pommel was a green jewel, and just like the necklace, it seemed to call to her too. Another shock of electricity shot across her skin as she held it in her hand and placed it on the table next to the necklace.

"What exactly are you planning to do?" She glared at him with all the hate she could muster. "Kill me so you can have the ring?"

"Not quite that pedestrian, my dear," Krogan replied. "I just need you to transfer the power back to the ring and break the bond. That way, we can finally have all three artifacts back together as they were meant to be. Now, stand in front of the altar," he instructed. "And take the dagger and the pendant in your hands."

Her heart beat a tattoo into her rib cage as she followed his instructions, picking up the dagger in her left hand and the necklace in her right. Heat began to spread, and the ring seemed to throb around her finger. "Arghhh!" She screamed as white-hot pain shot up her arms.

"Don't you dare let go!" Krogan screamed. "Not until it's done!"

She wasn't even sure she *could* let go—it was as if the necklace and dagger had melded to her hands. Even as she flexed her fingers open, they stuck to her palms. The pain intensified, making her double over and brace her elbows against the altar as she struggled to stop herself from passing out. The dagger and the necklace finally separated from her hands, and to her surprise, the ring slid right off her finger. Someone shouted her name as she felt her legs give out from under her.

"I got you."

Before she hit the floor, arms wrapped her up and pressed her up against a hard chest. The scent of minty chocolate told her who it was. "Sometimes the only way to change the future is to follow its path," she whispered. "That's what Gunnar said."

His entire body tensed, but he held her closer. "Sabrina ... I thought you were going to die."

"I—"

"Fools!" Krogan cackled loudly. "Now I'll have them all!" He slipped the ring on and raised the dagger and necklace triumphantly.

"No, no, no," Sabrina shook her head. "I thought that—" A deafening howl cut her off. She blinked as a large gray blur sailed overhead. "What in the—"

"Ransom," Cross said as he helped her get steady on her feet. "I can't believe it."

The large gray wolf had leapt over them and rammed straight into Krogan, and now they lay tangled in a heap. The mage let out a scream and reared an arm back, then plunged the dagger into the wolf's chest.

Sabrina screamed. "No!"

Cross held his breath, then something changed in his expression. "Hold on!" His arm snaked around her, tucking her in against him.

Everything happened so fast, she barely had time to blink. She felt that coldness around her, but then it was gone. "What the ..." She glanced around. They were at the edge of the force field dome the mages had created, sheltered under some cherry blossom trees. "Cross?"

He was kneeling down beside the gray wolf. "Stay still," he told the wolf. "It'll only hurt more."

Cross must have transported them away from the altar, but because of the dome, they could only get this far. "Stay here and don't move," he instructed. "I'll be right—"

He disappeared, and two seconds later, he was there again, along with her father and two other men. "Back," he finished.

"Dad!" she cried, hugging him. "Dad ..." He didn't move, so she hugged him tighter, but he remained eerily still, staring into nothing.

"The potion will wear off," Cross said. "But for now ..." He knelt down next to the wolf. It wasn't moving and its breathing was labored. "Thank you," he whispered, then grabbed the end of the dagger and pulled.

A loud crash muffled the wolf's pained cries. She looked back toward The Obelisk and saw that everything had erupted into chaos. There were several wolves attacking the mages, but aside from that, she saw all kinds of projectiles being hurled about—electricity, fireballs, rocks, park benches. She even saw the two Almoravid in the fray, holding their own. Krogan lay by the altar, all bloody and torn up, a hateful expression on his face as he realized their side was losing.

"Goddamn you!" he screamed. "We have the ring and the necklace, fall back!" Three mages formed a circle around him and began to chant.

What were they doing?

The red glass dome receded around them. "Cross, look!"

He looked up, then realized what was happening. "Fuck! He's getting away with the other artifacts." He glanced down. "I can't leave yet. I'm not done dressing the wound." He kept his hand over the gray wolf as bandages magically appeared over its chest.

A realization swept over her and Gunnar's words came back to her. "It's all right, Cross." She squeezed his shoulder. "It's all going to be all right."

"But they're getting away!"

"It's done," she said. "We've changed it. We changed the future, don't you see? I'm still alive. Everyone's alive."

"I—" His ocean-colored eyes went wide. "You're right. Gunnar said the ending wasn't set in his new vision." He got to his feet and looked down at the wolf. "This should help you for now, but we'll have someone see to you as soon as we can. Just hang on, Ransom." He raised the dagger up. "Thanks to him, we've at least managed to keep this one."

"But the ring ..."

"They still need all three together." His brows wrinkled together. "But now ... how could it ..." His expression changed.

"Cross? What's wrong."

"I think ..." He took a sharp intake of breath. "I just realized something ... but I'll have to wait until we're all done here to try and figure out if my theory is true."

"Looks like everything's going to be all right." She nodded back toward The Obelisk.

Most of the mages were lying dead on the ground, while the two who were remaining were tied together as Elise guarded them, her hands raised up, blue light crackling from her hands as she formed what looked like an electrified cage around them. Daric and Meredith, on the other hand, were going around checking that the mages were all dead. Duncan had an injured Julianna in his arms and gently laid her down on one of the park benches that hadn't been thrown around or burned up.

"Sabrina! Cross!" Astrid jumped over the railing to get to them, Zac behind her. "Thank God! It's all over."

Cross embraced his sister, then exchanged a quick backslap with his brother-in-law. "For now, anyway."

"Will he be all right?" Zac asked, glancing down at Ransom.

"Yes, I got the dagger out and dressed his wounds."

"Let's go get cleaned up," Astrid said.

"Saving the world's messy business," Zac said with a laugh as he kissed his wife on the cheek. "Now comes the fun part."

Astrid rolled her eyes. "Right. The cleanup. AKA, *my* job."

———

Cross had brought Sabrina, Ransom, Jonathan, the two Lycan bodyguards, and Julianna to the medical wing of The Enclave so the latter three could get checked up, then went back to The Obelisk to help with the cleanup. As Cross said, whatever spell or potion her father was under eventually wore off. Although Jonathan insisted he was fine, Dr. Blake nevertheless ordered he stay overnight for observation.

"I'm not injured," he grumbled as he lay back on the hospital bed.

Despite his grumpy disposition, Sabrina was just happy her father was all right. She gave him a kiss on the forehead. "Please, Dad, just stay at least until morning? I want to make sure there's no lingering side effects of whatever potion they gave you.

"Fine," he said.

In the next bed over was Julianna, who was being fussed over by her husband and decidedly *not* enjoying it. "For Christ's sake, MacDougal, you're worse than my mother!" She swatted his hands away. "The fireball just grazed me and the nurse patched me right up. I'll be fine in a couple of days."

"*Och!*" The Scotsman exclaimed. "You're my mate, and I'll hover over you as much as I want." There was a flash of grief in his eyes. "Darlin', I don't know what I'd do if I lost you."

The bed next to the quarreling—now embracing—couple was empty, which Sabrina guessed must have been reserved for Ransom. As soon as they arrived, Dr. Blake had him brought to the operating room to check on his injuries. Duncan explained that Lycans healed much faster than humans did, but it wasn't instant, and things like broken bones had to be taken care of right away, or else they might heal over wrong, and then they'd have to be re-broken and reset properly. Also, if the dagger had some magical properties, it might even slow down the healing.

Finally, at around two in the morning, Cross came back. Jonathan had fallen asleep, and Sabrina was curled up on the couch in the waiting room. "Everything okay?" she asked as he walked toward her.

"Yes. We're doing a debrief in the morning, but for now, the Alpha told everyone to go home and rest."

"Oh." She swung her legs off the couch and sat up. "I suppose I could go back to my loft. It would be nice to start wearing my own clothes again. What's the matter?" she asked when his brows drew together in a frown.

"I'll take you home, but do you mind if we stop by somewhere first?"

"Not at all." She got up and slipped an arm through his. "Where'd you have in mind?"

"I need to go see Gunnar."

"Let's go then."

In seconds, they reappeared in the darkened cabin. "Gunnar?" he called.

"I'm here." A lamp in the corner turned on, revealing Gunnar, sitting on the leather recliner. "Dad called and told me everything that happened. I figured you might drop by." He gestured to the couch, where a pot of tea and cups were already waiting. "Have a seat."

Cross led her to the couch, and they sat down. "Did you know?" Cross asked. "About what the ceremony was for?"

He shook his head. "Not really. Everything just kind of ... all melded together. Like hitting the fast-forward button while watching a movie."

Cross leaned forward, resting his elbows on his thighs. "Everything happened as you saw it, including the people who were there. But that ceremony wasn't their end game. It was just to break the bond the ring had on Sabrina."

"I realize that now." His face drew into a grave expression.

Cross tensed. "What now?"

"I ... Cross, I had another vision before you arrived."

"Of the future?"

"No, this was the past again." Gunnar's eyes glassed over. "Far in the past. I don't know why, it just feels so far back.

There's a man in a white robe, surrounded by others in red robes. They were in some kind of ancient temple, though everything looked brand new. He's on top of a tall platform, and there's a white marble altar in front of him."

"Then what happened?"

"Outside the temple, it's thundering. No." He raked his hands through his hair. "People running. Lycans running, their paws pounding on the ground. Then the man in the white robe raises his hand over the altar. There's a ring, a dagger, and a necklace. He cuts his palm and drizzles his blood over the artifacts, then puts on the ring. The men around him are chanting, and then he says something. I think he says, 'I will rise again.' Then ... that's it."

The silence that hung in the air was deafening. Sabrina reached over and took Cross's hand in hers.

"I think I know," Cross began. "I know what they want the artifacts for."

Gunnar turned to him, his face pale, and whiskey-brown eyes filled with fear. "They're bringing him back."

"Death and life," Cross said. "Magus Aurelius's enemies —the humans and Lycans—must have been on the verge of storming his temple. He used the ring to kill himself."

"So that they could revive him," Sabrina finished. A shudder ran down her spine, and she suddenly felt tainted, carrying the ring around. "That's why its power was so literal. Death and life. Kill something, then bring them back to life."

Cross's jaw hardened. "Krogan said something about Magus Aurelius's manuscripts. That's how they found out about the artifacts and his final intentions. That could be what he was talking about."

"In that case, we've only slowed them down." Gunnar ran

his fingers through his hair in frustration and buried his face in his hands. "Now they've got the ring back and they can bring him back."

"Wait." Cross shot to his feet and scratched his jaw. "When Sabrina used the ring, she was able to revive the plants and the mare right away. Why couldn't they have done it as soon as they got the ring? Or why haven't they done it by now? It's been hours since they escaped."

"I had my dead plants, and Georgie was right there," she reminded him. "If this Magus guy has been dead for thousands of years, there's nothing really left to revive."

Cross's brows snapped together before they lifted, his eyes widening. "Unless they had something else very powerful to increase the artifacts' powers."

"Double Alpha blood," Gunnar concluded. "We thought they were just using it to enhance the artifacts. I mean, obviously, that was just a side effect. It could be that was all they thought the blood could do."

"They didn't finish translating everything until recently," Cross said. "It makes sense Magus Aurelius only wrote down his plans at the end, when he was about to be defeated."

"We won't know for sure unless we read the manuscript ourselves," Gunnar pointed out.

"But it could be a working theory." Cross walked over to his brother. "I need to go and tell Dad and the Alpha."

Gunnar stood up. "Safe travels."

Sabrina, too, strode over to him. "We'll see you soon," she said before enveloping him in a hug. "And thank you. I figured out what it meant. The words you said to me before we left the last time, but tell me something."

"What is it?"

She looked him straight in the eyes. "Why the riddles? Why couldn't you just tell me the truth of what will happen?"

A dark cloud seemed to pass over him. "I've meddled with the future before," he said in a quiet voice. "And the consequences have been ... devastating. When I asked my grandmother, what was I supposed to do when I see these horrible things and can't stop them, she told me, 'Gunnar, the best way to use your gift is to advise people, not try to change who they are or change their minds. You must guide them, but ultimately, the only way to be truthful to fate is to let them make their own decisions.'"

Her eyes widened. "That's why your vision changed, isn't it? Why there wasn't an end. The future isn't set." The realization dawned on her. "I had a choice. To stay in Zhobghadi, or come back here. I made the choice."

Gunnar's mouth slowly turned up into a smile. "I guess we'll never know, really." He kissed her on the cheek and then clapped his brother on the back. "I'll see you soon."

They watched Gunnar retreat back into his room, both of them dumbfounded. "Am I right?" she asked Cross. "Was it that choice?"

He wrapped an arm around her. "When you think about it, he could mean any of the choices you or I made. Like when you decided not to take a second dose of the potion. Or when I decided to bring Ransom to New York. Or maybe it was when you chose to come into Wicked Brew that morning I ran into you."

"Ugh." Her fingers massaged at her temples. "I'm getting a headache just thinking about it. Is there any way you can skip meeting your father, and we can just go home?"

He flashed her a brilliant smile. "I'll leave him a voice message now, then we can go."

A short while later, they were in her loft apartment. "I still can't believe I'm back," she said. "And I can finally shower and wear my own clothes!"

He slipped his arms around her and pulled her close. "How about we save the clothes for later?"

Desire hummed deep in her. "Okay."

"Good, because I can't wait." He lowered his head and gave her the most passionate, bone-melting kiss she'd ever experienced in her whole life. In a split second, she found herself under him, on top of the bed, her clothes completely gone. *I guess there are some benefits of having a magical boyfriend,* she thought with a laugh.

He didn't kiss her as much as he devoured her—as if he had never tasted her lips before. She could feel the urgency in his kisses and his hands as they roamed her body. When he finally made love to her, she was moaning his name and clutching at him, her body moving in rhythm with him as they sought their release together. Her body exploded in pleasure and she moaned his name over and over again.

Afterwards, as they lay together in a sweaty, satisfied heap, he gathered her to his side and kissed her temple. "I'm not sure which choice led us to this path," he said. "Or maybe this was always where we were meant to be. I think that's what Gunnar was trying to say. We should let fate run its course. He didn't tell me you're my mate because he wanted to warn me to stay away. He always knew I would make my way to you."

"Hmmm ... maybe."

"I am glad about one choice I made."

Though she was sleepy and bone-tired, she made an effort to look up at him and gaze into those gorgeous azure eyes. "What's that?"

"When I decided to make you fall in love with me again."

She paused, letting his words sink in, then chuckled. "Oh, Cross."

"Why are you laughing?"

Reaching up, she brushed his cheek, feeling the warmth of her emotion for him, and for the child she now carried, burning in her chest. "I never stopped."

EPILOGUE

DESPITE THE EXCITEMENT OF YESTERDAY, SABRINA managed to wake up before Cross. Though he dragged her back to bed, thoroughly intending to make love to her all morning, she insisted on getting up and going to see her father. While he wanted to make up for all the time they'd wasted during the last three years, he couldn't begrudge her, not after what she had been through and finding out the truth about her mother. And to be honest, he wanted to make sure Ransom was recovering as well, since it was his fault the Lone Wolf was injured and dragged into this mess.

They dressed and got ready, then as soon as she finished the massive breakfast he brought for her, they went straight to the medical wing of The Enclave.

"You've spoiled me," she said when they appeared in the waiting room. "I don't know how I'm ever going to travel like a normal person again."

He chuckled and kissed her temple. "I'm sure you'll manage. You did find a way to get back here from Zhobghadi."

"Well, that was a private jet," she said. "So, I'm not sure if that counts as normal travel either."

Cross reminded himself to thank Deedee and Karim, and maybe, see if they could drop by for dinner sometime next week. For now, they walked into the recovery ward together.

Jonathan was already dressed and ready to go, seeing as Dr. Blake had given him a clean bill of health. "I'll go wait outside if you want to visit your friends first," he said, before leaving the ward.

"I want to go home too," Julianna whined. "I need a shower. And a cheeseburger."

"*Dinna fash*, darlin'," Duncan cooed. "Everything'll be fine and you'll leave when you're ready. And I have a surprise coming for you." He glanced over at the third bed, where Ransom was lying, still asleep. "Your friend's doin' fine," he said to Cross. "Looks like a nasty wound, but he's been sleepin' all this time, so he should be doin' some good healin'."

Cross and Sabrina made their way over to Ransom's bed at the far side of the ward. A blanket covered his legs, and he was naked from the waist up, the wolf tattoo above his hip. Bandages wrapped over his left shoulder and around his chest, and his skin was still ashen. But his breathing was normal, and he looked serene as he slept. "You really took one for the team," Cross mused. "I didn't think he'd do something like that."

"Maybe there's more to him than we think," Sabrina said, nudging his arm. "Bringing him along was a good idea."

"*Och*, now, here's my surprise," Duncan announced.

"Jules!" Isabelle had burst through the door and now dashed toward her sister. "Oh, my God, Jules," she cried.

"Duncan told me what happened, are you all right?" She hugged Julianna. "I thought—"

"Oh, for crying out loud," Julianna mumbled. "I'm fine. I'm a Lycan, remember? I may not have True Mate healing powers, but I'll be fine in a couple of days."

"The fireball burned a chuck of flesh off her left arm," Duncan said through gritted teeth. "She fainted from the pain."

"And they patched me up, but this thing"—she nodded at the bandage on her arm—"itches like the dickens. And don't even get me started on what generating new skin feels like."

"Thanks for watching over Kier," Duncan said to Isabelle, mentioning their infant son.

"Oh, no worries, he's fine. Whenever he cries, I just give him some food and he's good to go." She chuckled. "No wonder he's so chubby."

"He's *not* chubby," Duncan said indignantly. "He's—"

"Husky," Julianna and Isabelle quipped at the same, then they both burst out into giggles. "Anyway," Isabelle continued. "He and Evan are with Sofia now since I wanted to come see you. Oh, hey, Sabrina! Cross!" She greeted when she realized they were there. "Are you guys okay? Were you injured too?"

"No, we're good," Sabrina said. "But my dad was here, and we're taking him home."

"Oh?" She walked closer toward them. Her gaze dropped down to Ransom. "Is that your—" She stopped short, the smile from her face evaporated as she went visibly pale.

"Isabelle?" Sabrina cocked her head to the side. "Are you all right?"

Seemingly jolted out of her trance, she started. "I'm ... fine!" she said nervously, her hands waving in the air. "I just remembered something I have to—"

Ransom began to stir, his fingers twitching at his sides. His mouth opened, and he let out a low moan. "No ..."

If it were possible, Isabelle went even paler. "I should go see to Evan." Turning on her heel, she sprinted out of the ward.

"What's the matter with her?" Julianna asked. "She didn't even say goodbye."

Duncan shrugged. "Who knows? Maybe she ate something bad."

Cross looked down at Sabrina. Her face was scrunched up and eyes narrowed, as if she were concentrating. "What's wrong?"

"I ..." She worried her lip with her teeth. "Nothing. I mean, I'll tell you later. Let's go bring my dad home first."

They met Jonathan outside, who insisted they take a cab home instead of having Cross bring them back to his penthouse. And so, they did, though Sabrina complained about the traffic, mumbling to herself that they could have avoided this if her dad wasn't such a curmudgeon. Finally, they arrived at his apartment, and after getting him settled in, she and Cross strode out to the terrace.

"Where should we go?" he asked her. "Do you want to go home? Or maybe we could go to Paris or London?"

She chuckled. "I'll let you choose."

"I was hoping you'd say that." He threaded his fingers through hers and closed his eyes. "Oh, wait." Waving his hand over her, he created a warm, silk cloak that wrapped around her shoulders. "Now you're ready."

"Ready?" she asked, brows furrowing together. "Ready for—what?" She sucked in a breath as they arrived at their destination in a split second. "Oh. My. God."

They stood near the edge of a cliff, overlooking a fjord, its clear blue waters winding down between massive cliffs of chiseled limestone. The valley ahead had dots of green and yellow, signaling that the long slumber of winter was over, and nature was waking up again. *A new beginning*, he thought.

"Cross ... this is amazing," she sighed. "I've only seen pictures of this place."

"Now you can paint it for real." He turned to face her. "When all this is done, how about we build a cottage, right here?" Bringing her hands up to his face, he kissed each of her palms. "You can paint and I—"

"Can watch over our baby?" she finished.

Everything had happened so quickly, he barely had time to remember that she was, indeed, carrying his pup now. The realization floored him, and he had to steady himself at the thought. *I'm going to be a father.*

"Cross?" Clear violet eyes looked up at him, and the smile on her face warmed every corner of his soul.

"You're my fate, Sabrina. You and our child." Slipping his hand into the pocket of his jacket, he took out a ring and held it up to her surprised gaze. The stone in the middle was a large amethyst, surrounded by sparkling diamonds. "Will you marry me?"

"Yes," she cried without hesitation. "I will."

With shaking hands, he put the ring on her finger. "I love you, Sabrina."

"And I love you."

Her hands slid up behind his neck to bring him down for a kiss. Sweetness burst on his lips as the scent of apple cider and fresh snow surrounded him, permeating the air around him until he could only think, smell, feel, and taste her. For the last three years, he hadn't allowed himself to think of moments like this, couldn't even allow himself to dream of it because knowing that he could never have her had been pure torture. But now, he could not only dream it, but also live it. His beautiful dream come true.

———

There's one more story left in this series and it's going to be **BIG**.

Do we get to find out who Isabelle's mate?

Maybe.

All I can say is EVERYTHING COMES FULL CIRCLE.

And you'll find out in the last book

Heart of the Wolf - available at your favorite online bookstores.

I have some extra HOT bonus scenes for you that weren't featured in this book - just join my newsletter here to get access:

http://aliciamontgomeryauthor.com/mailing-list/

You'll get access to ALL the bonus materials from all my books and my **FREE** novella **The Last Blackstone Dragon.**

ABOUT THE AUTHOR

Alicia Montgomery has always dreamed of becoming a romance novel writer. She started writing down her stories in now long-forgotten diaries and notebooks, never thinking that her dream would come true. After taking the well-worn path to a stable career, she is now plunging into the world of self-publishing.

 facebook.com/aliciamontgomeryauthor

 twitter.com/amontromance

 bookbub.com/authors/alicia-montgomery